Playboy's
by

"I want you."

"I realise that," Olivia said cautiously. "There's just one problem."

"And what would that be?"

"Your relationship with my father."

Mac's brows lifted just slightly, then he scowled.

"He called this morning and said you might be stopping by."

"Did he?"

"Yep." She looked him straight in the eye. "Now, Mr Valentine, why don't you tell me why you're really here?"

Like Lightning
by Charlene Sands

ಶೀುಶಿ

"Thank you for coming to my rescue," Maddie said.

Trey spread his hand through her hair, coppery waves spilling over his fingertips, soft and smooth and silky. "You nearly gave me a heart attack, Maddie," he whispered. "I'm gonna need a better thank-you."

Maddie slipped her hand inside his shirt, stroking his flesh until his skin sizzled. Then she lifted her head and gave him the best thank-you of his life, a long, hot, sexy kiss that knocked the breath out of him.

"Was that better, Trey?"

"Better," he croaked, barely catching his breath.

Maddie stared deeply into his eyes and every shred of willpower he could muster wasn't enough for the intoxicating look of desire she cast him. "Ah, Maddie," he whispered, brushing his lips to her ear, "how am I supposed to keep my hands off you now?"

Available in August 2008 from Mills & Boon® Desire™

In Bed with the Devil
by Susan Mallery
&
High-Society Mistress
by Katherine Garbera

ᗡᏯᏰᏆᏰ

A Convenient Proposition
by Cindy Gerard
&
A Splendid Obsession
by Cathleen Galitz

ᗡᏯᏰᏆᏰ

Playboy's Ruthless Payback
by Laura Wright
&
Like Lightning
by Charlene Sands

Playboy's Ruthless Payback
LAURA WRIGHT

Like Lightning
CHARLENE SANDS

MILLS & BOON
Pure reading pleasure™

First published in Great Britain 2008
by Harlequin Mills & Boon Limited,
Eton House, 18-24 Paradise Road, Richmond, Surrey TW9 1SR

The publisher acknowledges the copyright holders of the
individual works as follows:

Playboy's Ruthless Payback © Laura Wright 2007
Like Lightning © Charlene Sands 2005

ISBN: 978 0 263 85911 9

51-0808

Printed and bound in Spain
by Litografia Rosés S.A., Barcelona

PLAYBOY'S RUTHLESS PAYBACK

by
Laura Wright

Dear Reader,

What would you do if someone set out to ruin your reputation? Take down your business? Destroy everything you've worked so hard to achieve? *Is your blood boiling yet?*

These are the questions I wanted to have my hero, Mac Valentine, face. I wanted to see how far he would go, how ruthless he would be in destroying the man who set out to destroy him.

Honestly, I've felt Mac's anger – that roaring sound of injustice that rings in your ears every time you think about how you've been screwed over. Maybe you have, too, and you want your payback. But after you have it, is the satisfaction of making that person pay enough? Does it heal you?

Let me know what you think about Mac and Olivia's story. And, if you want to share your story, I'd love to hear it. E-mail me at laura@laurawright.com.

All my best,

Laura

LAURA WRIGHT

has spent most of her life immersed in the world of acting, singing and competitive ballroom dancing. But when she started writing romance, she knew she'd found her true calling! Born and raised in Minneapolis, Laura has also lived in New York, Ohio and Wisconsin. Currently, she has set down her bags in Los Angeles, California, and, although the town can be a little crazy at times, Laura is grateful to have her theatrical production manager husband, two young children and three dogs to keep her sane. During her downtime, Laura loves to paint, play peek-a-boo with her little boy, go to the cinema with her husband and read with her daughter. She loves hearing from her readers and can be reached at PO Box 57523, Sherman Oaks, CA 91413, USA.

To Daniel, thank you for seeing me through
this book. You're the best!

One

"Congresswoman Fisher is on line two, Derek Mead is still holding on line three and Owen Winston is on line four."

Mac Valentine relaxed in his chair. His executive assistant, Claire, stood in the doorway of his modern, chrome-and-leather penthouse office, an expectant look on her grandmotherly face. She had been with him for eight years and she was somewhat of a voyeur when it came to watching him work. She especially enjoyed moments like this when he was about to crush someone. She thought of him as a ruthless, unflinching businessman, and on more than one occasion he'd heard her refer to him as a black-haired, black-eyed demon who held each one of his thirty-five employees to incredibly high standards.

Mac grinned. The woman was right. The only thing she'd left out was that if any one of those employees fell short of his expectations, if they didn't strive for the goal of making MCV Wealth Enhancement Corp. the first choice of not only the Minneapolis area, but also the entire Midwest, they were sent packing.

Behind her black frames, Claire's eyes glistened like a child waiting for dessert to be served. "Mr. Winston says he is returning your call, sir."

Mac palmed his BlackBerry. "Tell both the congress-woman and Mead that I'll return their calls. This won't take long."

"Yes, sir." Claire hovered in the doorway.

"And close the door when you go," Mac said evenly. "Today is not a school day."

"Of course, sir." Looking thoroughly disappointed, Claire left the room.

Mac pressed the call button and leaned back in his chair. "Owen."

"That's right," came the irritated voice on the other end of the line. "I've been holding for longer than I care to. What can I do for you?"

Satisfaction rolled through Mac at the slight tremor in the older man's voice. He turned his chair toward the wall of windows behind him and stared out at the view of the Minneapolis skyline. "I won't waste my time or yours asking why you did what you did."

"Excuse me?"

"Or force you to admit it," said Mac. "Attempting to ruin the reputation of a competing firm happens quite a bit in our game. Mostly with the older set. You guys get tired, lose your edge and the clients start looking elsewhere."

Mac could practically see Owen's face darkening with rage. "You don't know what you're talking about, Valentine—"

"You can't help it," Mac continued coldly. "You see these hotshots coming up the ranks with cooler heads and sharper minds and you start to worry that you're not going to be taken seriously anymore. And when you realize it's only a matter of time before you're forced out of business, you panic." Mac leaned forward and said without emotion, "You panicked, Owen."

"This is ridiculous," Owen sputtered. "You don't know what you're talking about."

Mac continued as if he hadn't heard. "A respectable man would recognize his limitations and retire, maybe play a round of golf in the morning followed by a nice nap in the afternoon."

"A respectable businessman, Valentine." Owen laughed bitterly. "A respectable businessman wouldn't give preferential treatment, key information or tips to certain privileged clients. A respectable man wouldn't give that information based on their client's long legs and large breasts."

It was the accusation of a desperate man, total BS, but the rumor had spread like the flu. "You are this close to a lawsuit, Winston."

"That sharp mind of yours would never allow these observations of mine to go on the record in a court of law. Such a long, drawn-out process. Even worse for your reputation, I would think."

It took a few seconds for Mac to respond, then a deadly calm crept over him like the blackening sky before a thunderstorm. "True enough," he said slowly. "Perhaps legal recourse isn't the right way to deal with you."

"Smart man. Now it's late and I have—"

Mac stood and walked across the room. "No, I suppose I'll have to come up with a different way to make you pay for what you've done."

"It's after seven, Valentine," said Owen tightly. "I have dinner plans."

"Yes, of course—get home to your family." Mac opened his office door and gestured for Claire. "Especially that lovely daughter of yours. What's her name again? Allison? Olive?"

Owen didn't answer.

"Ah, right…" Mac raised a brow at Claire. "Olivia. Beautiful name," Mac said as he watched his assistant go to her computer and begin a search. "Beautiful name for a beautiful woman, I'm told. You know, your daughter has a reputation for being a very good girl. Sweet, loves her father and steers clear of anything scandalous. Might be interesting to see how easy or how enjoyably difficult it would be to change that."

Claire glanced up, her expression a mixed bag of respect, curiosity and horror.

"You stay away from my daughter." The once cocky old man now sounded like an anxious pup.

"I'm not a religious man, Owen, but I believe the

phrase 'an eye for an eye' is appropriate here." Mac stalked back into his office. "I may be an arrogant, selfish prick, but I'm no fraud. I give every one of my clients two hundred percent, male and female alike. You went too far."

Mac stabbed at the off button on his BlackBerry and walked to the windows. The bleak, gray light of a hostile rainstorm hovered over the parking lot and street below, making Mac feel as though his threats to Owen Winston might be so powerful they could not only affect the sexual status of an innocent young woman, but the weather, as well.

"She owns No Ring Required."

Mac didn't turn around to address Claire's statement. "How do I know that name?"

"*Minneapolis Magazine* did a cover story on the business last month. Three women—a chef, an interior designer and a party planner—all top-notch business-women who have banded together to create—"

"A service for men who need the help and expertise of a wife," he continued. "But either don't have one or don't want one."

"That's right."

He turned around and nodded to his assistant. "Perfect. Set up an appointment with Olivia Winston for this week. It would seem that I'm in need of her services."

"Did you read the article, sir?"

"I don't remember…I probably skimmed it."

"These are hardcore, upstanding women who are well-respected in the business community. They are adamantly against any and all fraternization."

Mac grinned to himself. "Get that appointment for tomorrow morning. First thing."

Lip pulled under her teeth, Claire nodded and left the room.

Mac returned to his desk and thumbed through the files of the clients that had gone AWOL since Owen Winston's lies had surfaced two days ago. Who knew if they were ever going to return to his company or if their relationship with his firm was dead in the water.

Mac wanted to throttle that bastard—but violence was too quickly given and gotten over. No, it would have to be a rep for a rep. Owen had taken Mac's and Mac would take his daughter's.

Well-respected or not, Owen's little girl was going to have to pay—for the loss of revenue to MCV and its employees, and for her father's stupidity.

Two

Olivia closed her eyes and inhaled. "I'm such a genius...."

"How long are you going to make us wait, Liv?" Tess asked, her stomach rumbling loudly. "I skipped breakfast."

Seated at the table, Mary Kelley stared at the tall redhead's trim belly, her brows drawn together. "Sounds like a train's derailing in there. Very ladylike."

Tess gave Mary a teasing glare. "Give me a break, I'm starving." She pointed to the massive yellow diamond engagement ring on her pretty blond partner's finger. "Not all of us have beautiful men bringing us poached eggs and bacon in the morning."

Smiling, Mary touched her growing belly, her blue

eyes soft and happy. "Ethan's very concerned about feeding his child. If I don't have something to eat every few hours he freaks."

Tess snorted. "That's just a little too sweet for me."

Mary laughed. "Oh, c'mon. You'll change your mind about that someday. Guaranteed."

"Doubtful. I'm too much of a loner—and I like it."

"Well, then we have to get you to go out and social-ize more." Mary's eyes lit up. "Maybe you'll meet someone at Ethan's and my holiday engagement party at the end of the month. He has some cute friends."

"No thanks."

"You might meet up with the right guy."

Tess shook her head and laughed. "I don't believe in the right guy, Mare. Now, a truckful of not-so-right guys—that's something I believe in."

Mary poured herself another glass of milk. "You're not old enough to be so cynical. How many men have you dated at twenty-five?"

"Enough to know better," Tess said seriously, then turned to Olivia. "You and I are lucky to have escaped the noose for so long, right, Liv?"

"Oh, so lucky," Olivia drawled as she cut squares of brownie. Olivia tried to ignore the wave of envy that moved over her heart as she recalled the tenderness in Ethan Curtis's eyes that morning when he gave Mary a goodbye kiss at the reception desk before leaving for his office. He had looked so in love, so happy, so over-the-moon excited about their baby.

Olivia didn't begrudge her friend the beautiful man

and solid relationship, but she did wonder if it was possible for someone like her to have half of that kind of happiness. In her heart of hearts, she wanted a man—someone to cook for and love and make babies with, but odds of that kind of life coming her way weren't great. Even though she had grown up in years, she was still very much stuck to the past. In many ways, she was still that depressed sixteen-year-old who had just lost her mother to cancer, couldn't get her father to notice her and had escaped from her pain in the most foolish ways possible—parties and boys and sex.

The shame of what she'd done and how many boys she'd allowed herself to be used by hadn't diminished in the ten years since, but in that time she had grown extraordinarily tough. She had also become cautious and resolutely celibate. Today, her reputation was lily-white—she was a hard-nosed businesswoman who kept the secrets of her past to herself.

"All right," Olivia said brightly, setting two extra large squares of chocolate brownie before Tess and Mary. "These will keep your mouths occupied."

"I believe she just told us to shut up," Tess said with a grin.

Mary picked up her brownie and sighed. "But it was in the very nicest way possible."

"True," Tess said, her pale gray eyes raking the gooey chocolate square. "And for another one of these I will not only give up on the guy and marriage talk, but if asked, I will gladly roll over and pant."

"Before you do," said a husky male voice behind them, "just be aware that you have an audience."

Mary and Tess whirled around in their chairs, and Olivia glanced up. Filling up the doorway with a cynical, though highly amused, expression was a man with eyes the color of espresso. He was tall and broad and was dressed impeccably in a gray pinstripe suit and black wool coat. Olivia found herself clenching her fists as she felt an irresistible urge to flip up the collar of his coat and use it to pull herself against him. The feeling was so out of character that it frightened the hell out of her and made her stomach churn with nervous energy. In the past seven years, since her self-imposed exile from sex, her body had rarely betrayed her. Sure, there had been a few late nights with a good romance novel in her bed, but other than that, nada.

As she looked at this man, every inch of her screamed *Caution!*

"Mac Valentine?" she said, relieved that her voice sounded steady and cool.

He nodded. "I think I'm early."

"Only by a few minutes," she assured him. "Please come in."

As he walked toward them, his stride runway-model confident, both Mary and Tess stood and offered him their hands. "It's nice to meet you, Mr. Valentine," Mary said evenly. "We were just enjoying a midmorning pick-me-up."

"I understand."

"Chocolate is life's blood around here," Mary continued warmly.

"I wondered what that amazing scent was the minute I got off the elevator."

Tess patted Olivia on the back. "Well, that's our resident chef's doing. Olivia makes magic and we all get to enjoy it."

His gaze rested on Olivia. "Is that so?"

Olivia shrugged good-naturedly. "I've never been good at false modesty, so I'll just say, yes, I'm a damn fine cook."

Amusement glittered in Mac Valentine's dark eyes, and Olivia felt a shiver travel up her spine.

"And on that note," said Mary, packing up the rest of her brownie and half-full glass of milk, "Tess and I will leave you in Olivia's capable hands. Welcome to No Ring Required, Mr. Valentine."

"Thank you."

Tess shook his hand again, then when his back was turned grabbed another brownie, before following Mary out of the room.

Trying not to laugh, Olivia watched Mac take off his coat and lay it over an empty chair, then she gestured to the table. "Please, have a seat." She snatched the orange platter of brownies off the counter and held it out in his direction. "Would you like one?"

He glanced up at her. "Do I have to roll over and pant?"

"Only if you want seconds."

Mac Valentine's eyes flashed with surprise at her quick comeback. "I'll let you know." Then he took a brownie from the plate.

She sat beside him and folded her hands primly. She

didn't know exactly why this man was here, but she had a feeling he brought trouble with him—several varieties of trouble. "Now, your assistant didn't reveal much about why you're here today when she made the appointment. Perhaps you could."

"Of course." He sat back in his chair. "I need you to turn my home into something far more 'homey' than what it is."

"And what is it?"

"A lot of unused space."

"Okay."

"I have clients coming in from out of town, and I want them to feel as though they've visited a family man, instead of a…" He paused.

She lifted her brows. "Yes?"

His lips twitched. "Someone who has no idea what those two words really mean."

"I see." And she did. It wasn't the first time she'd worked with a clueless millionaire playboy.

"I think it would be best if you saw my house for yourself."

She nodded, her gaze darting to the untouched brownie before him. "All right. But you understand my main area of expertise is in the kitchen."

"I was led to believe you were a multitasker."

Why wasn't he eating her brownie? "I am, but if it's true homemaking you're looking for then Tess might be a better—"

"No," he said, cutting her off.

She paused and gave him an expectant look.

"I want you," he finished, his face hard.

"Yes, I can see that," she said cautiously. "There's just one problem."

"And what would that be?"

"Your relationship with my father."

His brows lifted, just slightly. "I have no relationship with your father."

"He called me this morning and said you might be stopping by."

"Did he?"

"Yep."

Mac studied her for a moment. "You have the reputation of being a soft-spoken sweetheart, did you know that?"

"Are you trying to tell me that I'm not living up to my reputation?"

That query produced a wry smile from him. "I think I'm going to have a bite of this brownie now."

It's about damn time, she thought as she watched him slip the thick dark cake between his teeth. He had large, strong-looking hands and thick wrists, and she felt a humming in her belly as she wondered what he did with his hands that garnered him such a roguish reputation.

Her father had left her with a big warning about Mac Valentine. But instead of being worried she felt as curious as a one-year-old with an uncovered wall outlet in her sights.

"Good?" she asked, pointing to the half-eaten brownie on the plate.

"Very good."

"I'm glad," she said evenly. "Now, Mr. Valentine, why don't you tell me why you're really here?"

Three

If there was one thing Mac Valentine could spot a mile away, it was a worthy adversary. She may have been only a few inches over five feet with eyes as large and as soft as a baby deer, but Olivia Winston's cleverness and sharp tongue clearly declared her as a force to be reckoned with.

He hadn't seen that coming.

But then again, there was nothing he loved better than a challenge.

He watched those brown fawn's eyes narrow, and knew she would wait all day for the answer to her question.

"Due to circumstances beyond my control," he began, "my financial firm has lost its top three clients. I expect this to change over the course of the next few months when they realize that no one else in this town can make them the kind of money that I can, and did. But in the meantime, I need some help from you in landing a few heavy hitters."

Olivia's gaze flickered to the tabletop. "Do you need my help rebuilding your business or your reputation?"

"I see your father has done more than warn you about me." She didn't confirm or deny this, so he continued, "My business is not in any danger, but yes, my reputation has come into question and I cannot—and will not—allow that to continue."

"I see." Her smile turned edgy. "So, you want these potential clients to stay at your house instead of a hotel?"

"They're the type who appreciate home and family and soft edges—" he waved his hand "—all of that."

"But you don't."

"No."

She stood and took the plate that was in front of him, the plate with half a remaining brownie on it. "I have a question for you," she said, walking to the sink and depositing the dish there. She was small, but all curves, and when she walked it was seduction with every step. She turned to face him, leaned back against the countertop and crossed her arms over her full chest. Mac felt his gut tighten at the picture-perfect sight of her. "You believe that my dad caused your clients to leave your firm, right?" she said, arching her brow.

"Actually it was the lies your father spread that caused my clients to leave," he corrected.

"If you think that, then why would you want to work with his daughter? Unless…"

"Unless what?"

She walked to him and stopped just shy of his chair. If he reached out, grabbed her around her tiny, perfect waist and pulled her onto his lap, what would she do?

Whoever said payback was a bitch hadn't seen this woman.

"Unless you want to use me to get back at him," she said in a voice so casual she might have been reading a grocery list.

He matched her tone. "Is that what he told you?"

"Yes, but he didn't really have to."

"And how exactly would I use you?"

She shook her head. "Not quite sure." When she sat this time it was across from him.

"But your father has some ideas?"

"He's worried about your…" She smiled, thin as a blade. "Obvious charms—I mean, you're a great-looking guy. But I assured him he didn't have anything to worry about."

Well, this was a first. "Really?"

She nodded, said matter-of-factly, "I let him know that I would never be interested."

Mac felt his brow lift.

She laughed. "I don't mean to insult you, but the truth is, I would never go for a guy like you."

"Why do you think I'm insulted?"

The question caught her off guard and she stumbled with her words. "I, well—"

"And what kind of guy do you think I am?"

She lifted her chin. "One who assumes he can have anything he wants and any woman he wants."

Mac was not a man of assumptions, he was a man of words and deeds, and this woman was starting to piss him off. "I go after what I want, Miss Winston, but the people and things that come to me come at their own free will, I can assure you."

"You're just that irresistible."

He sat back in his chair. "Do all clients of No Ring Required go through an interrogation process or is it just me?"

"You're not a client yet, Mister—"

"Ah, Olivia." Tess stuck her head in the office, a confused expression on her face. "Can I see you for a moment?"

"Sure." Olivia turned to Mac. "I'll be right back, Mr. Valentine."

He saw, with vicious pleasure, that she was caught off guard and he couldn't help but grin as he said, "I wish I could say I was looking forward to it."

"If you can't wait…" she began.

"Oh, I can wait." He reached for his coat, and snagged his BlackBerry from the pocket. "I'll make a few calls."

Olivia felt like taking the man's phone and crushing it under her heel, but she smiled and nodded. Once out in the hall, the door tightly closed behind her, she faced her anxious-looking partners.

"What are you doing in there?" Tess said in a harsh whisper.

"Talking to a potential client."

"Insulting a potential client, is more like it," said Tess dryly, her arms crossed over her chest.

"Tess, you don't know the situation—"

Ever the mediator, Mary took over, her tone calm and parental. "Whatever the situation is, Liv, we could hear you all the way from our offices, and it sounded like an attack. Can you tell us what's going on?"

Olivia blew out a breath. "He's not a normal client. Hell, I don't even know if he's going to be a client at all."

"Not after what I just heard," Tess grumbled.

"At ease, Tess." Knowing her partners deserved an explanation, Olivia offered them the simplest one. "He and my father are in the same business, and a few of Mac Valentine's clients have decided to leave him and hire my dad instead. Mac thinks my father went the un-ethical route and told the financial community that he was doling out preferential treatment and tips to his better-looking clients."

"Wow," Tess began. "And did your father do that?"

"I can't imagine. My father's always been at the top of his profession. But the point is, Mac Valentine believes it. He thinks my father is responsible for the loss of three of his best clients, and now he's hiring me to get even."

Tess frowned. "What?"

"How?" Mary said, perplexed.

"I don't know yet, but I intend to find out."

"I don't like the sound of this," Tess said, shooting Mary a warning glance.

"Does he have a legitimate request for us?" Mary asked.

"He's out to bag a few new clients to replace the ones he's lost, and he wants me to make his house homey and inviting on several levels to impress them."

Mary put a hand on Olivia's shoulder. "If you don't feel you can handle him, Liv, Tess or I will—"

"No. First of all, he only wants me, and secondly, I'm not about to run from this man. I'm a professional, and I'll get the job done without getting involved."

Mary put a hand to her belly. "Sounds familiar."

"If I don't take the job, I'm willing to bet this guy would find a way of letting it be known around town that one of NRR's partners isn't a true professional. We don't need that."

Both Mary and Tess begrudgingly agreed.

"Just be careful, okay?" said Mary, squeezing Olivia's arm.

"Always." She gave them a bright smile and a wave and returned to the kitchen.

Mac was just finishing a call when Olivia eased back into her seat at the table, an NRR contract for him to sign in her hand. She took a deep breath. "Sorry about that."

"For leaving the room or for the insults?"

"Look, I'm going to take this 'job' because I am a professional and have partners who are counting on me. I'm also more than a little curious as to what you're going to try and pull. But know this, Mr. Valentine, lay one hand on me and we're done, understand?"

Mac looked amused. "For someone who believes herself so unaffected by a guy like me, you're acting worried."

"Boundaries and rules—good things to have."

After a beat, Mac agreed. "I understand. Now, can we get down to business?"

Olivia slid the one-page contract and a pen across the table. "When would you like me to start?"

"I'm having the DeBolds to my home this weekend."

"The diamond family?" She was surprised. The DeBolds would be a huge score and, according to her father, incredibly hard to land as clients. Mac Valentine had guts and drive, she'd give him that.

"They don't have children yet, but they are very into family, and the lifestyle that accompanies it. I need to make them feel at home with me."

She nodded. "I understand."

"I want home-cooked meals, family activities," he continued. "I want them to see me as secure, a man who understands their needs and desires for the future."

"Okay."

"And I'd like you to stay at the house with us."

She paused and stared at him, hoping her gaze was a cold as her tone. "No."

"In a room upstairs, down the hall from the DeBolds."

"And where will you be?"

"I sleep on the first floor."

Out of patience, she stood from the table and shot him a hot look. "It's not going to happen."

He ignored her as if she'd never said a word, "I want you to be there with us from breakfast to evening."

"Yes, I know. And I will."

In his ever-present calm way, he studied her. "All right, we'll discuss that particular detail at a later date. Now, on to something more important—this contract I'm about to sign, it guarantees confidentiality, is that right? You will not reveal anything about my business, and whom I do business with?"

"Of course." She had loyalties to her father, but her loyalties to the business and her partners came first. "Do you have menus in mind or would you like me to plan something?"

"I'd like you to plan everything."

After signing the contract and issuing a rather substantial check to NRR, Mac stood, towering over her like a statue. The soft scent of fading aftershave drifted into her nostrils and it annoyed her that just a small detail like his scent made her feel off balance. She found herself staring at his lips as he said, "I would like you to come by my house tomorrow, see what you have to work with and what you feel needs to be changed."

She stepped away from him, trying to regain her cool composure. "How's 10:00 a.m.?"

"You have my address?"

"Yes." She looked up at him and grinned slightly. "And your number, as well."

"Clever." He held out his hand, and for just a moment Olivia felt this odd sensation to turn and run from him.

But she knew how ridiculous and childish that thought was, and she confidently placed her hand in his.

There were no sparks or fireworks that erupted inside Olivia at that first touch. Instead something far more worrisome happened; she had an overwhelming urge to cry, as though she'd been on an island alone for ten years and had woken up to see a boat a few miles off shore—a boat she knew in her gut she wasn't going to be able to flag down.

She broke the connection first.

"Until tomorrow then," he said evenly.

She watched him walk out of the kitchen and down the hall, the edges of his wool coat snapping with each stride. Yes, it had been a long time since she'd met a man who affected both her mind and her body, and it was pretty damn unlucky that he happened to be an enemy of her father's.

Thankfully, she had become quite good at denying herself.

Four

Mac had hoped Olivia Winston would be moderately attractive. After all, it would make his goal a little easier and more pleasant to achieve if the woman he was going to seduce was decent-looking. Unfortunately this woman was miles past decent—circling somewhere around blistering hot. She was also intelligent and passionate and pushed sugar. And if he had any hope of seeing his plan through to the end, whenever he looked at her he was going to have to force himself to remember the he and her father were at war. And that her unhappiness and disappointment and permanent scarlet letter would be his justice.

He slowed his car to a comfortable seventy miles per hour as he exited the freeway. But seeing her as an enemy to be taken down wouldn't be easy. Damn, the way she'd looked at him with those fiery coffee-colored doe eyes, as though she couldn't decide if she was intrigued by him or wanted to follow her father's advice and toss him right out on his ass. Mac turned onto Third Street, Minneapolis's restaurant row. Eyeing the line of cars in front of Martini Two Olives, he backed into an open parking space with one effortless movement. Light snowflakes touched down on his windshield as he spotted a tall, cool blonde through the window of the packed restaurant.

She smiled warmly at him as he walked through the doorway. Mac gave her a kiss on the cheek, and above the din of celebratory restaurant patrons, he said, "Hello, Avery."

"Well, Mac Valentine, it's been way too long," she practically purred.

They took a table at the bar and ordered drinks. When a scotch neat was set before him, Mac asked, "How's Tim? You two still in love?"

Avery blushed and smiled simultaneously. "Blissfully. And planning on starting a family next year."

Mack leaned back in his chair and took a healthy swallow of scotch. "I'm a damn fine matchmaker. My best buddy and my firm's geeky ex-lawyer."

"Hey, watch it with the geek stuff. That was years ago. I'm a knockout now."

He grinned. "Yeah. You're all right."

She laughed. When her laughter eased, she grew

serious, her pale blue eyes heavy with sincerity. "You are a great friend, and you did a good thing. We owe you."

"Yeah, well, I never thought I'd have to collect on that debt, but times are a little…unsure."

"Tim mentioned something…"

"He always sucked at discretion."

"What do you need? Anything at all."

"Do you still represent the DeBolds?"

She nodded. "My favorite clients."

"I've heard they're shopping for a new financial firm, and I'd like to show them what I have to offer."

Her fingernails clicked on her glass. "They might've heard the rumors, Mac…. And you know how they are about family, or lack of. They don't want to deal with—"

"I know, I know. That's why I'm planning to be everything they're looking for and more."

She looked unconvinced. "Five-star restaurants and over-the-top gestures won't impress them. If you really want them to take the firm seriously, you'd need to do something—"

He put a hand up to stop her. "Let me tell you what I have in mind, then you can decide to set it up or not."

"All right," she said and lifted the glass of red wine to her lips.

Given the kind of man he was, Olivia had expected Mac Valentine to live in a sleek, modern type of home made of glass or stainless steel or something impervious to warmth. So it came as somewhat of a shock to find that the address he'd given her belonged to a stately, though charming, mansion on historic Lake of the Isles Parkway.

After parking in the snow-dusted driveway, Olivia darted up the stone steps and rang the bell, noting with a smile the lovely way winter's ravaged vines and ivy grew up one side of the house in a charming zigzag pattern. The wintry November breeze off the lake shocked her with a sudden gust, and she was thankful when the door opened. A tall, thin man in his late sixties ushered Olivia inside. He explained that he was the handyman, then told her Mac would be down in a minute. Then the man disappeared down a long hallway.

Olivia stood in the spacious entryway of Mac's home, staring at a beautiful, rustic banister and staircase, and wondering why it felt only slightly warmer inside the house than out.

"Good morning."

Coming down the stairs like Rhett Butler in reverse was Mac Valentine. He was dressed simply in jeans and a white shirt, the sleeves rolled up to reveal strong forearms. Awareness stirred in her belly. She liked forearms, liked the way the cords of muscle bunched when a man gripped something, or someone.

"Find the place all right?" he asked when he reached her.

"Perfectly," she said, noticing that not only did he look good, but he smelled good, too. As if he'd showered in a snowy, pine forest or something. Realizing her thoughts had taken an idiotic turn, she flipped on her professional switch and said, "Shall we get started?"

His eyes lit with amusement, but he nodded. "Come with me."

As Olivia followed him through the house, she noticed that each room she passed was more warm and inviting than the next, with wood paneling, hewn beams and rustic paint colors on the walls. But there was a glaring problem that Mac didn't mention as they walked—every room, from bathroom to living room to the fabulous gourmet kitchen, was bare as bones. There were no furnishings, no artwork, no tchotchkes—no nothing. It was the oddest thing she'd ever seen. It was as though he'd just moved in.

"I'm sensing a theme here," Olivia said with a laugh as they stopped in the kitchen. "You, Mr. Valentine, are a minimalist of the first order."

"Not totally." He gestured to a massive stainless steel contraption on the counter. "I have an espresso machine."

Two perfect cups of steaming cappuccino sat on the counter beside it. Olivia took one and handed the other to him. "And that's a good thing, but it barely strikes the surface of a family home." Her hands curled around the hot cup, feeling warm for the first time since she left the car. "I have my work cut out for me. What's up with all this?"

He shrugged. "I never got around to buying furniture."

It was more than that, she thought, studying him. It had to be. He hadn't put his stamp on anything. Maybe he hated permanence or didn't trust it. Whatever it was, it would be her first order of business. "How long has it sat empty like this?"

"I bought the place three years ago."

She nearly choked on her cappuccino. "That's just wrong. Where do you sleep? Or more importantly what do you sleep on?"

"I have a bed," he said, leaning against the counter-top. "Would you like to see it?"

"Absolutely. It's my job to make sure it has that stamp of family charm on it."

"What do you think is stamped on it now?"

"Debauchery?" she said quickly.

He grinned. "There's one more room down here, and in this one, I did put down a few roots. Two, to be exact."

Curious, Olivia followed him down a short hallway and through a heavy wood door. She stopped when she saw it and just stared. The room was, in a word, fantastic. Olivia walked in and stood in the middle, thinking she could hear music playing. One wall was made entirely of glass and she felt instantly at one with the white wonderland outside. Snow fell in big globs off the many tree branches and landed in pretty little tufts below. Birds hopped in the snow, making three-pronged tracks, and squirrels passed nuts back and forth. Inside, to her right were a pair of comfortable-looking navy-blue leather arm chairs that sat before a massive stone fireplace. Mac sat in one of the chairs and motioned for her to do the same.

"So once in a while you force yourself to relax?" she asked, as the heat from the blazing fire seeped into her bones and called upon her to relax.

"A man needs a refuge."

"Well, this is great."

He glanced over at her. "Do you think you can do something with this house?"

"I believe so."

"Good." He dug into the pocket of his jeans, pulled out a card and handed it to her. "Get everything. From sheets to picture frames. I don't care what you spend just make it warm and family friendly."

She stared at the platinum card. "You want me to furnish the whole house?"

He nodded.

"Every square inch?"

"Yes."

"Don't you want your stamp on it at all? Choices in artwork? Television?"

"No."

"I don't understand. Don't you want to feel comfortable here?"

"I don't like feeling comfortable—too much can happen to a person when they get comfortable."

"I'll try and remember that," she muttered.

His voice grew tight and cold. "All I want is the DeBolds, signed and happy."

Olivia was tempted to ask him just where he'd gotten such a desperate need to win, but it wasn't her place to care. He looked so serious, so raw, so sexy as he stared into the fire. Just his presence made the muscles in her belly knot with tension, and she knew that no matter what she told her father, after today, the truth was she was attracted to Mac Valentine. Not that she was going to do anything about it, or allow him to use her in any way, but the attraction was undeniably there.

"I'll do my best to set the stage, sir," she said with just a hint of humor.

He looked over at her then, his eyes nearly black in their intensity. "I hope so."

Her gaze dropped to his mouth. It was a lush, cynical mouth and for a moment she wondered what it would feel like against hers. She turned away. "You need to understand something," she said as much to herself as to him.

"What's that?"

"I know you didn't hire me because I'm a dynamite cook."

He snorted. "That's a little self-deprecating."

"No, it's the truth."

He didn't reply.

"You're looking for revenge. I'm not entirely sure how you're going to go about making me pay for something you believe my father did, but be forewarned..."

"Okay."

She forced herself to look at him. "I'm not going to fall under your spell."

"No?"

She shook her head. "Instead, I'm going to watch you."

"Watching me...I like that."

"And if you get out of line, I'm going to shove you right back in."

"Olivia?" He raised an eyebrow.

"What?"

"What if *you* get out of line?"

The question stopped her…from thinking and from a quick reaction. Mac saw her hesitate, too, and his dark eyes burned with pleasure.

"I think social hour has come to an end," she said tightly, standing. "I have a lot to accomplish in a short amount of time, so let's get to work. Show me the bedrooms."

"All of the bedrooms?" he said with a devious smile.

"Yes."

He stood, shot her a wicked grin and said, "Follow me."

Five

"So?"

"How was your meeting with Valentine?"

Olivia hadn't been back in the office more than five minutes and Tess and Mary were already standing in the doorway to the kitchen, their eyes wide with curiosity.

"Fine," Olivia said from atop a stepladder. She was searching through an upper cabinet, going through brands of cookware. She wanted to buy just the right one for Mac's kitchen. "I'm checking out a few things, then I'll be gone for the rest of the day."

They walked over and stood beside the counter. Tess asked, "What are you up to?"

"I have to furnish his house. The place is practically empty."

"The whole house?" Mary said, fingering the stainless fry pan that Olivia had set on the counter.

"Why do you sound so surprised? We've done similar jobs before."

"True."

Olivia could practically hear Mary's brain working. She glanced down. "What?"

"Are you furnishing his bedroom, too?"

"Oh, for goodness' sake. You have too many hormones running around in there."

Laughing, Tess grabbed a mug from the dish drainer and poured herself a cup of coffee. "We're just worried about you, that's all. If everything you said about this guy is true, he's up to more than just having you refurnish his house to bag a big client."

"Of course he is. I told you both that."

Mary put the pan down, grabbed Tess's cup and took a sip of her coffee. "What if he's having you design the bedroom he's going to try and seduce you in?"

"What? You're both acting nuts. He may be trying to use me, but he's incredibly clever and creative and interesting in his thinking. Whatever he's planning has got to be far more elaborate than—" She stopped at the worried looks on her partners' faces. "What?"

"You like him," said Mary.

"Oh, come on."

Tess nodded slowly. "You think he's 'clever' and 'creative,' and you probably think he's hot, too."

Olivia laughed and stepped down from the ladder. "Of course he's hot. Anyone with eyes could see the guy is hot."

"Oh, dear," Mary began, one hand to her belly as if she were protecting the baby from hearing anything too scandalous.

"Not good," Tess agreed. "I think I should take over the job."

"Will you two chill out?" Olivia grabbed a pen from her drawer and began writing down the names of several pieces of cookware. "Mac Valentine may be great-looking and charming and all the other things I said, but I'm not an idiot. He is also an arrogant womanizer with no furniture and no moral compass."

Tess nodded. "Yeah, that's pretty much what that article I read last week said. But somehow they made it sound like it was a good thing."

"What? What article?"

"Tess, go get it," Mary commanded, then turned back to Olivia.

"Oh, you read it, too," Olivia said.

Mary shrugged. "I was going through all the old magazines for recycle and you know how once I see something I can't stop reading, blah, blah, blah…" Tess returned and handed the copy of *Minneapolis Magazine* to Olivia. Mary said, "It's from a few years ago. Page thirty-four."

Letting out an impatient breath, Olivia grabbed the magazine and quickly flipped through the pages until she found the right one. And she knew it was the right one—not by the page number on the bottom right-hand corner, but by the enormous photograph of Mac and another man sitting on a stainless steel desk, a killer view of downtown Minneapolis displayed out the windows behind them. The spread was called "Workaholic, yet Woman Friendly," and featured both men holding BlackBerries in one hand and gold bars in the other. The sight of Mac, looking both handsome and arrogant as hell, didn't bother Olivia at all. It was the picture of the other man who sat beside him that had her stomach turning over.

Tim Keavy.

Her heart pounded furiously against her chest and she broke out in a sweat. The one guy from high school who knew what she truly was, knew her most shameful secret. God, did this mean that Mac knew, too? Was he going to use it against her? Against her father?

Olivia brushed a hand over her face. So much for her calm professionalism around Mac Valentine. Damn him. She hadn't expected him to go this route. She'd expected a full-out seduction—not using her past against her.

She stared at Mac's dark, dangerous face. Was it possible that he didn't know, that this was just an odd coincidence? A nervous shiver went through her entire body. She was going to have to be extra vigilant now. Watch every move he made and be prepared for it.

For a moment she thought about quitting the job, but she didn't run away from difficult situations anymore. She was no coward. She rolled up the magazine, then grabbed her notes. "I've got to go."

"Just watch yourself, okay," said Mary.

"I will." And on her way out the door she tossed the magazine in the trash.

* * *

November snow in Minnesota was said to be only the warm-up act for what was coming in January, but as Mac pulled into his driveway, his tires spinning and begging for chains as thick flakes of snow pelted his windshield, he wondered if Christmas had already come and gone without his knowing.

He pulled into the dry haven of his garage and shut off the engine. For a moment, he just sat there. He'd left the homes of many women before, but never had he come home to one. Yes, Olivia was an employee so it should have made the situation feel less domestic, but it didn't. He found her too pretty, too passionate, too smart to be just an employee.

When he entered the house a few minutes later, he heard the clanging sound of pots and pans being put away, and walked the short distance to the kitchen. His body instantly betrayed him as he spotted Olivia bending down, stacking pan lids on a shelf inside the island. Her dark hair was pulled back in a girlish ponytail and her pale skin looked flushed from all the activity. She wore a red sweater that hugged her breasts and waist, and jeans that pulled deliciously against her firm, round bottom. Devilish thoughts went through his head…like how good it would feel to be there when she stood up, to wrap his arms around her waist, to feel her backside press against him, to slip his hands under that soft wool sweater and feel her skin, her bones and her nipples as they hardened.

She turned then, caught him staring at her and gave

him an expectant look. There was nothing new in it, she sported this look quite often, but today there was something more in her eyes, as though she seemed to be silently accusing him.

He dropped his briefcase and keys and walked into the room. She'd done wonders. The space was perfect, homey, yet surprisingly modern with its green, gray and stainless steel accents. She had actually created a family kitchen for him, based on his tastes. She was damn good at what she did, and he couldn't wait to experience the aspect of the job were she had the most skill: the cooking.

"Well, Ms. Winston," he said, trying to lighten the mood. "You're going to make some man a great wife."

But the joke was lost on her. Her brows drew together in an affronted frown. "That was an incredibly sexist remark."

"Was it?"

"Yes."

"Why? I was giving you a compliment. The room looks amazing."

"So, only a husband can appreciate it?" she said, holding an incredibly large frying pan in one hand. "This is my job because I love it, not because I chose something stereotypically female. Okay?"

"Sure." He eased the fry pan out of her hand and put it on the counter. "This is not a weapon."

She stood a foot away, looking altogether too attractive, even in her ire. "I don't need stainless steel to do harm, Valentine."

He nodded. "I believe you." He reached up and brushed a stray hair off of her cheek. Her skin was so soft it made him ache to keep touching her. "Tell you what, when I go out back later and chop firewood you can say that I'd make a fine husband."

Not even a hint of a smile. He had no idea what he might have done to make her so mad at him, but he knew he was in trouble.

"I doubt very much that you chop wood," she said, picking up a pot from the sink. "But even if you did it would take a lot more than watching you to make me think that you'd be a good husband."

"Why are you so angry with me?" he said finally. "I could sense it the moment I walked in. You look damn pretty, but clearly pissed off."

"I'm not angry!" she shouted, snatching a dishtowel off the counter.

"What is it? Have a conversation with your father today?"

"Listen, buddy," she said sourly. "I don't need to talk to my father to get fired up about you."

"Fired up?" he repeated, amused.

"That's right." She put the pot on the stove top. "I am fully capable of forming my own opinions about you."

He stepped forward, making her step back, her hips pressing against the granite island. "And what have you come up with?"

"That you're a man who likes women—"

He chuckled. "Damn right."

"You didn't let me finish." Her voice was low, as intense

as her gaze. "So much so that you can barely remember their names five minutes out of the relationship."

"I don't have relationships, Olivia." He wondered if kissing her right now was a bad idea or a brilliant one. But she never gave him the chance.

"Are you proud of the way you're seen by other people?" she said. "Someone who jumps out of one bed only to charm his way into another?"

"That's the question of a woman who is in desperate need of a man in her bed."

She stared at him, her cheeks red and her dark eyes filled with irritation, then she dropped her dishtowel and walked out of the kitchen. "It's getting late."

"I'll walk you out," he said, following her to the front door.

"Don't bother." She grabbed her coat and hat and gloves and purse and opened the door. "I'll be back first thing in the morning."

Then Mac saw the snow and remembered his drive home. "Wait. It's really coming down out there."

"Good night, Mr. Valentine."

"The roads are pretty bad."

She stepped out the door and went down the path, calling back, "I'm a Minnesota native, Mr. Valentine. I've driven in worse than this."

"Damn it to hell!"

Olivia glanced over her shoulder and winced when she saw that she'd backed over Mac's mailbox. There it was, stretched out in the snow, a sad, black pole with a missing head. What a fool she was thinking that just because she had four-wheel drive and an SUV she could avoid the realities of Mother Nature. She'd just wanted to get away from that man, out of his house and the questions about how others saw him, how he had jumped from one bed to the next and all of that crap that she'd tossed at him—questions she was really asking herself.

She put her car in gear and stepped on the gas. A sad whirring sound was followed by rotating tires.

"Damn snow."

She slammed the car back into Park. This job had gone from a leap of curiosity to just plain complicated. Never had she acted so unprofessionally, and even though Mac's motives for hiring her were questionable at best, her job was to execute without getting personal, without allowing her fears to drive her actions. Well, from this point on she was going to make sure that happened.

She cranked up the heat, then reached for her cell phone and dialed information. But before the automated operator picked up, there was a knock on her window. Startled, she turned to see Mac, in just his jeans and shirt, and she pressed the button for the window.

"What are you doing?" he asked.

"I've killed your mailbox, I'm stuck in the snow and now I'm calling a cab."

He cursed, the word coming out in a puff of breath. "You'd do better to call a tow truck. No cab's coming out in this. I could brave it and try to get you home, but I don't think that'd be very smart."

"No, it wouldn't," she agreed. "You should go back

inside." She rolled up the window, then reached for her cell phone and dialed the operator once more.

Mac knocked on the glass, hard this time. Again, she rolled down her window. "What?"

"You're going to freeze."

"Only if you keep making me roll down the window. Now, go in. You're the one who's going to freeze in that getup, and I refuse to be responsible for your getting pneumonia or hypothermia or something."

"You're acting like a child. Come inside."

"I'm not acting any way. I'm being sensible. It's not a good idea for me to go back in there tonight. Things got too heated earlier."

"True, but I think we could use a little more heat in that house."

"It's too cold for jokes." She sighed. She just wanted to get home, into the tub and have a hot soak, maybe watch a few reruns of *Sex and the City*.

But that wasn't going to happen.

"It's your choice," he said, his teeth chattering now. "Nice warm fire or freeze in the car."

She heaved a sigh. "Fine. I'll come inside…but I'm going to call for a tow truck."

He helped her out of the car, and she followed him through the drifts of snow to the walkway, then up to the front door.

"If the tow truck can't get to you tonight," Mac said as he opened the door, "you are welcome to stay in my room."

She stopped inside the entryway. She wanted to scowl at him, but instead she laughed. "Are you insane?"

"Actually I thought I was being pretty gentlemanly." He turned back and grinned. "And that's a rare thing for me."

"Can I use your phone? My cell doesn't work very well in here."

"Sure." He took her coat and hung it up, then covered her hands with his and slipped off her gloves. A shot of awareness moved through Olivia, from the hair on her scalp to the backs of her knees, and she looked up to find him watching her, his dark eyes intense. He took off her gloves so slowly it made her belly knot with tension, and when her fingers were finally released from the warm leather, he took her hands and squeezed them into his cold palms.

"You're freezing," she said.

"And you're warm." His fingers laced with hers, and her muscles tensed. "I don't think I'm going to let go."

Sadly, she didn't want him to, but she wasn't about to give in to herself or to him. He was using her, and she'd allowed herself to be used too often in the past.

Olivia pulled her hands away. "I'm going to make that call now."

"You're not getting your car out tonight, Liv," Mac said evenly. "Now I'm going to be bunking in one of the leather chairs by the fire since all the rest of the bedrooms haven't been furnished yet, so if you do stay, take my bed—or don't take it. Either way, I won't bother you."

She didn't know if she believed him, but what could she do? She needed the shelter for tonight. "Thank you."

He nodded. "Good night." Then he walked in the direction of the den.

Six

The guy at the first tow truck company hung up on her, the guy at the second tow truck company actually laughed when she'd asked if he could come out and excavate her car, and her third call had gone straight to a machine.

Olivia had known it would be somewhat of a long shot to get home tonight, but after the way her body had reacted to Mac's touch earlier—a very simple, not that overtly sexual a touch—she was really hoping.

She sat on the edge of Mac's king-sized bed, her shoulders drooping forward. She was tired and cold, and disappointed in herself for caving in and taking his room. A better woman might have stuck to her guns about not bunking in Mac's sparse, octagon-shaped room, maybe grabbing a few extralong towels from his bathroom and cuddling up on the carpeted floor of one of the empty guest rooms. But she was a wimp that way. She liked her creature comforts. She'd always wondered about people who liked camping. Strange noises and bugs for bunkmates…what was the attraction? Anyway, she was sleeping in Mac's bed tonight. She just hoped he'd keep his word and wouldn't venture out of the den to find her.

She pulled the comforter off the bed and wrapped it around herself. Then again, why would he leave such a lovely, warm spot by the fire? Olivia blew out a puff of air to see if she could see her breath. It was cold as hell in Mac's house, a ridiculous kind of cold that sank deep into your bones and could only be relieved by a hot bath. She didn't know what that handyman did around here, but first thing tomorrow, she was calling in a professional heating technician. Forget all the warm, family friendly furnishings. If the house felt like an igloo, the DeBolds were going to head straight for the nearest five-star hotel.

Olivia thought about lying down and trying to sleep, but when nature called, she threw off the comforter and dashed into the master bathroom. And there she saw it— surrounded by beautiful pale brown tumbled stone was a massive box of glass with a rain showerhead above and four body sprayers along one wall. Oh, she wanted to cry it looked so inviting.

Did she dare? Maybe just a quick one? Just to get warm.

Feeling a sudden burst of happiness at the thought, she flipped on the water and turned the temperature knob to the equivalent of "hotter-than-hell." After closing the door to keep all the beautiful heat contained, she got undressed. She was just about to step inside the shower when she heard a knock on the bedroom door.

Her heart dropped into her stomach. No, no, no. Not now. Why was he here? Did he have radar or a sixth sense that told him when there was a naked woman in his room or something?

She snatched a huge white bath sheet and wrapped herself in it, then she opened the door and walked out into the frigid air.

He was knocking again. "Olivia?"

She opened the door just wide enough to accommodate her head, but hid the rest of her from his view. "Yes?"

"So you took the room?"

"Yes. I took the room. Can we not make a big deal out of it?"

"Of course." He grinned. "Are you okay?"

"Fine. Just tired." *And cold.* "What's up?"

He didn't look convinced. In fact, he was trying to assess the situation as he spoke. "I put a frozen pizza in the oven if you're interested."

She shook her head. "Thanks, but I'm not very hungry. Just tired. Very, very tired."

"All right. Good night, then." Olivia thought that he was about to leave, that she was about to finally get warm, but then he paused and cocked his head to one side. "What's that?"

"What's what?" she asked innocently, as if she didn't know.

"Is that water running?"

"No."

His mouth twitched. "Are you taking a shower?"

"Not at this precise moment," she said with irritation, which caused him to grin, full-on and slightly roguishly.

"Taking advantage of my steam shower, are you?"

She rolled her eyes. "Oh, for God's sake."

"Hey, I don't blame you, the thing is awesome."

"Well, good…then I'm going to go—"

"Have all the towels you need?" he asked.

"Yes."

She looked expectantly at him. Time to leave, Mr. Valentine. What more was there to say? After all, he'd humiliated and humbled her, what could be left? But he didn't leave, he just stood there looking sexy in his black sweater and pants.

Olivia let out a frustrated breath. "I'm freezing, okay? I need a way to warm up."

His grin widened, his gaze dropped. "No, too easy."

"Good night, Mac," she said through gritted teeth. "Enjoy your pizza."

He chuckled and pushed away from the door frame. "All right. Enjoy your shower. But," he said as he turned to walk away, "if you find that you can't sleep or you get hungry, you know where to find me."

"That, I can promise you," she called after him, "will never happen."

Mac put another log on the fire, then rescued his bottle of beer from the rutted mantel before dropping back into his chair. The book he was reading was pretty dull, but he was halfway through it and he wasn't a quitter. Just as he was about to find out why early man and an anthropoid ape had almost the same number of cranial bones and teeth, he heard footsteps behind him.

"You suck, Valentine."

Mac chuckled and turned around. "Now why would you say something like—" The words died on his lips as he caught sight of her, practically glowing in the firelight. From the moment he'd seen Olivia Winston, serving up brownies and attitude in her office kitchen, he'd found her incredibly attractive. Tonight, however, she was breath-stealing.

Her white blouse was untucked and rumpled, and re-sembled a man's shirt with the cuffs falling loose about her hands. Her long, black pants seemed a little too big without the heels and belt, but it was her face and hair that had his pulse running a race at the base of his throat. With no makeup, she looked fresh, delectably soft, her flawless skin glowing a pale peachy color. Her long, damp, dark hair swung sexy and loose, and reminded him of a mermaid. It took every ounce of control he had not to take her in his arms and kiss her until she realized just how perfectly their bodies would fit together.

She walked over and dropped into the chair beside him. "My hot shower wasn't so hot."

"No?"

She tossed him a look of mock reproof. "And it's all your fault."

"I did inadvertently ask if you wanted me to join you," he reminded her, taking a swallow of his beer.

"That's not what I mean."

"No?"

"You made me stand at the door talking to you so long the hot water was almost gone by the time I got in there."

"I'm sorry," he said sincerely. "Let me make it up to you with a never-ending fire and a cold slice of pepperoni."

She looked unconvinced at first, then she shrugged. "Okay." She took a piece of pizza from him and practically attacked it. "Oh, the fire feels so good. Your room is freezing, Valentine. This house is freezing."

"It can get a little cold, I guess."

"You sound like you don't mind turning into an ice cube every time the sun goes down."

"I hardly notice. I'm really only here to sleep."

"Well, first thing tomorrow I'm calling a heating technician. The DeBolds may sell ice, but they don't want to sleep in it."

He grinned at her. "That was funny, Liv…clever."

She shrugged. "I have my moments," she said, reaching for a second slice of pizza.

Mac grabbed another bottle of beer from beside his chair, opened it and tipped it her way. "Something to drink?"

"Sure, why not?" She took the cold bottle from him. "Thanks."

"You bet."

"Sitting in a freezing house in front of a fire eating

cold pizza and even colder beer—this night couldn't get any stranger, could it?"

He sipped his beer, then said, "How about if I tell you that when I was around nine or ten I thought—well, I'd hoped—I'd grow up to be a comedian."

She turned to stare at him. "That would be stranger."

"Hard to believe, I know. I'd put on one of my foster father's suits and tell incredibly awful jokes to these three crazy dogs they had. I was really into toilet humor at nine."

"You grew up in a foster home?" Her tone had changed from cute sarcasm to barely disguised pity in a matter of seconds.

He hated that, and rarely told anyone about his less-than-ideal beginnings to avoid hearing just such a reaction. He didn't know why he'd just blurted it out to her. Inadvertently, yes, but still… Maybe he needed to ease up on the beer. "I lived in a few foster homes. No big deal."

"What happened to your parents?"

"My mother died when I was two, and my father was never really in the picture."

She bit her lip. "That's tough."

He shrugged. "It wasn't that bad."

"Was the foster father you borrowed the suit from a good guy at least?"

"He wasn't awful. Although he did come home early one night to see me knocking around in that suit and he was pretty pissed off."

"What did he do?"

"Went for the belt."

Olivia's mouth dropped open. "What a bastard. What a cowardly piece of trash. If I had been there I would've kicked his—"

Mac's dark laughter cut her off. "It was no big deal. It happened." Even though he said the words with cool casualness, he appreciated her passion and protective nature. "You know, twenty-five years ago, there wasn't this push for fathers to be loving and gentle. 'Hands-on' had a different meaning." He took a healthy swallow of beer. "Every kid got boxed by their dad, foster or not, once or twice while they were growing up."

She sat forward in her seat, and looked at him with a strange mixture of sadness and care in her eyes. "No, they didn't."

Sure, he'd had a few beers, but he understood exactly what she was saying, and who she was saying it about. His jaw twitched. Owen Winston may have disciplined with words, but he was certainly no saint. "Well, I learned my lesson," he said tightly. "I never touched his suits again."

They were both quiet for a while after that, both drinking their beer and staring into the fire. Mac's ire subsided, and he was close to sleep when he heard her say his name.

He turned his head. "Yeah?"

"What happened to the career in comedy?"

He chuckled. "Ended shortly thereafter."

She smiled. "Bummer." Her cheeks were flushed from the heat of the fire and she looked really beautiful.

"Or a blessing—depending on how you look at it."

Yawning, Olivia curled deeper into the chair. "Well, feel free to try out any new material you've got on me."

His body stirred with her words, but he said nothing. He wasn't going to push things. Whether she wanted to admit it to herself or not, she was growing interested in him, attracted to him, and someday soon he would have her in his bed. It wouldn't make nearly the impact if he took what she wasn't ready to give. Owen Winston needed to know that his sweet, innocent little girl had come to Mac all on her own.

Mac heard her breathing grow slow and even, and after a few minutes, he closed his eyes and allowed himself to sleep, too.

Olivia woke up in a daze. In front of her the dying fire crackled softly. For a moment, she thought it was morning, but with a quick glance to the windows to her left she saw that the inky blackness of night had yet to turn to the steely gray of dawn.

"Hey."

She looked over at Mac, who was sitting forward in his chair, his dark eyes seductive and hungry under heavy lids. "What time is it?"

"Around three."

She blinked a few times, feeling foggy. "I should go back to bed."

"But it's cold in there."

"Yeah." But she didn't move. She just stared at him.

Mac got out of the chair and went to her, sat on his

heels in front of her. The hot flicker in his gaze made every bit of Olivia's tired limbs feel on edge and alive.

He reached up to touch her face. She grabbed his wrist, that hard, thick, oh-so-masculine wrist, and he stopped and stared at her. Her heart thudded in her chest as he leaned in, his gaze hungry, his mouth so close. Looking back on that night, Olivia had wanted to blame the foggy tiredness in her brain or the cold and snow for what she did next. But she knew exactly why she went temporarily nuts. All the frustration she felt at her attraction to Mac, and all the years of pushing aside her feelings of need and desire, just seemed to explode in her face at that moment.

Her hand snaked around his neck and she pulled him down for a kiss. And not a peck kiss, either, but a full-blown, lip-nuzzling, teeth-raking, breath-stealing kiss.

Seven

"Holy—" Mac didn't finish the end of the curse as he took her in his arms and dropped back onto the rug, taking her with him.

Poised above him, Olivia welcomed the crush of Mac's mouth and the heat of his body against hers. It had been so long, almost ten years since she'd been touched like this, felt a man's lips on her, his warm breath mingling with hers. The delicious hard angles and clean scent of his skin thrilled her, and she pushed away any thoughts of how wrong the situation might be.

She threaded her fingers in his hair and gripped his scalp as he changed the angle of his kiss. Soft, hot, drugging kisses. All she wanted was to get closer to him, feel a new kind of heat, forget who she was for a few minutes, forget what he was after.

In one easy movement, he flipped her onto her back. The warmth of the fire made her sweetly dizzy and she arched against him. Sensing her need, Mac explored further. His hand moved down, under her shirt, and she felt his palm on her belly. Little zaps of fear warred with the almost desperate urge she had to feel his fingers brush over the skin of her breasts, hear his breathing change when he cupped them and felt the weight of them, feel the lower half of him grow thick and hard as his thumb flicked back and forth over her nipple.

Mac dragged his hand up, over her ribs and along the side of her rib cage. She arched and tilted her body toward his hand, silently begging him to go there, put her out of her misery or show her exactly what misery felt like again as he gave in to her fantasy.

He was no fool, he knew what she was asking for and he delivered with the utmost care. As he applied teasing kisses to her lower lip, his hand drifted from her ribs to her breast, and slowly—so slowly—he began to roll the hard peak between his thumb and forefinger. Olivia shuddered, and released an anguished sigh. Oh, such sweet torture. She felt as though she had just been plunged into a deliciously hot bath, and God help her, she never wanted to step out of it.

But somewhere, deep in the back of her mind, she knew if she didn't, she was going to drown.

He left her mouth and dipped his face into her neck, kissing and suckling her rapid pulse as the speed of his fingers on her nipple quickened. Back and forth, faster and faster.

Her legs were shaking now, almost uncontrollably, and she knew if he didn't stop touching her, she was going to climax. Right then and there without him even going near the hot, wet place between her thighs. And she couldn't do that—not now, not for him.

She pushed at his chest and sat up, her breathing as labored as if she'd just outrun a hungry animal.

"Why are you stopping?" His voice was ragged.

"You know why," she uttered softly.

He raked a hand through his hair. "Damn it, Liv, there's nothing wrong with being together like this, taking what you need when you need it."

She looked down at him, her body warring with her mind. "From you, there is." He looked so sexy lying there in the light of the fire with his hair tousled and a light shadow of beard around his full mouth. "From a guy who's just using me—"

"You're using me, too," he uttered darkly. "Don't pretend you're not. I could feel every moment you've denied yourself in your touch, in your kiss, the way your hips pushed against mine. You're starving, Olivia, and you want to feed so badly you're still shaking with it."

"I'm cold."

"Bull. It's hot as hell in here right now."

His words startled her. She did want him, but she wasn't altogether sure why. Was it to use him? Was it to make up for lost time and to finally feel a release in her body and a release of the past? Or was it because she was actually starting to like him?

Her body still hummed from his touch, but she ignored it and said softly, "I'm going to go back to your room now. Alone."

"Is that really what you want?"

Of course it wasn't, but she needed to step back and gain some perspective here. "Yes."

"All right. But if you get cold—"

She stopped him right there and stood. "A little cold might be a good thing right now." And without another glance in his direction, she left the room.

Mac woke up to the sounds of a snowplow and his doorbell chiming. Looked as though the streets were clear and his furniture delivery had arrived. He pushed himself out of his chair and stretched, the kinks in his back protesting. As he walked to the front door he wondered if Olivia was still asleep in his bed or if she'd slipped out at dawn.

He raked a hand through his hair. What kind of trouble would he be in if, after he let the furniture guys in, he went to wake her up, started at her ankles and worked his way up? He grinned, the lower half of him tightening at the thought. She might kick him out of bed—but maybe not.

Mac was still very deeply ensconced in that fantasy when he opened the front door. But when he saw who was on the other side, all softness and desire vanished, and his fangs came out. "Hell, no. It's way too early for this."

Owen Winston looked ready to murder him. "Where's my daughter?"

"You have a helluva lot of nerve coming here."

"Where is my daughter?"

Mac leaned against the doorjamb and raised one eyebrow. "In my bed."

The older man's eyes bulged out like a tree frog's and he lunged at Mac.

Eight

Olivia walked down the hall, an aching stiffness in her bones that came from sleeping in a chair for most of the night. If she'd had the day to herself, she might grab a massage and a whirlpool bath at the local spa, but she had a full plate today and a good soak in her bathtub when she got home tonight was about the best she could hope for.

When she got to the stairs, she heard voices below in the hall. "Oh, that's my cab," she called to Mac. "The tow truck company said they should be pulling out my car later this afternoon, so you don't have to—" She stopped talking. The voices she heard were angry and threatening, and she recognized them at once. One belonged to Mac, and the other, she was pretty sure, belonged to her father.

She raced down the hallway, but when she got to the entryway, all she could do was stare. There was her father, his back against the wall, looking like he wanted to kill Mac with his bare hands. And Mac, who was standing in front of him, only inches away, looked just as menacing.

"What the hell are you two doing?" she demanded. When neither of them answered, she walked over and stood in front of them, her hands on her hips. "Mac," she said evenly, trying to bring some sense of calm to the situation, and to the two fire-breathing men before her. "Take a breath and back up."

His jaw flickered with tension, but he didn't look at her when he muttered hotly, "Yeah. Sure. As long as your father here doesn't jump on me again."

"What?" Olivia turned to her father. "Jump on you?" When Owen didn't look at her, she put a hand on his shoulder and said in a voice laced with warning, "Dad, what are you doing here?"

Owen's lips tightened as he turned to look at her. "We need to talk."

"You could've called me."

"I tried to call you, but you weren't at home."

"Let's go outside." Embarrassed at her father's behavior, and the overly parental way he was treating her at that moment, Olivia tried to smooth things over with Mac. She felt really awkward looking at him, especially after their encounter last night, but she forced herself to. "I'm sorry about this—"

Mac put a hand up. "Don't worry about it, just get him out—"

"Don't apologize to him, Olivia," Owen said with a sneer. "He's a monster, a conniving—"

Before Owen could hurtle any more insults Mac's way, Olivia took his hand and pulled him out the door, calling over her shoulder, "I'll be back at ten for the delivery. If you'll just put a key under the mat…"

Not expecting a response, Olivia led Owen down the walkway toward her waiting cab. She was furious, and could barely contain her anger. She understood her father's need to protect her, but this was way over the top.

As soon as she believed herself to be out of earshot, she faced him, her tone grave. "Dad, seriously, what are you doing? Coming here and attacking a man in his own home?"

"He's no man, he's a—"

"He could have called the police. Hell, he still could…and I have to say I wouldn't blame him. What were you thinking?"

Owen suddenly looked very weary as he reached out to touch her hair. "I was trying to protect you, honey, stop you from making a huge mistake." His eyes clouded with sadness. "But it looks like I'm too late for that."

"Too late for what? What mistake…?" Then she understood why her father had come. She heaved a sigh. It was the same old thing—her father's desperation, and constant fear that she was going to turn out like his older sister Grace. Her poor aunt Grace, who had been way too wild, made way too many mistakes and had been totally incapable of picking a decent guy. Poor Aunt Grace who, after staying out until dawn partying with some jerk from the local college, had been killed in a car accident on her way home. She'd just turned eighteen the week before, and Olivia's father had never gotten over losing her.

Olivia understood her father's fears and his need to protect her, but she wasn't sixteen anymore. This over-protectiveness needed to stop.

Standing beside the open door of the cab, Owen was shaking his head. "That monster stood there in his doorway and smiled when I asked him where you were."

Oh, great. "What did he tell you?" As if she needed to ask.

"That you were in his bed." Her father said the words as though he had acid on his tongue.

So Mac had baited her father. What a shocker. God, they were both acting like such juvenile idiots....

"Is it true then?" her father asked, his brown eyes incredibly sad.

"Dad, I'm not going to answer that."

The cab driver opened his window. "You going to be much longer, lady?"

Olivia shrugged. "I don't know—maybe."

The man rolled his eyes and closed his window.

"Olivia, please," her father continued. "You're such a good girl. Don't act irrationally—and with a man who only wants to use you to get back at me."

"I'm not acting irrationally, Dad. And I'm not a girl anymore."

"I know...."

"No, I don't think you do." She bit her lip and contemplated broaching the subject about his fears and what the hell had happened so long ago. But his eyes still spit fire and he looked way too closed. "Listen," she said gently, "you knew I was taking this job, and that it would mean working closely with Mac Valentine."

"Helping my enemy."

"I have a company to run, too."

Owen seemed to consider this, then he said in a slightly calculating tone, "Okay, so you're helping him do what exactly? Go after new clients?"

Olivia shook her head. "That's confidential."

Owen looked livid. "The man is a conniving bastard who wants to hurt you, and you're worried about…"

She put a hand on his shoulder. "How long have I been living on my own, supporting myself?"

"Since you were eighteen." He pointed at her. "But that was not my choice."

"Exactly. I'm a grown woman who makes her own choices, and as I've told you before—respectfully—I don't have to answer to you or to anyone."

Owen wilted slightly, but it wasn't the first time he'd heard her speak this way. After her mother had died, and after Owen had emotionally checked out, Olivia had made decisions for herself. Some of them had been downright stupid, even reckless, but the majority, she'd been proud of—like her business.

Her father's gaze grew soft as he looked at her. "What happened to my little girl?"

"I left her back in high school." Olivia leaned in and kissed him on the cheek. "I have a busy day, as I'm sure you do, too." She got into the backseat of the cab and gave him a little wave before her driver backed out and pulled away.

Mac stood in the living room, watching Olivia's cab take off down the street. The glass on every window in the house was pretty thin, and he'd heard their entire conversation. Looked like he had gotten it wrong; Olivia may not be that sweet, naive girl he assumed her to be. But where her father didn't want to deal with it, Mac burned to know every detail of the past she seemed to be hiding—especially after last night.

Grinning, he left the living room and went into his study. Embers burned in the fireplace, and as he sat in one of the leather armchairs, his body twitched with the memory of Olivia in his arms, on top of him, underneath him. The way she'd responded to his touch, the silent, hungry demands. She'd felt pleasure before, but she'd been denied it for way too long. There was no need to push her, he realized. The demands of her body had started to take over her good sense and Mac was going to be there, totally available when it happened again.

After all, her father thought him to be a womanizing bastard, and Mac was ready to prove him right.

All in all a very successful day, Olivia mused, walking from one beautifully furnished room to the next. She'd quite outdone herself, and in record time, too. Each room complemented the next in leather and iron, glass and walnut.

She stopped in the living room and marveled at the classic, comfortable feel of the space. Not to mention the warm air puffing from the vents in the baseboards. She'd finally found a guy to come out in the snow and turn on the heat. A vast improvement in and of itself.

Though she'd purchased all the linens for the upstairs, the bedroom furniture wouldn't be arriving until early tomorrow morning. But they were close— well on their way to creating a very modern, very homey, very Mac-like environment.

"Ms. Winston?"

Olivia returned to the living room where Dennis Thompson, a local art gallery owner who looked rather like a short version of Ichabod Crane, was hanging several paintings she'd purchased for Mac's house.

"What do you think?" he asked, holding up two Josef Albers pieces, both in several shades of yellow. "On top of one another?"

She sat on the new distressed, brown leather couch to get a better view. "Hmm...I don't know. How about—"

"Side by side?" came Mac's voice behind her.

Dennis Thompson looked behind Olivia and beamed at Mac. "Perfect. I'll just go get my tools from the car."

Olivia turned, surprised. "You're home early, Mr. Valentine. Are you here to supervise?"

He was dressed in a tailored black suit and crisp white shirt, his tie loosened from his neck. "I came home for a late lunch or an early dinner."

"Oh, really?" she said with a grin. "I haven't stocked

the fridge yet and you ate the only frozen pizza, so what were you planning on having? The cocktail onions or that last, lonely bottle of Corona?"

He walked around the couch and sat beside her. "You're a pretty good chef, aren't you?"

"I like to think so." He smelled so good. She tried not to breathe through her nose.

"Well, then, can't you make something amazing out of onions and beer?"

"No," said Olivia succinctly, lifting an eyebrow. "Can I ask you something?"

"Shoot."

"When do you normally leave the office to come home?"

His lips twitched. "Oh, I don't know…"

"Approximately."

"Seven, eight…nine, ten."

She looked at her watch. "It's four-thirty—why are you here?" Her heart began to pound in her chest as she wondered for a moment if he was there to see her. After what happened that morning with her father, she wouldn't blame him. She just hoped he wouldn't spread the story around town. "Are you going to fire me?"

"No." He laughed. "That's over and done with." His voice turned serious. "As long as it doesn't happen again. I can't have your father showing up when the DeBolds arrive."

"It will not happen again," she assured him. "You have my word."

Satisfied with that answer, Mac leaned back and

crossed his arms over his chest. "I'm not exactly sure why I'm here. But I think the reason might be embarrassing."

"For you or me?"

"Me. Definitely me."

"Oh, well, then share, please."

He glanced around the room. "It's really warm in here."

"I know. I had the tech come this morning and it took him hours just to—"

"No, I mean what you've created here from the furniture to the artwork to all those little things on the tables and in the bathroom and on the mantels. It's all warm. I never thought I'd be comfortable with warm.…" He looked at her, surprise in his gaze. "As you start to make my house into a livable, family-friendly place I sort of want to be here to see it…and you."

Her muscles tensed at his words and she could almost feel the pressure of his lips on her mouth once again. Her reaction to him, her attraction to him, wasn't going away, she knew that. But she hoped that maybe the two of them could forget what happened last night and go on about their business.

When she found his gaze once again, Mac had that look in his eye, that roguish one that made her knees weak and her resolve disappear.

"Listen," she began, "about last night…"

"Yes?"

"I was half-asleep."

"Before or after you kissed me?" he asked huskily.

Right. Her brow creased with unease. "As clichéd as this is about to sound, it'll never happen again."

He grinned. "Are you sure?"

"Yes."

"We made sparks."

His words and the casual way he offered them made her laugh. "I won't argue with that. You're one helluva kisser, Valentine, but…" And on that note, she sobered. "You're also using me." She put a hand up as she saw him open his mouth to speak. "I know you think I'm using you, too, but I'm not. And last night, I didn't."

His grin evaporated. "Then why…"

She stared at him, wondered what he would say if she told him she was starting to like him—that even with the information she had about him and why he'd hired her to begin with, she believed he was good man. A damaged man—but, under that hard-ass exterior, a good one.

"Ms. Winston?"

Dennis Thompson had returned from his car and was standing in the doorway with his toolkit and another painting. "I'm sorry to interrupt, but before we can hang the rest of the pieces, we need you to tell us where you want them."

"I'll be right there," she told him before facing Mac again. "Now, we have guests arriving tomorrow after-noon, and I have to finish up here, then go home and plan a menu."

He nodded. "Have you decided to stay here?"

"Not yet."

"If you do, I won't bother you."

"I'm not worried about you starting anything." It was all she had to say. The flush on his neck and the stiffness in his jaw were obvious clues that he'd heard the slight emphasis on the word *you* and understood her meaning all too clearly.

She got up and was about to leave the room when Mac called her back. "Olivia?"

"Yes?"

"As far as the menu, I've invited another couple to join us tomorrow night, so there will be six instead of four."

"Okay. Anyone I know?"

He shook his head. "I don't think so. It's the DeBolds' attorney and her husband."

"Got it." She tossed him a casual, professional smile, then left the room.

Nine

If someone called Mac Valentine an arrogant jerk to his face, he usually agreed with them before kicking them out of his office. He was arrogant. But in his defense he believed he was the best at what he did and that unshakable confidence was the only way to stay at the top of his game. Today, at around three o'clock in the afternoon, he'd had that theory tested and proven correct by one of the clients who, just a few weeks ago, had been running scared after Owen Winston's foolish attempt to discredit him. After waiting for twenty minutes in the lobby, the client had sat before Mac and had practically begged him to take him back. Whether the man still believed that Mac had given preferential treatment and tips to his other clients or not, being at a competing firm had not proved lucrative and he wanted back in.

Mac pulled into his garage feeling on top of the world. When one client returned, he mused, the others would surely follow—they'd leave Owen Winston and other financial firms and come back to where they belonged.

He cut the engine and grabbed his briefcase and laptop. Today's success would by no means deter him from getting revenge on Winston. And in fact, he actually felt a stronger desire to follow through on his plans with Olivia. By the end of the weekend, he thought darkly as he stepped out of the car and headed into the house, he would have it all: Owen's little girl and a powerhouse of a new client to add to his roster.

The heavenly scent of meat and spices, onions and something sweet accosted his senses when he walked through the door. Home sweet home, he thought sarcastically, walking into the kitchen. But once there, he promptly forgot everything he'd just been thinking, plotting and reveling in. In fact, as he took in the sight before him, he realized he had little or no brain left. "You look…"

Olivia stood before the stove, stirring something with a wooden spoon. "Like a wife?"

He saw the lightness, the humor in her eyes, but couldn't find a laugh to save his soul. He cleared his throat, his gaze moving over her hungrily. "I was going to say, breath-stealing—but I suppose you could look wifely, as well."

She wore pink. He hated pink. He'd always hated

pink. It was for flowers or cotton candy. But Olivia Winston in pink was a whole different matter. The dress she wore was cut at the knee and cinched at the waist, and pushed her perfectly round breasts upward, just slightly—just enough so that she looked elegant, yet would also drive a man to drool. Her long dark hair was pulled up to the top of her head, causing her neck to look long and edible, and her dark eyes, still filled with humor, reminded him of warm clay beneath long, black lashes.

And she had wanted him to forget about the other night? Get serious. All Mac wanted was to pull her against him, ease the top of her dress down, fill his hands with her, play with one perfect pink nipple while he suckled the other. His groin tightened almost to the point of pain. He wondered, would she moan as he nuzzled her? Or would she cry out again, allow herself to climax this time?

"Well, thank you for the compliment," she said, gathering up several bottles of wine. "Would you mind setting those things down and giving me a hand?"

"Sure. What do you need?"

She nodded in the direction of the island. "Wineglasses. Can you grab them and follow me?"

He picked up the spotless glasses that were laid out on a towel on the island and followed her into the dining room.

"Well, what do you think?" she asked, setting the bottle down on an impressive black hutch.

This woman wasn't fooling around. She was damn good at what she did, and it showed in every detail.

She'd set the table with unusually modern-looking china, gleaming stemware and silver silk napkins. But the most impressive part was the centerpiece, which sat in the middle of a round walnut table. It looked as though she'd brought the outdoors inside with cut branches from his yard, white candles and small silver bells.

He set down the wineglasses and released a breath. "It's perfect."

"Good." She checked her watch. "Your guests will be here in thirty minutes. You'd better wash up and change your clothes."

"I have time."

She gave him an impatient look. "It would be rude, not to mention awkward, if you weren't here when the doorbell rings."

"Careful, or someone might think you're the woman of the house," Mac said with amusement, wondering how long it would take to kiss that pink gloss off her mouth.

Reaching for the dimmer switch on the wall, Olivia lowered the lights a touch. "For all intents and purposes this weekend, I am."

His gaze swept over her. "Did I tell you how much I like the color pink?"

"No, you didn't," she said primly, putting her arm through his and walking him toward the stairs. "But we really don't have time for that now. I have a dinner to get on the table, and I won't allow anything to burn."

He grinned. "Of course, can't have things getting too hot now, can we?"

She glared at him, raising one perfectly shaped eyebrow. "I think a shower would be good for you."

He nodded and said with sardonic amusement, "Yes, dear," then took the stairs two at a time. She was right. He needed a shower, a really cold shower. Hell, he thought, chuckling to himself, he might do better diving into one of those piles of snow burying his lawn.

Harold DeBold was one of those guys people just liked the minute they met him. Hovering somewhere around forty, he was very tall and thin, and had pale blond hair and wintery blue eyes. He reminded Olivia of a surfer, relaxed and free-spirited. His wife Louise, on the other hand, was dark-skinned, dark-eyed, completely city-sexy in her gorgeousness and totally high-strung. But she also seemed sincere, and when she was told that Olivia was going to be their chef for the weekend, instead of thinking it odd that the person Mac had hired to help him was not going to stay in the kitchen and/or serve, but was going to eat and socialize with them, she'd acted as though it were the most normal thing in the world—even adding that she was thrilled that Olivia was going to cook some down-home Minnesota fare for them.

"Honestly," the woman said to Olivia, curling her diamond-encrusted hand around her wineglass. "I feel like all I've eaten for days is foie gras, caviar and squid ink. I'm over it."

Chuckling, Harold told Mac, "We've been in New York for the past week."

They were waiting for the DeBolds' attorney and her husband to arrive as they sat in Mac's den, which had been completely transformed into a contemporary, masculine, but family-friendly retreat with his two existing leather chairs and several other pieces of dark blue chenille furniture curled around the fire. Cozy rugs dressed the hardwood floor, and lights had been installed outside to showcase the wintery-forest view from the floor-to-ceiling windows.

Mac reached over and topped off Louise's wine. "You two were in Manhattan for a week and you didn't get around to pasta?"

Louise snorted. "Unfortunately, no."

"Next time you go, let me know," Mac said seriously. "There's this tiny hole-in-the-wall in Little Italy that you've got to check out. The spiciest pasta puttanesca—not to mention the best-tasting parmesan cheese I've ever had."

"Cheese." Chuckling, Harold said with dramatic flair, "City folk think that all us backcountry Wisconsinites get to eat is cheese, so they refuse to take us anywhere that might serve it. Instead, they figure they've got to impress us with all those fancy, unpronounceable, unrecognizable *foods*." As he said the last word he mimed air quotes.

Olivia held out a tray of hors d'oeuvres. "Well, everything you're going to eat tonight is as easy to pronounce as it is to eat."

Louise sipped her wine and said, "Thank God."

Harold took one of Olivia's famous blue cheese

jalapeño poppers wrapped in bacon and practically sighed when he ate it. "Oh, my," he said to Olivia, his blue eyes so warm she couldn't help but wonder if he was flirting with her just a little bit. "If these are any indication of your culinary skill, then you might never get me to leave."

Louise agreed. "These tomato basil tarts are over the top."

Olivia smiled, pleased that her fun and flavorful finger food was such a hit. "Thank you."

"Are you self-taught, Olivia?" Louise asked.

"I actually went to culinary school, then I worked for several chefs in town before starting my business."

Harold's brows drew together. "And what kind of business is that exactly? Catering? Or are you a personal chef?"

Olivia looked over at Mac, who was sitting in a dark blue wing-back chair by the fire. He didn't appear concerned by the question, and even winked at her, so she was as honest as she needed to be. "Myself and two other women provide catering, decorating, party planning...those kinds of services to clients."

"And are your clients mostly clueless men or women?" Louise asked, her eyes dancing with humor until she realized she was including her host in that question. She offered him an apologetic smile. "Of course, I didn't mean you, Mac."

Mac laughed. "No apology necessary—I know where my skills lie and they're not in the kitchen."

"Mine, either, sadly," Louise said on a sigh.

"All it takes is a little practice," Olivia told Louise sympathetically.

Harold shook his head wistfully. "She has tried, Olivia."

"Hey, there." Louise gave him a playful swat on the arm.

The doorbell chimed over the laughter in the room, and Mac stood. "I'll get that. Must be Avery."

When Mac was gone, Harold turned to Olivia. "My lawyer and her husband are great people, and are usually very punctual."

Olivia smiled warmly. "We're in no rush tonight."

"I like that attitude," Louise said, snatching up another tomato tart. Male laughter erupted from the front hall, and Louise rolled her eyes. "Boys. We just found out that Mac went to college with Tim, fraternity buddies or something."

It was as if time slowed after Louise had said the name *Tim,* and Olivia couldn't seem to find her breath. Even the room spun slightly. "Tim?" she managed to say. "That's your attorney's husband?"

Louise may have answered her, but Olivia's ears were buzzing. It wasn't him. It couldn't be him.

"Sorry we're late," came a voice that Olivia recognized at once. She swallowed. What was in her throat? It felt like a rock. She wouldn't turn around—couldn't turn around. He was coming and she felt frozen to the couch.

"Avery couldn't decide on which shoes to wear," he said dryly.

"Don't you blame me, Tim Keavy, you know it was your fault." The woman sniffed and added, "The Vikings game was on."

"Typical." Mac chuckled. "Avery, Tim, I'd like to introduce our amazing chef for the evening."

No.… She didn't want to.

"Olivia?" Mac said.

She wasn't ready.…

"Olivia?" Mac said louder, sounding puzzled now.

Her heart slamming against her ribs in a noxious rhythm of fear and dread, Olivia turned around to see the one person in the world who knew her secret—the boy who, nine years ago, had walked in on an affair between a teacher and a student. A boy who had made a young Olivia Winston feel like trash from that day forward.

Ten

For a moment, Mac wondered if Olivia was having an anxiety attack. Her face was as pale as the snow outside the window, and her eyes looked watery, as though she desperately wanted to cry, but wouldn't allow herself to go there in front of guests.

What the hell was wrong with her? Had the DeBolds said something to upset her while he was gone? The quick, almost fierce anger that rose up inside of him surprised him, as did the protective impulse jumping in his blood.

Protecting Owen Winston's daughter was hardly the plan.

His gaze shifted, and he saw Tim staring at Olivia, his lip drawn up in a sneer. It was a look Tim usually reserved for people who didn't perform to his standards, from office staff to the guy who continued to put whipped cream on his espresso at the local coffee shop. Mac didn't get it.

He watched Tim walk toward her and stick out his hand. "Wow," he said coolly. "Olivia Winston. Small world."

"Microscopic." Olivia rose stiffly and clasped his hand for about half a second. "Hello, Tim."

"How do you two know each other?" Mac asked, though the tone of his voice sounded slightly demanding.

"We went to the same high school," Tim stated flatly.

"How funny," Louise remarked with a dry laugh, clearly not seeing the discomfort between the two. "You knew Olivia in high school and Mac in college?"

"That's right," Tim said.

Mac watched as Olivia seemed to get herself under control. With a smile affixed to her face, she walked over to Tim's wife and held out her hand, "Hi, I'm Olivia. Welcome."

"Avery Keavy. It's so nice to meet you." Avery had the good sense to leave the high school talk alone, and instead gestured to the coffee table and assorted hors d'oeuvres. "These look amazing. I'm sorry we're late."

Olivia picked up a tray and offered a stuffed mushroom to Avery. "It's no problem. Dinner's almost ready. In fact, I'm going to check on it right now. If you'll all excuse me…" After she placed the tray on the buffet, she excused herself and headed for the door.

"Need any help?" Mac called after her.

She turned then and glared at him. "No. I've got everything under control, Mr. Valentine."

Mac had never seen anyone look at him with such full-on revulsion, and he had no idea why. And her palely masked anger didn't end there. It continued all through dinner. Not that the DeBolds or the Keavys really picked up on it, they were way too focused on the food—which was perfection. But Mac saw every little glare she tossed his way as he served himself another helping of her mouthwatering brisket and smashed red potatoes, and wondered why the hell she was so upset at him. It couldn't be just because he was responsible for inviting Tim to the house. What was the big deal, so he knew her in high school?

Maybe he'd have to go to Tim for the information if Olivia wasn't going to speak to him. He looked over at Tim. The guy was just going with the flow. He didn't even look at Olivia.

"Pecan pie is one of my favorite desserts," Harold was saying to Olivia, his plate nearly empty.

Olivia gave him a warm smile. "I'm so glad. Would you like a second piece? How about you, Louise?"

"Absolutely." Louise held out her plate. "And I'm not even going to ask you to force me in to it."

Avery dabbed her mouth with her napkin. "Will you force me then, Olivia?"

"Of course," Olivia said, keeping her gaze fixed on Tim's wife. "I demand that you hold out your plate, Avery."

Avery gave her a small salute. "Yes, ma'am."

Avery and Louise broke out into laughter as they

passed around the fresh whipped cream to top their pie. Mac, however, was too distracted to find humor in the situation. When he should've been selling himself to the DeBolds, talking about how he could change their financial future, he was staring at Olivia, wondering what was wrong with her and how he could fix it. It pissed him off. Why did he care if she was angry with him?

After the brown-sugar coffee and pecan pie had been completely devoured, Avery thanked both Olivia and Mac for their hospitality and she and a very unsocial Tim took off. The DeBolds, feeling a little jet-lagged and extremely full, requested an early night, as well, and retired to their room.

The night had been a successful one—on the business front at any rate. The DeBolds seemed content and happy with Mac and with his home, and wasn't that the first step to having them as clients? With the DeBolds in bed, Mac had to deal with Olivia, who had fled to the kitchen as soon as both couples had gone.

When Mac entered the room, Olivia was camped out over the sink, washing dishes at a frenetic pace, taking out her anger on a serving platter.

"Great dinner," he said, walking over to her, leaning against the counter next to the sink.

"Yes," she said stiffly. "I think you've impressed them."

"I hope so."

"Yep. One step closer to getting the big fish on the hook."

He didn't respond to her sarcasm. "Do you need any help?"

"No."

He exhaled heavily. "Are you going to tell me why you're so angry with me?"

She continued to scrub the life out of a white platter, and Mac wondered if talking right now was a stupid idea. Maybe she just needed to cool off with her soap and hot water. But then she dropped the platter in the sink and turned to face him, anger and disappointment in her dark eyes.

"I knew you were out to punish my father and use me in the process," she said. "But I had no idea how far you'd go."

"What are you talking about?"

"Are you kidding me?"

"No."

"Tim Keavy," she snapped.

"What about him?"

She shook her head. "Don't do that."

"Do what?"

"Don't act like you're clueless. It doesn't suit you. You're a shark, be proud of it."

"You're nuts, lady." He gritted his teeth and pushed away from the counter. "All I know is you two went to the same high school."

"Right." She glared at him, her nostrils flaring. "So how does this go? You think by outing my sordid past to my dad, he'll back down on whatever he has on you? Apologize?" She shook her head, then walked past him out of the room, saying, "It'll never happen. My father's even more stubborn than I am."

He followed her. "Where are you going?"

"To my room."

"You're not leaving?"

"I'm going to give this job everything I have, get you the clients you want, then get the hell out. You'll have no ammunition if you're looking to ruin my business reputation along with my personal one."

"You're talking crazy," he said, following her up the stairs and down the hall to the guest room. She had chosen the one on the opposite side of the house than the DeBolds, and Mac was thankful he didn't have to whisper.

When she got to the door, she said, "Good night, Mac," then went inside.

When she tried to close the door behind her, he wouldn't let her. He held the door wide. "Listen, you can't just throw all that garbage in my face, then walk away."

She released her grip on the door, put her hands up in the air. "What do you want to say, Valentine? That you didn't know your best friend from college knew me?"

"Damn right," Mac said hotly, walking into the room and closing the door behind him.

"I don't believe you."

"I don't care if you believe me or not, it's true."

Standing just inches from him, she held her chin high as she stared hard into his eyes. "It's going to take a lot more to humiliate me and screw with my father than tossing my past mistakes, my past humiliations, back in my face."

He grabbed her shoulders. "I'm not doing that."

"Bull."

"I don't give a damn about your past."

"I do!" she shouted, her voice cracking with emotion. She dropped her gaze, bit her lip and cursed. When she looked up at him again, she looked like a kid, so vulnerable it killed him. "I hate that part of my life."

Tears sprang to her eyes.

"Stop that." He gave her a gentle shake, for the first time feeling the guilt that came with his plan. "Stop it, Olivia."

This wasn't how it was supposed go. He was the one who was supposed to make her miserable, then send her back to her father in shame. He should be reveling in the fact that he had access to information about her past that would make her father suffer.

"Damn it." He hauled her against him and kissed her hard on the mouth. "I don't care what happened before, and neither should you." He nuzzled her lips, then nipped at them, suckled them, until she gave in, gave up and sagged against him.

"There's nothing wrong with this," he said as his hands found her lower back and raked upward. "Or this." He dipped his head and kissed her throat, suckling the skin that covered her rapid pulse, grinning as a hungry whimper escaped her throat. "Nothing to be ashamed of, Olivia."

"You don't understand," she uttered, letting her head fall back.

He held her close, his lips brushing her temple. "Help me to, then."

"I…can't. I made a promise to myself…."

He rubbed his face against her hair. "When you were a kid?"

"Yes," she whispered.

"You're a woman now." He nuzzled her ear, nipped at the lobe. "Everything's different."

On those words, she froze. "That's the thing," she said, her voice hoarse. She drew back, her eyes filled with regret. "Nothing's different. Not at all. I refuse to make any more stupid mistakes with men who just want to…" She didn't finish, just shook her head.

"Olivia."

She disentangled herself from his grasp. "Two more days. That's it. That's all you're getting from me, so do your worst because after this weekend is up you're going to be done. Done with me and done with my father."

"We'll see about that," Mac said darkly before turning and leaving the room.

Eleven

And the winner of the worst night's sleep contest was…Olivia Winston.

Standing over the stove, she made sure her pan was hot, then carefully cracked an egg into the hole she'd made in the slice of crusty bread. Three cups of extra-strength coffee and all she wanted to do was go back to bed. But maybe that had nothing to do with being tired as much as it had to do with hiding. For someone who had gone into this job thinking it would be easy-peasy, she sure was going through a lot of difficult, trying moments. Not to mention, some sexually charged moments that she couldn't get out of her head. She'd really underestimated Mac and his desire to bury her father, and she'd overestimated herself, and her needs, in the process. She'd wanted to find out just how Mac was going to get back at her dad, and had basically given him the goods to make it happen.

She flipped the bread. To make matters worse, she wanted more—more of him, more of his touch, his kisses. She was weak and a total disappointment.

She felt him in the kitchen even before she saw him, and wanted to kick herself for the giddiness that erupted inside her at the thought of seeing him again.

"Good morning."

She spared him a quick smile. "Morning." He looked good, Saturday-morning sexy in expensive black sweats and dark tousled hair.

"Sleep well?" he asked, pouring himself a cup of coffee.

"No. You?"

He chuckled. "I slept okay."

"Yeah, guys can sleep through anything. Your brains turn off—so lucky."

"Maybe our brains turn off, but that's about it." Despite his hard, unyielding business-guy attitude, he had this obvious sensuality, this slow, tigerlike laziness that made him seem always ready for bed. "Honestly, the effects of what happened in your room last night are still with me this morning."

She ignored the pull in her belly. "Me, too—but maybe in a different way." She laid another slice of bread in the hot pan and cracked an egg. "Listen, Mac, I don't know if I believe what you said last night about Tim—if you set that up or not—but I can't worry about it anymore. I've spent too many years worrying about the past. Can we just let everything go and concentrate on what we're trying to accomplish with the DeBolds?"

"Let *everything* go?"

"Yes. Do you think you can do that?"

"Do you really think *you* can do that?" he countered, his eyes glittering with heat.

Before she could answer, Harold and Louise walked into the kitchen, all smiles and dressed like models from a Hanna Andersson catalog. "Morning," Harold said, taking a seat at the island.

"Morning," Mac said good-naturedly. "Sleep well?"

"Perfect," Harold said. "Something smells good, but that's not surprising."

Olivia glanced at Mac, who was watching her over his steaming cup of coffee, then she turned to her guests. "Eggs in a blanket, bacon and good, strong coffee."

"Are you trying to fatten us up?" Louise asked, sitting beside her husband.

"Of course," Olivia said on a chuckle, setting two cups of coffee before them. "But only so you have all the energy you need for what I have planned today."

"And what do you have planned?" Mac asked, seeming to suddenly realize he'd never discussed plans with her.

Olivia looked at them all brightly. "Ice skating."

Mac practically choked on his coffee. "Ice skating?"

Louise, on the other hand, looked as though she were about to explode with happiness. "Did you hear that, Harold?"

"I did. I did."

Clasping her hands together like a little girl, Louise cried, "I haven't been skating in ten years."

"Well, then maybe it's not such a good idea—" Mac began, but Louise cut him off.

"Not a good idea? No, no, no—it's perfect. Harold and I had our first date on a skating rink. Rounder's Pond—it was in back of my grandfather's property, a beautiful kidney bean shape and surrounded by trees. Do you remember that, honey?"

"Of course." Harold smiled at his wife, then looked over at Olivia. "You have made my wife very happy today. Thank you."

"My pleasure." Olivia beamed as she turned back to the stove. "Now, let's get you two fed."

Mac came to stand beside her.

She whispered over the DeBolds' loud chatter, "You look panicked."

"And you look happy about that," he muttered.

Laughing, she took two perfectly cooked eggs in blankets out of the pan and placed them gently on plates. She whispered, "Buck up, Valentine. Ice skating is perfect and fun, and I've planned a lovely picnic afterward with hot chocolate."

"I don't skate, Olivia."

"Well, you lucked out then." She handed him the two plates and smiled. "I'm a great teacher."

He'd been good at sports. Not the school kind. You had to spend more than a year living in one place to get on an organized team, but he'd killed at street basket-

ball and alley soccer in every community he'd been sent
to. He'd never tried hockey though, and before today had
assumed that hockey, or anything involving skates, was
a little like trying to understand German when all you
spoke was Spanish. But he'd jumped into it with both
blades. It took him about twenty minutes to really feel
his balance, but after that, he was like a demon racing
on the ice, even getting an impromptu hockey game
going with Harold and some of the guys on the lake.

After an hour, he retired himself and joined Olivia on
the bench. She was dressed all in white and looked very
pretty. She'd spent much of her time with Louise in the
center of the lake, teaching the woman how to execute
perfect little turns and spins and other girlish things
Mac didn't have a clue about—but he'd sure liked
watching her in between plays.

"Well," she began, her cheeks pink from the cold
and exercise, her eyes bright with humor. "You sure
took to that like a baby to a bath."

"You think so?"

"You had the moves, Valentine. I was very impressed."

Instead of throwing away her compliment with a
laugh, he felt an odd sensation in his gut as if he'd eaten
something past its expiration date. And he knew exactly
what that feeling was—he'd felt it once or twice in his
life and it worried him. He liked this woman.

He blew out a breath, turned to watch Harold and
Louise as they skated casually around the lake. He had
to get rid of this feeling, stop himself right here, right
now, before he did something stupid like abandon his

plans to make her father pay. He had one more night—tonight—to get her in his bed, then they were done.

"And I'm impressed," he said in a voice he normally reserved for his employees, "with your skills off the ice."

"What do you mean?" she asked, looking confused.

"You did well." Mac gestured toward the DeBolds, who were laughing and holding hands as they weaved in and out of the other couples in the "slow lane." "They look happy."

"They do," she agreed.

"Funny that you picked the very thing they did on their first date."

"Not funny at all."

He stared at her. "You knew?"

She smiled.

"How—"

"Romance breeds comfort, comfort breeds trust," she explained, taking out a thermos of hot chocolate and pouring them both a cup. "And that's what you're looking for, right? Trust in you and your skill?"

He shook his head. This woman was unbelievable. He'd had no idea how far she'd go to help him. Honestly, he hadn't expected much with her knowledge of what his true motivations were, but she'd really come through for him. Too bad he couldn't offer her a position in his company. He asked her, "How could you find out something like that? Even if you researched them, something so personal…"

She laughed as she handed him the steaming cup of

chocolate. "You really didn't know who you were hiring, did you? Silly man."

"Maybe not—but I see it now. I see you."

"Yeah? What do you see?" she asked, sipping her chocolate.

"You're a damn good wife."

"Thank you."

"And if I wasn't completely against legal unions, I might be compelled to make you marry me."

She laughed again, clearly thinking that every word he'd just uttered was a nonsensical joke. Mac wasn't so sure.

"That's very flattering, Mac, but you know I'd have to turn you down."

"Really?"

"Yep." She looked away, sipped her chocolate.

"You want me to ask why, don't you?"

"Nope."

"Fine," he grumbled. "Why?"

She turned back to face him, the humor in her gaze now gone. This time he saw the sad reality of a woman who knew and understood him—it wasn't pretty to look at.

"What?" he said. "Go ahead, say it."

"I don't think you'd make a very good husband."

Nothing shocking there. "Well, I don't know. Last night you thought—"

"That was passion, desire," she interrupted.

"You can't have passion and desire in a marriage?"

"Of course, but those kinds of needs are only *part* of

it." She nodded toward the middle of the lake. Louise was now teaching Harold how to do a spin. He looked like an idiot, Mac thought. An idiot in love.

"Look at them," Olivia said wistfully. "They're friends, true companions. They really like each other."

Mac pressed his lips together. Not that he wanted to admit it—and he wasn't about to, out loud at any rate—but he liked Olivia. He thought they made a pretty good team.

"They're coming back," Olivia said, pulling Mac from his thoughts. "And after a full morning of cold and exercise, I'm betting they're hungry."

"I know I am," Mac said softly, his gaze resting on Olivia.

She shook her head at him, but he saw that flash of hunger in her eyes—the same one she'd worn last night when he'd touched her, kissed her.

Screw friendship. Maybe what they had wasn't long-lasting, but it was real, and there was going to be a moment when she allowed herself to take it. And if he was on top of his game, that moment would come tonight.

At four o'clock in the afternoon on Saturday, Olivia was dealt some bad news. She was in the kitchen, pounding chicken breasts into thin paillards, when Mac walked in and announced, "Harold and Louise want to ask the Keavys to come over after dinner tonight for cocktails."

Olivia's heart dropped into her stomach with anvil-like heaviness. She continued to smash the chicken, but with slightly more vigor. "Okay."

"Avery's the DeBolds' attorney. It's good to have her here. I think it will get them talking and asking questions tonight, and I need that to happen. They're leaving in the morning, so—"

"You don't have to explain, Mac," she said tightly, not looking at him. "This is your home. You don't need my permission to invite someone here."

"I know that." He sighed, pushed a hand through his hair. "Damn it, I care about your feelings, okay? Too much, but there it is."

"You don't need to worry about me." She needed him to just stop talking about it, stop asking questions. But that wasn't Mac's way. "I'm a professional. I will not allow my feelings to distract from the goal of this evening."

"Screw that. What happened with Tim? Did he treat you badly? Not show up on a date? Was he…all over you on a date? What the hell happened between you two?"

"Nothing."

"I'm trying to be sensitive here, Olivia, because I can see that whatever happened in the past is upsetting to you—but it was high school. That's a long time ago."

Her head came up and she glared at him. "You've got to stop with the questions. This is none of your business, Mac."

"I know, but if it interferes—"

"It won't. I swear I'll be the perfect hostess tonight—I was just caught off guard before."

He looked as though he wanted to say more, ask more, demand more, but after a moment he turned and started to leave the room.

Thinking he was gone, Olivia faced her meal-in-progress once again, feeling tired. All she wanted to do was throw her ingredients into the garbage and go home, forget about Tim, forget about Mac. She put down her mallet, took off her plastic gloves and put her head in her hands.

"Olivia."

Her heart sank. Damn him, why hadn't he left the room like he was supposed to? He'd seen her break down, lose it a little, and that wasn't good. She felt him beside her.

"I'm just a little tired, that's all," she said.

"Come on. It won't go further than this room, if that's what you're worried about. I swear I won't use anything you tell me. Talk to me."

She looked up and melted at the concerned look on his face...she could almost believe it was genuine.

He reached for her, wrapped his arms around her. "Give me something, Olivia."

Maybe it would be easier if he knew, she thought. Then it would all be out in the open—he wouldn't have to dig for information. But...there was a part of her that didn't want him to know, didn't want him to see her as Tim had seen her, and maybe still did—as trash, as a little tramp who had been so starved for love she'd slept with her teacher.

"He knows something about me," she began, letting her head drop onto Mac's shoulder. "A mistake I made. And he didn't like me for it, simple as that." She couldn't go further than that, she just couldn't....

"Simple as that, huh?"

"Yes."

"I don't believe you."

She stepped back, lifted her head and gave him a bold smile. "I have chicken to prepare."

"Olivia…"

"Everything will be fine tonight, Valentine."

He reached out and brushed his thumb across her cheek. "You're sure?"

His touch was like the best kind of comfort food and she wanted to wrap her arms around him again and beg him to take away her anger over a past she couldn't find a way to change. But that job belonged to her alone. If she ever wanted to feel comfortable about men and sex and love again, she had to deal with her past herself. "Now, I want you to get out of my kitchen and go be with your guests. It's your last night to impress the DeBolds, and I'm going to make sure you do."

Mac regarded her without smiling. "It's their last night, and it's your last night."

She nodded, then faced the counter again and got back to work. She wasn't sure when he left exactly, but when she turned around to get the arugula from the fridge, he was gone.

Twelve

The amazing thing about Olivia Winston was that once she made up her mind not to care about something or someone, it came rather easily. When Tim and Avery joined them after dinner for drinks and a few games of Pictionary, Olivia put her nerves aside and became the professional she knew herself to be. She was in her element: a small, elegant, relaxed, family friendly get-together with great desserts and just enough spirits to make everyone smile. She and Tim had managed to successfully ignore each other and the DeBolds were happy and acting exceptionally warm and familiar with Mac.

An all-around success.

"We've had such a good time," Louise said, sipping

a second cup of Olivia's delicious hot-buttered rum as they relaxed beside the fireplace in the den.

Harold nodded in Mac's direction. "You're a class act, Valentine."

"Thank you, Harold." Mac tipped his glass in the couples' direction. "It's been a pleasure having both of you here. Maybe we can do it again over the summer."

Harold grinned warmly. "Maybe. Maybe."

Avery had excused herself to go to the ladies' room, and perhaps Tim had felt uncomfortable without her, but he, too, excused himself to have a cigar on the porch.

While they were gone, Olivia asked Louise about her New York trip and if they'd seen any Broadway shows, and as she listened to the woman's hilarious accounts of a show they saw about underpants, she saw Mac get up and follow Tim out of the room.

Her stomach rolled over, but she forced her attention back on Louise.

He was a guy. A hardheaded guy who went after what he wanted regardless of the consequences. And right now what he wanted were answers.

He knew where his friend had gone—the balcony off the kitchen—and headed straight there.

Out in the inky darkness, a light snow was falling and the air felt still and frigid. Tim was simultaneously puffing on his cigar and shaking from the cold.

Mac stepped out onto the balcony, barely feeling the below-zero temperatures. "I couldn't stand those things when we were in college and I can't stand them now."

Laughing, Tim said curtly, "Then why are you out here?"

"I need to talk to you."

"About what?"

"About her. What did you do to her?"

His nose was red at the tip, his ears, too. "What? Who?"

"Olivia," Mac said impatiently. "In high school. What happened between you two?"

"Oh, man…" Tim shook his head.

"Come on."

"I don't want to go into this," Tim said, tossing his cigar over the balcony and into the snow.

"You will go into it," Mac said through gritted teeth. "Or I'll make you dive into that snow and fish out the cigar using only your teeth."

Tim stepped back, chuckled. "What's with the violence?" He was trying to be funny, and although the clown act had worked on their frat brothers in college, it was going nowhere tonight. When Tim realized that Mac was having none of his BS, he shrugged his shoulders. "Oh, hell. Fine. It was a long time ago, junior year. I'd just finished soccer practice and I was getting a few things out of my locker. I heard a girl and a guy in an empty classroom. It was late, after five." He shrugged again. "I thought it was a couple of kids fooling around and I was going to jump out and scare the crap out of them." Mac raised his eyebrows. "It wasn't a couple of kids. It was Olivia."

"And?"

"And the math teacher."

Mac cursed.

"Yep."

"So, you didn't jump out?"

"Hell no!"

Mac could see why Olivia felt embarrassed about something like that. But hell, everyone did stupid things when they were kids. One question remained though. He stared hard at Tim. "I don't get it. Why is she so angry at you?"

Tim blew out a breath. "I didn't exactly keep the news to myself."

Anger smashed through Mac like a tidal wave. "What? You told someone about what you'd seen?"

"A few people actually." He quickly reacted to the hard look on Mac's face. "C'mon, it was high school. If you can't talk trash about the school skank, what fun is—"

Mac stopped him with a deadly glare. His voice low, he asked, "What did you call her?"

Swallowing hard, Tim dropped his gaze and tried to play it off with humor. "C'mon, man, it was a long time ago."

Mac stared at Tim as if he were seeing him for the first time—and he looked a like a major ass. He said evenly, "It was a long time ago, but you clearly haven't grown up one day since then. You need to leave, Keavy."

"What?"

"Right now."

"You've got to be kidding."

"Do I look like I'm kidding?"

"I don't get you, man." Tim hugged himself against the cold and swayed from foot to foot. "Why do you care about this? She's your employee, not your…" Tim stopped moving. "Holy sh—"

"Don't," Mac warned menacingly.

"You like her. Wow. I haven't seen you really get into a woman since…" He searched his memory. "I was going to say college, but you really just played around then, too."

Mac scowled. "I'm going inside now. I'll think up something to tell Avery, then you need to get the hell out of my house."

"Look, Mac," Tim started, changing his tune as he looked almost sincere, "I was a kid…"

"We're done here." Mac left his former friend in the cold and went inside.

"Door County, Wisconsin, is the sweetest spot in the Midwest. Beautiful wildlife. It's kind of a kitschy area with friendly people who don't try to get in your business—it's my kind of place. We bought some land six years ago and built our dream home." Louise sighed as she sat in front of the fireplace and sipped her buttered rum. "Traveling is fun and always a great adventure, but nothing feels better than going home, you know?"

Olivia nodded, but she didn't exactly feel that way about her two-bedroom apartment. Sure, it was pretty and bright and had a decent kitchen, but it wasn't exactly her dream home.

"When are you going back, Louise?" Avery asked, curled up like a pretty blond cat on the sofa, while Harold inspected a book on architecture that had been on the coffee table.

"Tomorrow morning. We want to be there in time to start decorating for the holidays. Harold and I have this thing for Christmas trees. We go to the lot ourselves and pick out one for every room in the house."

"Every room?" Olivia asked disbelievingly.

Louise laughed. "Yes."

"It's beautiful," Avery said knowingly. "And that pine scent everywhere…"

"You know," Louise said to both Avery and Olivia, "we're having all of Harold's family for Christmas." She lowered her voice. "He has an enormous and very judgmental family."

"I can hear you, honey," Harold said, flipping through the pages of his book. "I'm sitting right here."

With an impish smile she continued, "They have always taunted me about not being able to cook and take care of my man, so this year I have vowed to create the best Thanksgiving dinner anyone has ever seen." She paled. "I have no idea how I'm going to manage it though. Unlike you, Olivia, I have zero skill."

"It's not that difficult," Olivia assured her, trying to be as supportive as she could. Anyone could learn to cook, but in her opinion Thanksgiving dinner was not the best place to start. "The simpler the better. All you need are a few recipes."

"A few?" Louise repeated nervously.

Olivia laughed. "Before you go in the morning, I could give you a little lesson in—"

Suddenly, Louise's face brightened, her eyes rounded and she burst out, "That's a wonderful idea."

"Great," Olivia said. "So, meet me in the kitchen say around—"

"No. That's not what I mean."

Confused, Olivia shook her head. "I'm sorry...I don't understand."

Louise grinned widely. "You're done working for Mac tomorrow, right?"

"Yes."

"Then come with us to Door County."

"What?"

Louise looked beyond excited, like a kid, sitting forward in her seat. She put her mug on the coffee table. "Stay for a few days and teach me how to cook. In style, too—the kitchen is awesome, and I have every tool...every tool I have no idea how to use."

Still in shock, Olivia just muttered, "Wow. I don't know."

This time, Harold jumped in. "Why not? You travel for your job, right?"

"Right, but—"

Louise laughed. "I know I'm not a bachelor looking for help, but couldn't you extend your client base to include clueless, helpless females, too?"

Olivia glanced from Harold to Avery to Louise. They were all smiling. Why couldn't she do this? She was done with Mac, and she'd love to see Door County and help the DeBolds. She shrugged and smiled herself. "Okay. I'll have to check my schedule, see if I've been booked. But if not, I'm all yours."

"Great." Clasping her hands together, Louise turned

to her husband and hooted. "I'm going to wipe those evil, know-it-all smirks off your family's faces."

Harold's lips twitched. "They don't smirk, darling."

It was at that moment that Mac entered the room. He spotted Avery and gave her a terse glance. "Avery, your husband's not feeling well. You'd better take him home."

Avery looked concerned. "What?"

"Tim needs to go."

A small flicker of concern tapped at Olivia's insides. What had gone down between the two of them to make Mac look so annoyed and Tim rush out? What was said? Her heart dipped as she wondered what Tim had revealed.

"He's waiting for you by the front door," Mac told Avery brusquely.

"Oh. Okay." Slightly confused, Avery stood and offered a quick goodbye to Olivia and the DeBolds before leaving the room.

Without another word about it, Mac turned his attention to the threesome remaining. His eyes were cool and detached, but he was forcing a grin. "You all look excited about something."

"Is Tim all right?" Olivia asked.

"He'll be fine," Mac stated quickly and without an ounce of emotion.

Louise looked serious for a moment. "I hope so."

Mac nodded, then glanced around expectantly. "So, what did I miss?"

Louise didn't hesitate to switch topics, "We're talking about Harold's family and how they're going to drop their jaws when I cook and serve them Thanksgiving dinner."

"Looks as though my wife has hired Olivia to teach her how to cook," Harold informed him on a chuckle.

"Really?" He looked at Olivia, his jaw set.

"Could be. If I'm free." He didn't look pleased, but Olivia couldn't tell exactly what was going on behind his eyes. Was it whatever had happened with Tim or the prospect of Olivia working for the DeBolds that had him fuming?

"Where are you going?"

"To our home in Wisconsin," Louise said, but Mac was still staring at Olivia.

"When?"

"Tomorrow."

"No." Mac said the word so darkly and succinctly that everyone stopped and stared at him.

"What's wrong?" Olivia asked Mac.

Mac recovered quickly, his tone now ultraprofessional as he addressed her. "You and I haven't finished our business yet."

"Huh?"

Harold and Louise exchanged glances, and Harold cleared his throat. "I'm sorry, Mac. We didn't know."

It was then that Mac realized he was about to alienate the clients he wanted so badly to score. "No, no," he said, chuckling, back in total control now. "I'm the one who's sorry. My business is so all-consuming these days, I didn't get a chance to ask Olivia to continue on."

"All-consuming," Harold repeated with understanding. "Well, that's why we agreed to come here, isn't it?

And why we're considering transferring our financial holdings to you."

"Well," Mac began, "my new project with Olivia doesn't have to start immediately. But I would like a chance to talk with you both, show you the plans I have created for your future. Do you have room for one more in Door County…?"

Harold seemed to like this idea and nodded in agreement. "Kill two birds, is that it?"

Mac nodded.

Olivia sat on the floor fuming. She did not appreciate Mac's interference or his interloping ways, but before she could even get a word out, Harold was talking again—sounding pumped up and making specific plans.

"Okay," he said. "So while the women are in the kitchen—"

"Hey, watch yourself, Harold," Louise warned good-naturedly, going to sit beside him on the couch. "Make sure you don't add a 'where they belong' to the end of that sentence."

He patted her leg. "Never, darling." Then he turned back to Mac. "While the women are in the kitchen plotting against my family, you and I can do some ice fishing and talk about how you're going to make us richer than we already are."

"Richer, more secure and totally protected."

Harold beamed. "I like the sound of that."

Olivia knew she had zero control over her immediate future. The DeBolds had found a perfect situation, and as they sat there grinning they had that rich person's, "we're going to make it happen no matter what anyone says" look on their faces.

Olivia stood and started gathering plates and cups, knowing full well that Mac was watching her, feeling like he'd won, like he had more time to get her into bed. She swallowed thickly at the thought, trying to ignore the pounding of her heart.

The only thing that could save her now was if her partners had booked another job for her.

Thirteen

All the excited chatter about Mary's upcoming engagement party came to a screeching halt when Olivia walked into No Ring Required's modern kitchen and announced her plans to fly to Door County the following day. Seated at the table, Tess and Mary listened intently as Olivia explained that she was going to Wisconsin to teach Louise DeBold how to cook Thanksgiving dinner, and that Mac Valentine was going along, as well.

Mary cupped her mug of tea and tried to be the rational one. "Okay, I personally think it's great that we're expanding to include women who don't have, or who choose not to grow, the stereotypical 'wifely' gene, it's just…" Her voice trailed off.

"I'll finish for her," Tess stated boldly, pulling her red

hair into a loose bun. "The fact that your former client, Mac Valentine, is going with you is a little bizarre."

Olivia sat beside Mary. "I know, but Harold DeBold wants to get to know him better and hear his plans for their financial future before he'll give Mac his business. So, you see, it's really two separate gigs going on here."

"Uh-huh," was all Tess said.

"Going out of town seems to be where trouble starts," Mary said, touching her belly.

Olivia frowned at her. "You don't consider little Ethan or Ethanette here trouble, do you?"

"No, of course not. I just mean, when you're out of town you're not in your comfort zone and you look to someone else for comfort—that is, if you're attracted to that someone else." She leaned forward. "Are you? Are you attracted to that someone else?"

"I refuse to answer on the grounds that this one—" she pointed behind her to a looming Tess "—might sucker punch me, or something."

Tess laid a hand on Olivia's shoulder and said sweetly, "I'm fair. I'd at least have you turn around before I hit you."

Mary laughed, and Olivia grimaced. "This is partly your fault, ladies."

"How is it our fault?" Tess demanded, sitting across from them.

"Maybe someone should've booked me for another gig starting today."

Tess snorted. "Maybe you need to stand up to this guy and tell him to take a hike."

"Maybe I will." Both women looked unconvinced, and Olivia sighed with frustration. "Look, you two, the only comfort I'll be cooking up is in the kitchen, okay?"

Tess and Mary continued to vocalize their opinions and concerns for the rest of the day. Then later, when Olivia returned home to pack, the phone call to her father didn't go much better....

"You are insane to go anywhere with that man," said Owen Winston angrily.

She had him on speakerphone, and was packing a suitcase while they talked. "Dad, I didn't call for advice, I called to let you know that I was going to be out of town for a few days."

"To the diamond DeBolds house in Door County." He made a noise that sounded awfully like an out-of-tune French horn. "Door County is a place for couples on vacation. Did you know that?"

Yes, she did, and it probably worried her more than it did him, but she wasn't about to let her father know that. "Will you go by my apartment and feed my fish...once a day? Will you?"

He heaved a sigh. "Of course. We don't want them to suffer."

She laughed at his sarcasm. "Will it hurt your masculine pride if I tell you that you're acting like a drama queen?"

"Livy, tell me you're not falling for that bastard."

She stopped packing. "No falling."

"Good. And tell me you're not going to—"

"Stop. Dad. Please don't go there." This was it.

Maybe this was it. The opportunity for her to tell her father the truth. Not the details, but the basics of what she'd done in high school, so that if Mac ever did approach her father with the information it wouldn't come as a shock.

"I'm sorry, Livy," he said, sounding sad and maybe a little lonely. "I love you and I just want…"

"The best for me, I know—I get it." She bit her lip, thought about how to say it, how to begin…then she remembered how Mac had promised not to use her past against her by going to her father, and she found an excuse to leave it alone, or at the very least, put it off until maybe she and her father were face-to-face.

She tossed a few sweaters into her suitcase and said, "I love you, Dad, and I'll see you on Thursday."

Fourteen

Mac enjoyed the solitude of a private plane. He had a rule: if he was going to be in the air for more than an hour, he always chartered a Gulfstream. He glanced around with an assessing gaze. The DeBolds' Citation was smaller than what he was used to, but comfortable enough once he was seated. He was curious to see how it felt once they got it in the air, as eight-seaters could act a little unsteady at times. The interior was ultraplush, though, outfitted with soft leather and thick carpet, and the very capable steward, Tom, had set out glasses and a bottle of sparkling water.

Just outside the plane Mac heard Tom greet another passenger. Mac glanced up from his laptop, annoyed at the jolt of excitement that ran through him when Olivia Winston came aboard.

"Morning," Mac said.

She gave him a friendly smile. "Hey." She took the single seat across the aisle from him. "Are we early?"

"I don't think so."

His gaze moved over her, from the soft chocolate-brown sweater to the jeans that stretched temptingly over her thighs and hips when she sat. His hands itched to touch her. It had been too long and he could hardly wait to have her—in his arms and in his bed. Up until this point, there had been too many distractions, and he'd been unsuccessful in his attempts to seduce her. Now that they were going away together…

The steward came out and addressed them, his large blue eyes and round face filled with practiced friendliness. "Welcome aboard, Ms. Winston, Mr. Valentine."

"Thank you," Olivia said warmly.

"Is there anything I can get you?"

"Not for me, thanks." She turned to Mac. "Anything you need, Valentine?"

He grinned at her and uttered, "Nothing that Tom can provide."

She rolled her eyes at him, then glanced back at the steward. "We're fine, thank you."

He nodded. "We'll be leaving in just a few minutes. Please fasten your seat belts."

Tom was about to head for the cockpit when Olivia called out, "Excuse me."

"Yes, Miss Winston?"

"Aren't we missing a few passengers?"

The steward looked confused and just a tad annoyed. "I'm sorry?"

"The DeBolds?"

"Oh, no, miss. They went home last night, and sent the plane and myself back for the two of you."

Olivia looked at Mac, then back at Tom. "Why?"

"I don't know, miss."

The man stood there. And Mac, growing tired of both Tom's put-out attitude and Olivia's questions, decided to step in. Sitting on the tarmac wasn't his idea of a good time. "Thank you, Tom. Now, let's get this lady in the air, shall we."

Looking relieved, the man nodded. "I'll inform the captain."

When he was gone, Olivia turned to Mac, her dark eyebrows drawn together in a frown. "Why wouldn't they call us, have us all leave together?"

Mac shrugged. "Why does it matter?"

"I'm just curious. It's a little odd."

Below their feet, the engine sprang to life with an easy vibration.

"I have a feeling they're trying to get us together," Olivia remarked, fastening her seat belt.

"We are together."

"You know what I mean, Mac."

"Ah, yes." He grinned at her over his laptop. "And what if they are? Would that be so wrong?"

She glared at him. "What is it with married people?

Why do they always feel like they need to make more couples?"

"Maybe they want others to experience their blissful state."

"Do you really believe that, Valentine?"

"Nope."

She laughed. She had a great laugh, throaty and youthful, and he had an incredible desire to always keep her laughing, keep her happy.

"Listen, Valentine, I think we need to try and remember why we're here." She was leaning back in her seat, her head tilted toward him.

"And why are we here…?"

"To work," she said, humor dancing in her eyes. "Or in your case, to work and exact revenge on my father through poor little me."

He couldn't help it—he smiled at her, and she returned it. She was something else, no wilting flower. Why did it excite him that she understood exactly what he was after and wasn't afraid to take him on?

"Speaking of revenge…" she began, her eyes suddenly not meeting his.

"Yes?"

"Did your friend give you any helpful ammunition the other night?"

Mac's jaw tightened. "No."

She was quiet for a moment, then said, "Tim didn't tell you about…what happened?"

He stared at her, hard and intense. "Listen, Olivia, I told you before, I don't care what happened in your past. I don't need to use BS hearsay from a former friend to get what I want from you."

"Former friend?"

"I'm not sentimental. I don't value friendships. And if someone crosses me, goes too far, I have no problem walking away."

She nodded. "I'll remember that."

A slow grin moved over his lips. "Now, let's get back to talking about why we're here."

"Right. To work."

Mac sighed. "I'd hoped you'd forgotten."

She laughed. "Nope. And odds are Louise and Harold are going to throw more of this—" she gestured around the interior of the cabin "—our way."

"More private planes, more romantic destinations...sounds like hell on earth."

"You don't want to take any of this seriously."

"No."

She sighed and looked away. "Well, I do. And if you have any sense you'll focus on landing this client, not getting me into bed."

Damn, he liked her—he liked her attitude, her spirit, her brains, the way she moved and how her eyes always spoke for her. But there was no way he was going to allow his feelings to interfere with the facts. He wanted payback. Of course he wasn't about to use her past or Tim's account of it against her. He would only work with what he had now—his desire for her, and to take Owen's daughter to his bed. Mac would have what he wanted: revenge and a woman he desired above all things.

The plane backed up slowly, getting in position to taxi. "Not to worry, Olivia," he said with a tone of arrogant confidence. "I'm fully capable of landing both you and the DeBolds."

Comprised of a sprawling log house, orchard and barn, the DeBolds' home was truly one of the most unique places Olivia had ever seen and she was completely enchanted by it. On fifty private acres, just a half mile north of Sturgeon Bay, the custom log home was already being dressed for the holidays. When Mac and Olivia arrived, a crew of ten or so men and women were working outside, affixing garlands, wreaths and twinkle lights to trees, doors, rooftops and anything else that didn't move.

Olivia gave a low whistle as she stepped out of the Town Car that had picked them up from the airport. "Okay, I grew up in a very nice house with very nice furnishings—most of which you couldn't touch—but this…this is spectacular."

Mac helped the driver with their luggage, told the guy that he could handle it from there, then gave him a hefty tip.

As the car pulled away, Olivia stood in the driveway and just stared at the house, transfixed. "I wouldn't think that anything so big could feel so warm and friendly, but it does." She leaned down and picked up her small carry-on, as Mac had the rest of the luggage. "I think I know where I'm retiring to."

"Really?" Mac said, sounding surprised.

"Yes, really." She followed him up the walk to the front door. "This is my fantasy home. If they have horses, I'm just going to tie myself to one of the fence posts and cry squatter's rights."

"I don't get it. I mean, it's 'cute' in a country bumpkin sort of way, but—"

"Yeah, I know it's not like that glass and stainless steel penthouse of yours in Manhattan, but—"

He stopped, shot her a sideways glance. "How did you know about my apartment in Manhattan?"

"Oh, Mac," she said on a laugh, "you never stop underestimating me. Great place, by the way, very James Bond meets Times Square."

"Thanks," he muttered as they reached the front door. "I think."

"But this place is way cooler. What could you possibly not like here?"

"It's just a little too much like a bed-and-breakfast," he said, dropping the bags onto the DeBolds' massive monogrammed welcome mat.

She snorted. "You're such a guy."

Before she could stop him, Mac snaked a hand around her waist and pulled her close. "Damn right."

Olivia gasped, and even though it was twenty degrees outside, heat accosted her skin like a blast from an oven.

"But, hey," he said gently, gazing down at her, "if you like this place, that's all that matters. I'm more than willing to accept patchwork quilts, sunflower wallpaper and raspberry-colored bathrooms if you'll share it with me."

The soft, sweet way he was looking at her made

Olivia almost believe him. And yet she chose sarcasm over sincerity. "Interesting. Sounds like you've been to a B and B a few times before. You've got the description of every bed-and-breakfast I've ever heard about down pat."

"I've been sent to a few Web sites in my time."

"By a few ladies?" His lips were so close, looked so good—and she could remember exactly how they felt.

"Women seem to think 'homespun' is romantic."

"And it's not?"

He slowly shook his head. "Not to me."

Power pulsed from him, strength and sexuality, too. It was a hard combination to resist. And again, she questioned herself, questioned why she needed to resist at all. Why couldn't she just have fun here and not hold back? She was an adult, maybe a foolish one, but hey...

"I'll probably kick myself later for asking this," she said, "but what is romantic to you?"

"Well, this doesn't suck." He grinned mischievously, then glanced up.

Olivia followed his gaze and spotted a sprig of mistletoe hanging from a beam over the porch. "Now this is just awkward," she began, laughing. "What if the mail carrier and the UPS guy got here at the same time—"

"Ah, shut up, Winston." He cut her off with a growl, then covered her mouth with his. His nose was cold, but his lips seared with heat and need, and Olivia melted into his embrace.

"You smell good," he whispered against her lips.

"It's the snow."

"No."

"Pine trees."

"No," he said, applying soft kisses first to her top lip then to the bottom one. "It's you."

Her breath caught in her throat as he kissed her again, hot, sweet kisses that made her forget where she was. Like a blind woman, searching, hungry, she slipped her hands inside his coat and ran her fingers over his trim waist to his back, then upward. The muscles in his shoulders flexed, and she gripped at them, squeezed at them as she tipped her chin up to get closer. She just wanted to get closer to him.

It was at that moment the front door opened. Like a guilty child with both of her hands stuck in the forbidden cookie jar, Olivia jumped away from Mac.

Pulling the door wide, Louise looked from Olivia to Mac, just a touch of confusion on her perfectly made-up face. "Did you ring the bell? We didn't hear anything."

Olivia quickly said, "We…just arrived." She looked at Mac to corroborate this, but he only stared at her, his eyes rife with amusement. Of course he wasn't going to be any help.

A broad grin on her face, Louise said, "That's odd. One of the decorators came inside to tell me you were here."

Which meant that said meddlesome decorator probably also mentioned what Mac and Olivia were doing out on the porch.

As Louise ushered them inside, Olivia muttered a terse, "Oh, man," back at Mac, which only made him chuckle.

"Harold," Louise called up a beautiful log staircase. "They're here." Then she turned back to Mac and Olivia. "Have a good flight?"

Trying to brush off any residual embarrassment, Olivia forced a smile. "It was great, thank you."

They followed Louise into a massive, two-level great room with hardwood floors, exposed beams and a rock fireplace that stretched all the way to the cathedral ceiling. The open floor plan was spectacular, allowing visitors to see the living room, dining area and huge chef's kitchen, with a rectangular black granite island, from the entryway.

"You have an amazing home," Olivia remarked. "I'm completely in love with it, and this area."

Louise beamed. "Well then, you'll have to get out of the kitchen while you're here and experience Door County fully—or our property, at the very least. We have horses and orchards, and cross-country skiing is a blast."

From beside her, Mac touched the small of her back. "Horses, Olivia."

"Yes, I heard. Very exciting," Olivia said, stepping away from him so her cheeks—and several other parts of her—wouldn't go up in flames from his touch.

Above them, a creaking sound echoed on the landing, and a few seconds later, Harold trotted down the stairs. He had a big grin on his face when he saw them. "Welcome, welcome," he said warmly, shaking Mac's hand, then Olivia's. "Good to have you both here."

"We're looking forward to the stay," Mac said. "Great place you have here."

Olivia shot him a look as Harold said, "Thank you."

"So, I suppose you both would you like to get settled before lunch?" Louise asked

"I'm a big unpacker," Olivia joked. "So, that would be great."

Harold looked at Louise, who looked at him with big eyes, then she turned to Mac and Olivia. "We wanted to have you stay in the house, but we're having the rooms fixed up for Harold's family, and of course they're very particular about what they want."

"Easy, honey," Harold said on a chuckle.

"Anyway, we have two small guest houses on the property, and we've had them made up for you."

"Guest houses?" Olivia said, feeling a little worried. Guest houses were a little like hotel suites. Staying in the house was far safer. "Are you sure we're not putting you out?"

Louise laughed as though this were the silliest idea she'd ever heard. "I'm going to get lunch ready. Not to torment you, but so you'll be able to see my skill level— or lack thereof—and Johnny, our groundskeeper, will take you across the pond to the guest houses."

Across the pond. Right.

Those guest houses had better be a good fifty yards away from each other, she mused as Harold called for Johnny over the intercom. It took no more than thirty seconds for the tall young man to show up, an easy smile on his thin face.

After thanking the DeBolds for their hospitality again, Mac and Olivia followed Johnny down a long flagstone path and around a small pond, which was tree-lined and frozen solid.

When Olivia saw the adjoining guest houses, her heart leaped into her throat. They were too close, only separated by a wall, for goodness' sake. But when they were ushered inside the first house, her heart sank. Decorated from top to bottom in luxurious whites and creams, soft rugs and warm lighting, Olivia knew she was in trouble. The large one-room suite screamed romance, from the small fir tree, which was dressed in white lights, to the massive stone fireplace, to the four-poster, king-sized bed with down pillows and terrycloth robe draped across the comforter, to the double whirl-pool tub not ten feet away.

Olivia put her hands on her hips and sighed. "Oh, yeah, they're trying to hook us up."

Beside her, Mac chuckled. "Want to come and see my room? Maybe it looks even more like a room at a bed-and-breakfast than yours does."

She didn't think that was possible, and she uttered, "Some other time."

"Promise?"

When she glanced up at him, saw the wicked gleam in his dark eyes and the curl of a smile on his extraor-dinarily handsome face, she felt her knees grow weak and knew it was only a matter of time before the rest of her followed suit. Because seriously, how much could a girl resist?

Fifteen

"I'm really sorry about lunch. I was trying to impress you, and I ended up almost killing you."

If someone were looking at Louise DeBold from the outside they'd see a confident, beautiful, sharp woman who owned every room she walked into and didn't need accolades from anyone to feel her value. But as she stood in front of Olivia, a semicooked turkey sitting on a platter of greens, she looked as though she'd shrunk in both stature and self-confidence.

Olivia took the platter from her and set it on the island. "You didn't know the turkey was undercooked."

"I would if I'd have cut into it."

Olivia laughed. "True."

Ripping off her apron, Louise sighed. "I think I might be hopeless."

"You're not."

"Harold's family is going to have a field day with this." She sat at the island. "I don't fail at things, Olivia, you know? I was an appraiser for ten years—the top gemologist in the country. Everyone came to me...." She stared at the turkey as though she'd just gone to war with it and had come back bruised and defeated. "I can't fail at this."

"You won't," Olivia assured her. "Now, get that apron back on and come over to the cutting board. We're going to try this again."

"All right."

"Poultry is a tricky thing," Olivia explained as she took another small bird out of the fridge and laid it in the sink. "I like to compare it to a relationship."

At this Louise perked up. "How so?"

"If it's not seasoned right or given enough heat, it will fail. Not to mention become boring and bland."

"Wow."

"That's right," Olivia said as she pulled out the bag of giblets and other delicious innards from inside the turkey. Then she washed it inside and out and patted it dry with paper towels.

"So," Louise began tentatively, "if I may be so bold as to ask, are you and Mac good poultry or bad poultry?"

Olivia took a second before answering to assess the warming feeling that had seeped into her belly. "We don't have a relationship."

"So, earlier on the porch…"

"Was a moment of insanity."

Louise sighed. "God, I love those."

Olivia laughed, she couldn't help herself. "Mac and me…it's complicated."

"Uncomplicate it, then—just like you're doing for me with this damn bird. Dress it, season it well, stick it in the oven on the right temp and baste, baste, baste."

Olivia pointed at her. "You've got this down, Louise."

"I like you, both of you," she said, seasoning the inside of the turkey with salt and pepper. "It would be fun to do this again."

"It would, but it might be a separate thing. While Mac is an amazing money man, he wants nothing to do with relationships."

"You never know, Liv." She paused, looked up. "Can I call you that?"

Olivia smiled. "Of course."

"Harold was a total player when we met," Louise said as she dug under the skin, loosening it from the breast.

"Really?"

"Uh-huh."

"I can't imagine it."

She stuffed the breast with sprigs of sage and thyme. "Well, it's true. Different chick every night. And look at him now." She slathered the top of the bird with butter. "Today, he brought home all this beautiful wood. He wants to build a baby crib, all by himself."

"Baby crib—are you…"

She smiled as she walked over to the sink to rinse her

hands. "My point is, you just never know what people are capable of until you give them the chance. Now, let's put this thing in the oven and get to work on the stuffing."

When Mac walked into the kitchen two hours later, Harold in his wake, the scent of Thanksgiving nearly bowled him over. He spotted Olivia at the sink with Louise, watching over the diamond queen as she carefully poured steaming boiled potatoes into a stainless mesh bowl. They looked very cozy, the two of them, almost like friends.

Harold elbowed him in the ribs and whispered, "I know it may be sexist, but look at our girls, wearing aprons and cooking their men some supper. Almost makes a guy want to grunt and scratch himself."

Chuckling softly, Mac said, "Almost." But he was hardly laughing inside. His reaction to Harold's comment worried him. *Our girls*—the phrase should've washed over him, meant nothing, hell, meant less than nothing. But the idea of Olivia belonging to him in any real, meaningful way made his heart ache strangely.

Now, as a kid he'd been put in and taken out of home after home until he was close to fourteen. Thanksgiving and family really hadn't meant anything sacred or special. So maybe it was that when he looked at Olivia with Louise in the kitchen, being all domestic and looking content—and with the smells of a happy home curling through his nostrils—it had triggered something. Something he might want at some point in his life.

At some point, but not now…

"I love this part," Louise was saying as she smashed the hot potatoes with something that looked like a branding iron. "Gets out all your aggressions."

They hadn't noticed Mac and Harold yet.

"Don't I know it." Laughing, Olivia poured the hot cranberry relish into a bowl. "The key to good cooking is to make simple food with really fresh ingredients."

"Something smells good in here," Harold said, walking past Mac and slipping his arms around his wife's waist as she continued to beat the potatoes into submission.

Glancing over her shoulder, Louise smiled. "Yes, a proper lunch. Even if it is two o'clock."

Mac looked over at Olivia. She was watching the happy couple, her eyes melancholy. Then she noticed him looking at her and offered him a gentle smile. Mac's body stirred. What would happen if he walked over and put his arms around her, kissed her neck as she stirred sugar into those plumped-up cranberries? Would she want to get lost in the fantasy that the DeBolds had created and were slowly but surely sucking them into?

"So, did you two have an interesting talk?" Louise asked Harold and Mac.

"Interesting doesn't begin to cover it," Harold said, releasing Louise from his grasp. "This guy is too damn smart. Why Avery didn't introduce us sooner, I'll never know. The amount we could've been saving in taxes…" He shook his head.

"So do we have a new financial advisor then?" Louise asked.

"It would seem that way."

Olivia glanced at Mac, gave him a tight-lipped smile. It could've been congratulatory or sad, he didn't have a clue.

"We'll have to give Avery a call," Louise said, "and have her draw up the papers."

Harold nodded. "Right."

Mac's jaw clenched at the mention of Avery. He hadn't spoken to either her or Tim since he'd tossed the latter out of his house the other night. He'd have to work out his relationship with Avery, but he was done with her husband. Mac glanced up and saw Olivia watching him, curious. He forced his mood to lighten and winked at her. Then he addressed Harold.

"Not so fast," he said, joking with Harold. "You know I'm only taking you on as a client if you can play a serious game of pool."

Harold raised his brows at his wife. "Can you spare me for a few hours after dinner?"

"You've been challenged, honey," she said. "I don't see how you can't go." She held up her bowl of potatoes. "But right now, you're going to sit at the table, eat the meal we've prepared and then promptly tell me what an amazing cook I am."

"Done." Harold growled, kissed her neck. "Then after lunch, I want you to lie down for a while, okay?"

"What about our guests?"

"We're fine." Olivia carried stuffing and cranberries to the long pine table. "I have a book and Mac always has work to—"

"No way," Louise said severely, her dark eyes narrowed. "Didn't you say you loved horses, Olivia?"

Mac took a basket of rolls from Olivia's hands and nodded before heading to the table. "Yes, she did."

"Perfect. The horses need some exercise." As if she had just solved an enormous problem, Louise smiled contently and they all sat down at the table and marveled at the delicious-looking pre-Thanksgiving feast. "A ride in the Door County snow is a must-do for every couple."

Olivia's head came up with a jerk. "Louise…"

"I meant, every*one*." But the giggle that followed completely and obviously negated her quick correction.

They weren't a couple, but as far as Olivia was concerned there was nothing more romantic than horseback riding through the snow with Mac, dipping under naked, brittle branches, galloping across an open field iced with white. For the first time since they'd arrived, Olivia understood what Mary had meant about the dangers of getting out of her element, her comfort zone, and hanging around with a guy she could see herself kissing until she was both sweaty and naked.

As she slowed her chestnut mare to a brisk walk, Olivia breathed in the cold air. She turned to look at Mac. He was like something out of the movie *Camelot*, in a modern wool coat and scarf, of course, but he had rugged, thick dark hair, and that one-with-the-horse thing going on, and she didn't even try and stop herself from imagining him sitting in front of her, her arms wrapped around his waist as they gave the mare some serious exercise.

The sky was starting to lose its afternoon warmth when Olivia stopped in the middle of a snowy field and took in the faded colors of the sunset. "Come on, Valentine, tell me this doesn't beat the Manhattan skyline by a mile."

His horse, a proud gray palomino, was a little frisky and Mac had to circle him around Olivia and her horse a few times to get him to calm down. "I don't know," he began. "What's so amazing? Fifty acres of trees, natural springs and killer views. I don't get it."

She laughed at his lighthearted sarcasm. "So, are you headed home tomorrow?"

"What?"

Their horses puffed out warm breath into the cold air. "You bagged the DeBolds. It's a done deal. Harold as much as said he was ready to sign on the X when we were at lunch."

"He was ready to sign back in Minneapolis."

"What?" Olivia said, confused, studying him.

A hint of a smile curved his lips. "Harold and Louise would've signed papers before they left Minneapolis if I had pushed for it."

"Then why didn't you?"

He chuckled. "C'mon, Liv. You know why I'm really here."

Catching the spark of challenge in his eyes, Olivia took a shivering breath. "You have a huge new client, and you said that one of your former clients has come back. Do you really still feel the need for payback?"

He regarded her with amused impatience. "I feel the need for you. The payback is just a bonus."

His unguarded, hungry look sent chills running through her body. Saying nothing, she turned her horse around and headed back toward the barn. With a click of his tongue, Mac spurred his horse forward to catch up with her.

When they were riding side by side again, he said, "I know you're as curious as I am."

"About what?"

"What my skin would feel like against yours."

"Mac…c'mon…"

But he wouldn't stop. "How long you could hold out before you begged me to kiss you somewhere other than your mouth. What it would feel like when I pushed inside of you, climaxed with you."

His words went straight to the core of her, and she swallowed against the tightness in her throat. She was in trouble here or she was about to allow herself a good time…she wasn't sure which. "I am curious, but I'd hoped I could hold out." She saw the gentle slope of the barn up ahead, looking like a wood-hewn salvation. She forced herself to look at him, into those dark, wicked eyes. "Honestly, I'm not so sure I can hold out—or want to anymore."

A flush that had nothing to do with the cold crossed his cheeks. "Well, that's an admission."

"Yeah."

They rode back to the barn in silence. Around them, the air swirled with new, fresh snow, and the sky grew gray as afternoon came to a close. Inside the stables, Johnny was nowhere in sight, and after climbing down and tying up his horse, Mac reached for Olivia, helping her off her horse and onto her feet.

"I'm going back to the room to take a shower before dinner," Olivia said quietly, trying to disentangle herself from his grasp.

But Mac held her firm.

She looked up at him. "What are you doing?"

"Holding you until you stop fighting."

Running on instinct, Olivia tried to push away from him, get free of the rousing feel of his body against hers. But it was no use. She growled her frustration. She wanted him. There was no more denying it, to herself or to him. Damn it, why should she have to deny herself? Sure it might be a mistake, he might be a mistake, but so what? She was old enough now to deal with her stupid choices.

She stared at his mouth, that full, hard mouth that could crush her with his words, yet make her want nothing more than to leave all past mistakes and promises in the dust. "What are you waiting for then?"

His hot gaze swept her, but he said nothing.

She laughed out of sheer insanity. "Kiss me, damn it!"

He laughed, too. But he quickly sobered, let his head fall forward against hers. "Olivia, understand that if I kiss you now, I'm not going to be able to stop."

"I don't want you to."

"And I want you more than I've ever wanted anything in my life." He pulled her against him and gave her a deep, all-consuming kiss on the mouth.

Olivia could barely breathe when he released her, grabbed her hand and uttered hoarsely, "Come with me."

Leaving the horses tied up, Mac led her down the center aisle of the stable, all the way to the end, then off to the right, down another corridor. When he spotted an empty stall, he pulled her inside and closed the door.

Clean, sweet-smelling hay blanketed the floor, but Olivia barely registered the fact as Mac pulled off her coat and took her in his arms. His kiss began soft and slow, light pressure on her lips as he swayed back and forth to music she couldn't hear. Then the pressure increased until she opened for him, gave him access to her tongue, until she murmured "so good" and other ridiculous utterances, until she wrapped her arms around his neck and kissed him back so intensely she felt as though she were drowning.

He left her mouth and dipped his head, nuzzling her neck, nibbling at the thin flesh over her pulse, making her blood race in her veins. It had been so long, and she couldn't wait to feel his skin on her skin, the weight of him as he pressed into her. Just the thought of having him inside her had her feeling weak and hot and wet.

Somehow Mac got Olivia onto her back, but the change of position barely registered. All she knew was that one moment she was standing, and the next, her body was cradled in a soft nest of hay.

"What if someone comes…?" she uttered breathlessly. "Sees us…"

Positioned above her, Mac unbuttoned her shirt. "I don't give a damn if anyone sees us."

She refused to recall the last time someone had seen

her with a man. This was different. This was right now. It was almost as if she needed to do this—this way— and she felt no shame in her actions.

His hands found her belly, and she sucked air between her teeth at the sheer pleasure of him touching her naked skin, so close to the center of her, where she ached. She wanted him to just get to it, send his hand lower and put her out of her misery. Hell, she was already so worked up it would only take ten seconds— maybe less.

But Mac wasn't going there, not yet.

She wore a bra that clasped in the front and he easily took care of it, casting aside the two pale pink wisps of fabric. The fading light of afternoon filtered through the small square window above them, and Mac looked down at her and shook his head. "You have no idea…"

"What?"

"How long I've wanted to see you like this, and touch you. And now, I feel like I should take time to just…marvel."

She laughed, but it was almost a pained sound. "You do and I'll kill you."

He gave a quick, husky laugh, then bent his head and dragged his mouth over one of her breasts, then the other, applying soft, irritatingly slow kisses over the skin around her nipple.

Feeling as though she was about to explode, Olivia reached up and threaded her fingers in his hair, tried to pull him down.

"Patience, Liv," he whispered, the heat of his breath sending sparks to every nerve ending.

Olivia waited, the muscles in her legs contracting, her toes pointing until finally she felt him, felt that electrifying sensation of hot, wet tongue against her hard, sensitive nipple. Her breath came out in a rush and she thrust her hips in the air. Sensing the urgency in her body, Mac lapped at the hard peak, finding a rhythm, groaning when he heard her moan as his free hand moved down…down her belly, over her hips and under the slip of cotton.

"No," he uttered hoarsely, his fingers burrowing between her thighs. "Olivia, you're too hot, and way too wet. I don't know how long I can wait."

"And you wanted me to be patient," she uttered.

He found the entrance to her body and thrust his middle finger inside of her. It was too much. She sucked in air, shivered and bucked against his hand. She almost didn't know what to do. Her hands fisted hay, and the way he was moving inside her, pressing against that deep, sensitive part of her, she felt tears drop onto her cheeks, down to her neck.

"What is it?" he whispered, concerned. "Does this hurt?"

"No," she uttered. "No. It's wonderful."

He kissed her cheek, her lips, her neck.

"Make love to me, Mac. Please. Now." She couldn't control her body and all she wanted was him, inside of her. She clawed at his shirt, tore a few buttons and unhooked the others, then pulled it off of his chest. He was so beautiful, the way the thick muscles of his chest rose and fell with each breath he took. With greedy hands, she found his zipper and tugged.

"Olivia, wait."

She shook her head, annoyed. "No. For what?"

"I don't have anything—not here."

"No...." Her heart sank, and her mind raced for a solution. "Can't you just let me feel you, for a moment?"

"I think I only have a moment in me," he said hoarsely. "But I'll protect you, if you want that."

She nodded, wriggling out of her jeans and underwear, not giving a damn about the risks. Mac, too, pulled off his remaining clothes and wasted no time, slipping his hands under her, lifting her hips and burying himself deep inside her.

Olivia saw stars, actually saw them on the back of her closed lids. For just a moment, she let the delicious feeling of Mac inside her wash over her, then as he began to pull out, she woke up from her daydream. She gripped his hips as he thrust back inside of her, opened her legs and wrapped them around his waist, rocked with him, moaning, scratching at him, knowing she had little time left and feeling simultaneously frustrated and desperate for release.

Then Mac leaned down, caught one hard nipple between his lips and suckled deeply. She lost it. Pumping furiously, she gave in to the fire and ice of her climax, crying out, whimpering as Mac bucked and thrust inside her, the sweet feeling rolling through her.

On a curse, Mac pulled out and hovered above her.

Hardly a second elapsed before Olivia reached for him, wrapped her hand around him and stroked the thick, pulsing length of him until he sucked in air, thrust against her hand and climaxed.

He dropped down beside her on the hay, breathing heavily, his brow damp, and wrapped his arms around her. They lay there in silence, both breathing heavily, both damp with sweat, watching the last lights of day fade into the early gray of evening.

Olivia wanted to stay with him, keep him against her, but she didn't know where they stood now and that made her feel uncomfortable, as though she wanted to steal away by herself and think things through. "I want to stay," she began. "But I need to help with dinner."

"I know. Listen, Olivia." In one quick, effortless movement, he rolled her on top of him and cupped her backside possessively. His eyes blazed with a sincerity she'd never witnessed before. "You have nothing to worry about from me."

Her throat tightened with emotion as she looked down at him. "Oh, I think I have a lot to worry about with you. Just not in the way that you mean."

Chuckling, he squeezed her backside. "You might be right about that." He leaned in and kissed her gently on the mouth. "To speak in your language, sweetheart, this was just an appetizer. And I fully intend to enjoy the next course and the next and the next...."

Sixteen

Men didn't normally notice table settings or flower arrangements. They were usually hungry when they sat for dinner and just wanted to fill their bellies with whatever it was that smelled so damn good.

Sounded cavemanish, but it was true.

Mac was no exception as he sat beside Olivia at the DeBolds' dinner table, his plate piled high with fettuccine Alfredo and garlic bread. He was perfectly content at that moment. "You should be very proud of yourself, Louise. This is amazing."

Across the table, Louise looked at her husband and grinned. "Thanks, but I think my teacher should get all the credit."

"No way," Olivia retorted, twirling pasta on her fork. "You did this all by yourself. I just supervised."

Harold put an arm around his wife. "All by yourself, honey?"

"She's exaggerating."

"I am not!" Olivia insisted, laughing.

Just hearing Olivia's voice made Mac's body stir and he turned and stared at her. Dressed in a pair of funky black pants and a white sweater, she looked like a sexy ski bunny. He had every intention of being with her again tonight. As he'd said, their encounter in the barn was like a warm-up for the real thing. They'd both been too worked up, unable to take their time and really enjoy each other. Tonight, however, he was going to make her climax over and over again.

Olivia was talking to Harold, her eyes bright and happy. "And she rolled out the pasta herself."

"You did?" Harold said to Louise.

Blushing, she confirmed it. "I did."

Harold kissed her cheek, then said, "We have a pasta machine?"

Louise laughed. "Yes. Who knew, right?"

In between bites of pasta, Olivia said, "Tomorrow morning, we'll work on a few breakfast dishes that will have your in-laws apologizing for ever doubting your culinary skills." She grinned widely. "Think crab cakes benedict with lemon and parsley hollandaise, eggnog French toast and pancetta—"

"Forget apologizing," Harold interrupted merrily.

"They'll want to stay here all the time with that kind of menu."

Louise blanched. "Hmm, maybe we'd better rethink the cooking thing."

Everyone laughed, then Harold said, "Too late, honey—they're going to want to be here more often anyway when…you know."

Mac watched all three of them grin and wondered what was up, what he was missing. "Are you three going to let me in on the joke?"

"No joke," Harold said, looking at his wife in a soft, sweet way. "Louise is pregnant."

"Wow, congratulations," Mac said, reaching across the table to shake Harold's hand.

The proud father-to-be actually blushed. "Thank you."

"Do you really think your family will want to be around more?" Louise asked, a worried expression crossing her face.

"Not my family," Harold clarified. "My mother."

"Oh, Lord."

"She'll be ecstatic, sweetheart."

"She'll be meddlesome."

Finished with her pasta, Olivia dabbed her mouth with her napkin. "Well, she'll be here, and from a girl who hopes to have a child someday and has no mother to get frustrated and annoyed with for visiting too often, I say, 'you're lucky.'"

The news that Olivia's mother was not in the picture didn't come as a shock to Mac. When he was gathering information on Olivia and her father, he'd seen the

obituary. But hearing her talk about it, the trace of
sadness in her voice, did something to him, made him
feel protective. He knew what it felt like to lose a parent,
and he didn't enjoy seeing her upset.

Louise was smiling sympathetically at Olivia. "I'm
sorry. I had no idea. When did you lose your mother?"

"In high school."

Mac didn't know what made him do it, but he put his
hand over hers under the table. It felt good, right.

"That's awful." Shaking her head, Louise looked over
to her husband. "No matter how insane your mother
makes me, I'm going to grin and bear it for this little one."

Harold downed the last bite of his garlic bread. "Glad
to hear it, sweetheart." He turned and winked at Olivia,
who smiled in return.

As the foursome chatted and ate, Olivia did the
strangest and most enchanting thing. She rotated her
hand under his so that they were palm to palm, and
every once in a while she gave him a gentle squeeze.

Olivia pierced a freshly made popcorn kernel with a
needle and pulled the yellow fluffy bit onto the string
until it met with its cranberry neighbor. As the stereo
belted out Judy Garland's version of "Have Yourself a
Merry Little Christmas" and the fire crackled and spit,
she sat on a thick, oval rug in front of the tree, trying to
teach Mac how to make garland for the little Christmas
tree in her suite. It wasn't easy. The guy was a financial
genius and one helluva kisser, but when it came to a
needle and thread, he was all thumbs.

Mac crushed the popcorn kernel as he stuck the needle into it. Cursing, he tossed the remaining bits into the fire. "This is BS."

Olivia laughed. "Come on. No swearing when Judy Garland is singing."

"Why not? I feel sad and it's a sad song."

"It's not a sad song," she corrected. "It's an emotional song."

"Same thing."

She settled back against the base of the chenille chaise and sighed. "This was kind of me and my mom's song."

He looked at her as though she'd just stuck her needle in his side. "Okay, you can't go there when we were joking around, it makes me look like a jerk."

She smiled. "You're not a jerk." Realizing what she'd just said, she made a face, then laughed. "I can't believe I'm saying that."

He raised a sardonic eyebrow at her. "You're very funny when you're melancholy."

"My mom loved a good laugh, so she'd appreciate the dark humor in this conversation."

"When did she pass away? I know you said something at dinner…."

"When I was in high school." It was amazing that the words were still so difficult to say, and Olivia felt the urge to leap up on the bed and burrow under the covers.

"So, you were…what? Sixteen?"

"Yep."

"That's tough on a teenage girl. Mom's gone and

Dad is…" He paused, cocked his head to the side. "Dad is what?"

The direction of this conversation was starting to worry her. Mac was a sharp guy and he was putting the pieces together as he watched her. Sixteen, mom's gone, girl looks for comfort… "Dad was devastated—understandably—and he couldn't manage to do much but breathe." He was staring at her, studying her. "What?"

"Owen left you to fend for yourself, didn't he?"

Her jaw tightened. "No. He was grieving."

"So were you, Olivia."

She looked away, into the fire, her throat feeling that all too familiar tightness. She didn't want him, of all people, pointing out that her father had emotionally abandoned her for a time. It wasn't his place.

"How did you grieve, Liv? How did you manage all by yourself?"

"I wasn't by myself, damn it!" she shouted hoarsely. Fine, he got it. She hadn't been alone—she hadn't allowed herself to be alone. She'd found a substitute for the missing affection from her father, and a way to push back the pain. She grabbed her garland and a cranberry. "I went a little crazy for that first year and a half. But I got back on track, okay?"

He nodded. "Okay."

"I don't want to talk about this anymore."

"Done." He gestured to the bowl. "Can I have some more of that popcorn?"

He granted her a soft smile, and she felt the tension in her muscles relax. She let her shoulders fall and she released the breath she'd been holding since their conversation had begun. "Here you go," she said, handing him the bowl.

"I'm going to try this again."

She watched him stab at the popcorn, one piece, then two, then three. She shook her head and took away the bowl of popcorn before he crushed every piece to bits. "I'm thinking that this activity might be a little too sweet for a guy like you."

"Damn right it is," he said, reaching for a cranberry instead. "But I figure the sooner we finish decorating this tree the sooner I can kiss you."

She laughed. "Smart man. So, did you do any of this kind of thing around Christmas when you were a kid?"

"Nope. Not until I was fourteen, anyway."

"What happened when you were fourteen?"

"I was taken in by a college professor and his wife. They weren't the home-and-hearth type, but we had nice, relaxed holidays."

"Not the home-and-hearth type…"

He'd strung five cranberries on the string and looked quite proud of himself. "What I mean is they weren't the kind of parents who baked pies, sang me to sleep or tried to give me advice about girls. But I didn't mind that—I'd had enough of people trying to make me into something I didn't want to be. These people were teachers, question askers, and they made me think. They inspired me to work my ass off. They were the reason I ended up going to Harvard."

Interesting, Olivia thought. It explained so much

about him. Why his whole life was his work—and why he'd do anything to protect it. "Did they end up adopting you?"

He shrugged. "In their way. I lived with them until I was twenty-one."

"Are they still around?"

He shook his head. "She died a year after he died."

"I'm sorry," she said softly. "It must be hard to be alone."

He stabbed another red cranberry, then glanced up at her through his thick lashes. "I'm not alone right now."

She'd never met a man like this one, never been so affected by anyone. In a matter of a few minutes he had her feeling sad, frustrated, unsure, angry, protective and now, aroused. "Does growing up the way you did make you want kids, or not?"

There was no flash of revulsion or even dislike for the idea in his gaze, only a look of frank sincerity. "I can't imagine being able to love anyone that much. I don't think I'm capable of it—you need to see love from a very early age to be able to learn how to give it."

It surprised her that he'd given the idea so much thought. "It helps, probably, but I don't think it's a necessity. I think love can be learned, just like history or reading."

"Or chemistry?" he offered, amusement dancing in his eyes.

She nodded. "Exactly." Then she leaned in and kissed him on the mouth. A soft kiss at first, coaxing him to open for her, taste her. And when he did, she sighed. He'd eaten some of the popcorn when she hadn't been looking because his lips were slightly and deliciously salty. "I'm not going to wait for you to finish your garland."

"Sweetheart," he uttered huskily, "I was about to throw the whole damn tree out the window."

The tip of his tongue ran across her lips in one silken stroke and she smiled, touched his face with one hand. He had the slight scratch of a day's worth of beard, and the rough feeling acted like a drug on her. She angled her head and kissed him hard, reveling in the wounded, turned-on sound he made as he returned her kiss, then nipped at her bottom lip.

"I've come prepared tonight, Ms. Winston," he said, his eyes blazing with hunger.

"I hope you've come doubly, maybe even triply, prepared."

A hoarse chuckle escaped his throat. "I'm glad we're on the same page because there's no way I'm letting you out of my bed before sunup."

He was just about to kiss her again when there was a soft knock at the door. Mac cursed brutally. "I might have to kill the person on the other side of that door."

He pushed to his feet, stalked to the door and flung it wide. Johnny. He looked embarrassed.

"I'm sorry to bother you, sir," he said, then caught sight of Olivia. "And you, Miss Winston—but Mr. DeBold needs to speak with Mr. Valentine immediately."

When Mac first arrived and saw Harold DeBold sitting on the couch in his living room having a beer, he wasn't sure what the man wanted to see him about. Maybe he was freaked out about becoming a dad and wanted to talk about it, or about Louise. Or maybe he wanted their financial plans to change immediately to include the child.

Then Mac noticed another beer on the coffee table, opened, sweat beading on the bottle, and for the first time since he'd met the DeBolds his confidence in having them as clients waned.

Harold gestured for Mac to sit. "I apologize for interrupting your evening."

Mac wasn't up for pleasantries—not tonight. "What's this about?"

"I didn't know Olivia's father was Owen Winston." Mac frowned.

"He's a legend in the financial world," Harold continued.

Mac didn't like where this was going. He stared at Harold steadily. "Is there a point to this?"

Sensing Mac's irritation, Harold pointed to the bottle on the coffee table. "How about a drink? It's a great little microbrew from—"

"Harold," Mac interrupted tightly, "with all due respect, I don't want a goddamn thing except to know where you're going with this Owen Winston thing."

Harold grinned at that, then nodded. "I just got off the phone with him, Mac."

"You called him?"

"No. He called me."

"Looking for his daughter?"

"He wanted to warn me about you." Harold took a heavy swallow of beer. "But he also doesn't like that you're here with his daughter, that's for sure."

Mac grabbed the bottle of beer from the table and drained it. Then he stood. "Thank you for your time, Harold."

"You know, it was ballsy of you to hire her."

Mac shrugged. "It was calculated."

"Okay, then it was ballsy of her to take the job."

Ballsy…? Maybe the better word was unethical. Strange. Olivia had called him immoral once, but he'd never broken his client's trust—not like she just had. "I assume we're done here?"

"Of course. I don't want to keep you. But, Mac…" Harold stood, regarded him seriously. "I don't believe in rumors or the pissed-off ramblings of a jealous rival. I go on what I see. You have our business." He shrugged. "I just thought you should know."

Mac should have been thrilled—or hell, satisfied—but all he felt was the urge to shove his fist through a wall.

"Thank you, Harold." Mac shook his hand, then walked out of the room and out of the house.

Outside, the bitter wind slammed him in the face, small bits of snow pelting him from all sides. But he hardly felt it. From day one, he had been out to screw Olivia Winston, both physically and emotionally, and had ended up being screwed himself.

He spied her cottage, the lights of the Christmas tree inside glowing through the large bay window. She was a sly one, he had to give her that. But her little betrayal was going to pale in comparison with what he had planned for her next.

Seventeen

Olivia had little practice at seduction. She'd never been to a Victoria's Secret store or trolled the bookstores looking for the most recent printing of *How to Please a Man*. Instead, she was relying on the good old-fashioned art of being naked on a bed to get Mac right where she wanted him. And that would be on top of her...

On the other side of the room, the fire blazed in the hearth, warming the room and subsequently her skin. She was a little nervous. This was major exposure, total vulnerability, every flaw out there to be judged and inspected. For a moment, she contemplated greeting Mac from under the covers, but decided against it.

The door opened and Mac walked in, bringing a blast of frigid air with him. He was back so soon. Must've been nothing all that important with Harold, she thought, just guy talk. She shifted on the bed so she was lying sideways like one of those women in a Botticelli painting. Then he looked up and saw her. When he realized that she was nude, a flush of heat rolled up his neck. In one easy movement, he closed the door, then went to the edge of the bed.

Olivia's heart beat strongly in her chest. "Everything good?"

He nodded, his eyes dark and intense as he stared down at her. "Perfect." He unbuttoned his shirt and removed his pants. "Exactly what I was hoping for."

Anxious excitement played in Olivia's belly as Mac crawled toward her like an animal at feeding time. When he had her in his arms, he paused for a moment and just looked at her, her skin, her breasts. Then he leaned forward and took one soft peak into his mouth.

Olivia sucked air between her teeth and melted back onto the bed. This was what she'd wanted, what she'd hoped for tonight. She couldn't wait to have him inside of her. She closed her eyes and reveled in the feel of Mac on top of her. His skin, the way his muscles flexed and hardened as he moved down her body, planting kisses on her ribs, then her belly.

As he moved downward, Olivia smiled. She knew where he was going and she reached for his hair, fisted his scalp. His head dropped between her thighs. She felt his hands between her legs, pressing them apart, his fingers raking up her skin, opening the hot, wet folds. Her rational mind fell apart, and all that was left in her brain was the place that registered pleasure. And then he was licking her, soft, quick laps that had her legs trembling with excitement. Her fingers gripped his hair as he continued suckling her, as she bucked against his mouth. She could barely hold on. The feeling was too strong, too intense.

"Oh, Mac…I'm going to…"

He must've heard the desperation in her voice, knew she was on the brink of climax, because he lifted off of her, grabbed the foil packet that had been in his jeans and sheathed himself.

He entered her with one hard thrust. Olivia cried out, her body wracked with heat and energy as she took him fully. He slipped his hands under her hips and squeezed her closer, then pulled out and slammed back into her again. Olivia felt the initial thunder of climax coming over her and her body reacted. She bucked under him, her hands searching for his chest, her nails digging into the flesh over his muscle.

He bent his head, covered her mouth with his in a deep, all-consuming kiss. Olivia started to whimper, the core of her shaking and pulsing until her body could no longer contain the hot, decadent energy inside and she erupted. Her head dropped to one side, then the other as she cried out in several painful-sounding screams that seemed to rip right through Mac.

He pounded into her, over and over, until she thought he might rip her apart. But when she straightened her legs and spread them wide, he stiffened, groaned and thrust deeply inside of her, bucking, pounding, until he gave in and took his own release.

In the moments afterward, Mac stayed on top of her, his hips flexing and shuddering with the aftermath of release. But as soon as her arms went around his neck and threaded into his hair, Mac pulled himself away and off the bed.

Olivia stared after him, her body still achy and warm from his touch. "What's wrong?"

He sat there, his back to her. Then from deep in his chest, he started laughing. It was not a pleasant, happy sound, but dark and ominous.

"What?" Olivia asked softly.

Mac glanced over his shoulder, his gaze eerily satisfied. "I had no idea you were as ruthless as me."

A waft of cold air moved through her. "What are you talking about?"

"I have to say I'm impressed."

"Impressed with what?" He didn't look like himself. He was dark and sad, and Olivia suddenly felt very naked. Covering herself with a throw, Olivia asked, "What is wrong with you?"

"During my drink with Harold he informed me that he had just gotten off the phone with your father."

Olivia's heart sank. "No...."

"To warn him about me."

Olivia swallowed hard.

Mac stood and threw his shirt on. "I wonder how he knew I was with the DeBolds."

This was not happening, Olivia thought with deep

frustration and disappointment. How could she have made such a mistake? How could her father be such an ass? "I'm sorry. I told him where I was going, but—"

"And that I was going, too, right?"

"Yes, but—"

"I remember you calling me immoral…."

"Mac, I know you're angry and I get why. And I don't blame you. But if you look at the situation for what it is, I did nothing wrong here."

He put his pants on. "Really. How do you figure that?"

She came up on her knees, the throw pressed to her chest. "We're not working together on this trip. Our job ended when I left your house. I'm working for Louise, and I had every right to tell my father where I was."

"Where you are, yes. Not where I am." He put on his coat. "Good thing Harold and Louise don't believe lies spread by tired, envious, unscrupulous old men."

"Stop that." She hated what he was saying because now she was starting to believe it was true.

Dressed and ready to walk out, Mac paused and looked at her. His gaze was filled with disrespect. "I believe we're even, don't you?"

"*We're* even?" she repeated. "Who are you referring to, Mac? Me and you? Or you and my father."

His lips thinned dangerously, then he shrugged as if he couldn't care less. "Take your pick."

"Well, you did nothing to me," she said tightly. "I'm not hurt or humiliated. You wanted me and I wanted you. I'm done obsessing about my past, about mistakes I've made. I enjoyed every moment of us."

For one second—just a split second—his eyes softened. Then the walls closed once again and he uttered a terse, "Well, perhaps that's where the revenge lies then. There's no more *us* to enjoy."

He closed the door behind him, and Olivia just stared after him. An hour ago, that door had been the heaven's gate her lover had walked through. Now, it represented the enormous barrier between them.

She dropped back onto the bed. She had told him the truth. She felt no shame in the choices that she'd made. She had wanted Mac as much as he had wanted her, and though they were never going to be together this way again, she had no regrets for making love to him one last time.

Because, no matter how much he despised her now, she felt sure of one thing—that's what it had been for her.

Love.

Eighteen

Morning-afters were usually filled with headaches or heartaches. Olivia's was filled with both. She had struggled to get through the two-hour breakfast lesson with Louise, overcooking the hollandaise, then dropping the pan to the floor when the woman had mentioned that Mac had indeed left late last night—on his own plane, of course.

If she were a more carefree woman, Olivia mused, stepping out of the DeBolds' limousine and gathering up her bags, she'd just chock the whole thing up to a great fling, and the reason she had finally let go of her shame about the past. Mac had made her feel good— nothing wrong with that. She was an adult now, and she deserved pleasure, even if the man giving it would never love her back.

"Have a safe flight, Olivia," Louise said, waving from the window of the limousine.

Olivia shouldered her bag, then waved back. "Thanks for everything."

"No—thank you. I'll let you know what happens on Thanksgiving."

Her evil smile made Olivia laugh. "Give 'em, hell, Louise."

The woman smiled and waved again, then rolled up the window and the car pulled away. Olivia walked toward the plane and boarded. As she sat in her leather bucket seat waiting for takeoff, she thought about herself and Mac and their backgrounds, and how their pasts had totally dictated their present. He'd been abandoned, and had learned to survive in the only way he could. And he had survived—he'd gone to the top of his profession. She'd been abandoned, too, but unlike him, she hadn't fought—instead, she'd refused to deal with her pain and had looked for help in the wrong place.

So she understood his anger, and the fear behind it.

She fell asleep thinking about him, and woke up in Minneapolis with a neck cramp and a small twinge of hope that maybe she'd see him again. She got her car from long-term parking and drove home. For the first time in a long time, her apartment felt warm and safe, and for the rest of the night, she ignored the blinking light on her answering machine and settled under her comforter to watch *Bridget Jones's Diary*.

Tomorrow was a huge day. She had menus to execute

and staff to boss around. Ethan and Mary's holiday engagement ball had been in the works for weeks, but it was the last thing Olivia wanted to think about. Celebrating her friend's happiness was a must-do, of course, and she'd never shirk her duty, but because of who Ethan was, the event was going to be a blowout. The whole of Minneapolis was going to be there, and she couldn't help wondering if maybe that meant a certain financial genius was going to show up....

Olivia pulled the covers up to her chin, aimed the remote at the TV and pushed Play.

Ah...Colin Firth.

Mac's lungs were about to explode, and his legs felt shaky, but he didn't stop running.

It was coming up on 5:00 a.m. and he'd been in the gym of his office building on the treadmill for over an hour, trying to get his brain to shut down. Unfortunately, it looked as though his body was going to go first.

He stabbed the off button on the machine and reached for his towel. Damn it, he thought, walking unsteadily to his private locker room. When he'd left Door County two days ago, he'd counted on the fact that he wouldn't have to see Olivia Winston for months.

It wouldn't be nearly that long.

Mac hated tuxedos about as much as he hated over-the-top parties, but he was a slave to business, and after learning that one of his former clients was going to be at Ethan Curtis's engagement party tonight, he'd reconsidered the invite. Ethan Curtis was marrying Mary

Kelley, Olivia's business partner, so she was definitely going to be there.

He'd broken things off with many women in his time, and had never given a second thought to seeing them again. It was just this woman—she made him feel like a weak animal, a constantly hungry animal. He had to get her out of his system.

He stripped and headed for the shower. Maybe the best way to get Olivia out of his head was to force himself to see her again, be reminded of her betrayal. Or maybe he was just kidding himself and tonight was going to be just as hellish as the past two nights had been.

The top floor of the world-famous building rotated at the pace of one revolution per hour—that way the guests who were partaking in food and drink wouldn't get dizzy and lose their lunches in the first five minutes.

A wise plan by the architect, Olivia mused as she left the kitchen after inspecting each and every serving platter before it went out. She spotted Mary talking to Tess by the window and headed their way. Her blond hair piled on top of her head, Mary was wearing an off-the-shoulder gray silk dress, her protruding belly stretching the material in a lovely, earthy way. And looking especially glamorous in a brick-red minidress and matching heels, her red hair loose and blown straight, was Tess. Olivia watched as No Ring Required's resident hard-ass reached out and touched Mary's stomach, her smoky eyes shining with warmth.

"Well, well, well," Mary said when Olivia approached, her gaze running over Olivia's strapless chocolate-brown pencil dress. "Can I say it again, Miss Winston? You look hot."

Tess snorted. "That word should not be coming out of a pregnant woman's mouth."

Laughing, Mary remarked, "How do you think I got this way in the first place?"

Pretending to cover her ears, Tess said, "Okay, too much information."

Feeling self-conscious for a moment, Olivia smoothed the fabric of her skirt and glanced around at the party, which was packed and in full swing. She'd dressed carefully for Mary's engagement party. After all, she was wearing two hats—guest and worker—so she had needed to find the right combo. And then there was the not insignificant fact that Mac might be coming. She wasn't going to lie to herself and pretend that seeing him hadn't affected her choice in wardrobe.

"Did you see your father yet?" Tess asked, pulling her from her thoughts.

Olivia shook her head. "Where is he?"

"Over at the bar."

Olivia had been trying to get hold of her father for the past two days, but he'd been in Boston on business and hadn't returned her calls.

"So," Mary said cozily, "before Ethan steals me away, are you going to tell us how Door County went?"

"No."

Tess lifted a brow at Olivia's succinct reply. "Uh-oh."

"Was I right?" Mary asked gently. "About going out

of town together? Did you two…hmm, how to put this delicately…"

"Forget delicately," Tess interrupted. "Did you get busy with the guy?"

Olivia felt red all over. "C'mon, Tess. Jeez."

Tess gave Mary a look. "That's a yes."

"Tess," Mary said, warning in her gaze, "I hope you've learned from this—never go out of town with a guy you find attractive."

"Please…he'd have to slip something in my double espresso and carry me off for that to happen, and God help him if he did that." Tess was looking around the room as she spoke, and in a matter of seconds her whole demeanor changed. Her skin went white as milk and she stared, fixated on something.

Both Mary and Olivia saw the change and turned to see what was affecting Tess in such a way, but in the sea of people, they couldn't tell who or what was the cause.

"What's wrong, Tess?" Olivia asked.

"I swear I just saw…someone I knew a long time ago."

"Old boyfriend?"

"I suppose you could call him that. He looks so different—it can't be him."

Mary attempted to lighten the mood. "Did he look better or worse?"

"He looked bored and aloof, and utterly gorgeous." She kept searching the crowd. "It can't be him." She turned back to them, color returning to her cheeks. "Seeing people from the past is an awkward thing."

It was all she said, but Olivia knew it had to be more

than feeling awkward. Tess had actually looked panic-stricken. But Olivia didn't get to inquire further because at that moment Ethan walked over to them and slipped his arm around Mary's growing waist. "Can I take my girl? There's a coat check up front calling our name."

Mary rolled her eyes. "You are such an exhibition-ist, Ethan."

"It's one of the reasons you love me, right?"

She smiled at Olivia and Tess, then kissed her soon-to-be husband. "Of course, honey."

When they'd walked away, indeed toward the coat check, Tess quickly excused herself, too, saying that she was going to see about something.

Then, Olivia spotted her father speaking to two men by the bar and she headed his way.

Standing near the jazz band, Mac watched Olivia dance with her father. She looked beautiful tonight, and even though he'd tried to put her out of his mind, his body remembered everything. Clearly, it was going to take a helluva lot of time and effort to forget her.

She caught his eye then, and blanched. She hadn't expected him, and she looked both hopeful and worried. His hands itched to touch her, kiss her. If he had any pride, any sense, he'd walk away from the situation and never look back. But he was an idiot.

Pushing away from the stage, he walked toward her just as the song was ending.

Owen spotted him, too, and gritted his teeth as Mac walked up. "What are you doing here?"

"Retrieving an old client," Mac said easily.

"Oh, yes, I saw you talking with Martin Pollack. I suppose he's willing to overlook your—"

"Stop, Owen. This story of yours is growing so old there's mold on it. Everyone knows you lied, they're just waiting for you to admit it."

"I'm not admitting anything."

"Suit yourself. I don't give a damn anymore." He looked at Olivia. "You look beautiful tonight."

"Thank you." Her eyes glittered with warmth, and something else…something he couldn't quite name.

"Are you having a good time?"

"Not really."

Owen stared at her. "Let's go, Olivia."

But Olivia wouldn't take her eyes off of Mac. "It's okay."

Mac was confused. "What is?"

"If you need to do it, I understand. You have me and my father here."

"What are you talking about?"

She smiled, a little sadly. "The great revenge. What it's all been for."

"Oh, Liv…" Mac shook his head. She didn't get it. She thought when he'd walked out the other night he was still bent on payback. She didn't understand that what she'd done had pissed him off as a man—not a businessman.

"What did you do to my daughter?" Owen said menacingly.

"Dad, that's enough," Olivia said.

But Owen wasn't listening. "If you hurt her—"

"I'm serious, Dad. You've caused enough trouble." Olivia glared at her father. "One more word about Mac, and our relationship will be irrevocably damaged. Do you understand me?"

Owen looked shocked. "Olivia."

A surge of need moved through Mac. It was so powerful it took him completely by surprise, and he reached for Olivia's hand and lifted it to his mouth. After he kissed the palm, he spoke to Owen, but he looked into Olivia's chocolate eyes. "You have an amazing daughter, Winston. Beautiful and brilliant. I tried like hell to make her pay for your mistakes, but she'd have nothing to do with me."

Owen said nothing.

Mac released Olivia's hand. Revenge was a useless thing. He was done. He nodded at Olivia, said good-night and walked away.

Nineteen

The party wasn't supposed to end until midnight, but Olivia just couldn't stay any longer. She asked Tess to cover for her, then grabbed her coat and headed for the elevator. Just as the doors were about to close, her father slipped inside.

"Dad, I said good night to you...." She knew she sounded peevish, but she didn't care. She wanted one thing right now and any interruptions were unwelcome ones.

"Sweetheart, I just had to tell you that I'm so proud of you."

"For what?" she asked impatiently.

"Keeping that snake away from you."

That was it. Olivia reached out and pulled the emergency stop button. The elevator came to a jolting stop, and her father looked at her like she was crazy.

"What's going on?"

"I love you, Dad, but I'm not doing this any longer. Get this straight, I'm not Grace—"

"What?"

"I'm not your sister. I'm not Grace. Her life is not mine." She looked at him, her gaze serious. "What I am is a grown woman who is not going to cater to her father's fears about a life he can't control."

Owen's neck reddened. "Olivia…"

"My personal life is my own. Period." Owen looked very stuffy in his tuxedo, very impervious, but she went on. "Now, about Mac. You're going to leave him alone. Bottom line is, I love the guy, and if we can both get past how we met and why we were brought together, I think there might be a future in it for us."

Her father looked horrified. "No.…"

She took a breath and softened at the look of despair on his face. "What do you have against him, other than the fact that he wanted to punish you for lying to his clients?"

For a second, Owen looked as though he was going to deny it, then he dropped his gaze and stared at his shoes. "Getting old isn't graceful or easy. People treat you like you might break, like you can't take the heat—they think your mind isn't what it used to be."

Olivia touched his arm. She loved her father—even with all his faults, and there were many. She rolled up on her toes and kissed him on the cheek. "Do the right thing, Dad. You're a great money man, a legend—everyone thinks so. Just be that for as long as you can." She reached out and flipped down the emergency stop button. The elevator descended. "The truth will come out eventually. Don't make this foolish mistake be your legacy. Take care of it."

Owen was silent for a moment, then he nodded.

The doors opened to the lobby and Olivia stepped out. "I have somewhere I need to be. Good night, Dad."

He gave her a tight smile and uttered a soft, "Good night, Olivia," before the elevator doors closed again.

When Mac walked into his house an hour later, he felt like he didn't belong there. Every piece of furniture, every color on the walls, had been picked out by her. Why was it then that she herself wasn't here? Olivia belonged here, she belonged to him.

"Damn it," he muttered, going down the hall to his room. He was going to take a shower, then head over to Olivia's apartment. He was so tired of fighting for the stupid, inconsequential things in his life. He was going to fight for something real now. He was going to make her talk to him.

"I'm trying this again."

Instinctively, Mac prepared himself for a fight. Then the voice registered in his brain and he let it fall to the side as he looked up. There on his bed, lying back against his pillow, was Olivia. She was fully dressed, her dark hair tousled and loose, and she had a worried smile on her lips.

Mac stared at her. "How did you get in here?"

She held his gaze steady with hers. "I still have the key. You forgot to ask for it back."

He shook his head slowly. "I didn't forget."

The expression in her eyes turned hopeful and she said, "Mac, about tonight...and the DeBolds..."

He cut her off. "No."

But she was insistent. "Yes. I need to say this to you again." She pushed off the bed and walked over to him, stood before him. "I didn't think. I shouldn't have said a word about where I was. It was bad business, and I've learned from it. You could've lost the DeBolds—"

"Stop." He grabbed her arms and pulled her against him. "I don't give a damn about the DeBolds. Hell, I could've lost you." His gaze moved over her face. "From the very beginning, I put you in an impossible situation. I was a first-rate ass."

She bit her lip and her eyes misted over. "I have to tell you something. I talked with my father, and—"

"Sweetheart, I don't care," he said, truly meaning it. He'd never believed he was capable of the feelings he was having, the intensity of his feelings for her. "I don't care about any of that anymore. The only thing that matters to me is you, making you happy, making you smile, having you in my bed every morning. I'm tired of fighting, of doing battle." He reached out, brushed his fingertips across her cheek. "The only thing I'm going to fight for now is you...us."

Olivia could hardly believe what she was hearing. This was not the impenetrable tycoon she'd known when she had signed on to be his wife-for-hire. This was the loving, forgiving, generous man she'd hoped and prayed would walk into the room tonight and smile at her, accept her apology and go forward with her.

"Ever since I laid eyes on you, my life means something, Liv," he continued, taking her face in his hands. "Screw the money and the need for more, and more power to go with it. This is something good. You and me. I don't know what to do with it, but I know one thing, I'm not letting you go."

"Oh, Mac…"

He leaned in, kissed her on the mouth, a possessive, branding kiss that had her catching her breath. "I love you, Liv. I love you so much I ache."

"I love you, too." She laughed, pressed her forehead against his. "God, we're such idiots. Our intentions going into this thing were so stupid."

"True, but if they hadn't been we never would have found each other."

She nodded. "Or the way out of the past."

"Damn right." He kissed her again, a deep kiss that had her melting into him. Groaning with need, he murmured against her mouth, "Sweetheart, stay with me, love me. I want you to be mine forever."

Olivia smiled, her heart so full and happy. "Yes." She couldn't believe she was hearing him say that he loved her—it was a miracle.

Mac looked up then, his eyes burning with desire. "I'm going to marry you."

Olivia tried to fight back the tears, but it was useless. She nodded, and choked out, "Okay."

He brushed away the tear from her cheek. "Make babies with you."

"Yes. Yes." She threw her arms around his neck and held on tight. From a shameful past that had held her hostage for so long, to a light, loving future with the man of her dreams. How was it possible? She was so lucky.

Mac took her mouth in a slow, pulse-pounding kiss. "I love you, Mrs. Valentine."

"Sounds strange, doesn't it?" she whispered against his mouth, feeling so vulnerable, yet so loved.

He shook his head and nibbled at her lower lip. "No way, sweetheart. Sounds just right."

* * * * *

LIKE LIGHTNING
by
Charlene Sands

CHARLENE SANDS

resides in Southern California with her husband, Don, and two children, Jason and Nikki. Her love of the American West stems from early childhood memories of story time with her imaginative father. Tall tales of dashing pirates and dutiful sheriffs brought to life with words and images sparked her passion for writing. When not writing, she enjoys sunny California days, Pacific beaches and sitting down with a good book.

She loves to hear from her readers. Charlene invites you to visit her website and enter her contests at www.charlenesands.com.

To my fun-loving friend, Pam Frendian!
Thanks for your continued love and friendship
through the years.
And to Ellen Lacy, my dear friend
who loves to read as much as I do.
Here's to Tuesday mornings and those
wonderful beach days!
I am truly blessed to call you both friends.

One

"**I** do." Trey Walker uttered the words slowly, both awed and a little bit frightened. In a million lifetimes, he'd never dreamed he'd say these words. Especially not to Maddie Brooks, the auburn-haired beauty standing beside him, her wide eyes filled with gratitude. They stood under an arbor of lush traveling vines in the small garden area behind his house at 2 Hope Ranch.

"I do, too," she offered, as a gentle breeze blew by, messing her hair enough to give her down-home girl appearance a sexy edge.

Trey swallowed hard, intrigued by the young woman who'd be living with him for an unforeseen length of time. In truth, the petite green-eyed female scared the hell out of him with her innocent looks and wholesome demeanor. She was the exact sort of woman Trey avoided—the kind that said "KEEPER" in big bold capital letters. But damn it all, if Trey hadn't needed her, or rather if 2 Hope Ranch hadn't needed what she had to offer, Trey would never have agreed to this.

"So you agree to the terms?" She repeated softly, her voice a mere whisper on the wind.

"I do, Maddie. There's no need to sign a contract. My word is good as gold."

Maddie nodded a bit tentatively as she swiveled her body around, glancing at the property, her slender hands set in the back pockets of her denim jeans. Trey looked his fill, enjoying the view of a perfectly formed backside. He was one to appreciate a good-looking woman, and Maddie was all that—even in her range-dusty work clothes.

When she turned back around, Trey snapped his head up to meet her gaze. Again, her words were soft as morning dew and Trey got the feeling she was as reluctant about this arrangement as he was. "I'll move my things in tonight, and tomorrow I'll set up my office in the old barn. The animals all seem to be doing fine. I think this might just work out."

Trey squeezed his eyes shut momentarily. He grunted a reply and held out his hand. A handshake in this part of Texas was more than enough to bind an agreement.

Maddie lifted her right hand from her pocket and slid her palm into his. He shook the hand quickly before the impact of her touch could register to any other part of his body, other than his addled brain. "It's a deal then."

She bit down on her lip drawing his attention to a heart-shaped mouth so pink and ripe that Trey was certain the Almighty had made her lips expressly for kissing. Too bad, Trey thought with regret, because he'd already set Maddie Brooks strictly off-limits. She was his business partner now, of sorts.

She would rent out one room in his house, use the old barn as her office and treat her animal patients there. Not only would 2 Hope Ranch gain from the rental fee, but Maddie had also agreed to treat all of Trey's livestock for free. It was a deal he couldn't refuse. His ranch had encountered more than a few setbacks lately and Trey just plain needed the revenue. He'd had no choice really and neither had Maddie. Her veterinary office had burned clear down to the ground just days ago and Trey's was the only ranch within miles that had an extra barn and a ranch house big enough to accommodate her without any problem. There was no denying Trey had plenty of room on the grounds as well as three empty bedrooms inside his house. Trey had taken in her animals, first thing, when they'd been rescued by the fire department in Hope Wells. The yellow Labrador Maggie was healing from a wound of birdshot while the border collie, Toby, had been injured when hit by a car. Two rabbits suffered from ear mites and various other small pets were now housed inside Trey's smaller, older barn. Hell, he couldn't have the animals suffer. They needed a home, but he hadn't bargained on Maddie coming to live with him. No sir.

Uncle Monty had pulled a fast one talking him into this arrangement and Trey wasn't at all certain his uncle hadn't had matchmaking on his mind.

Maddie graced him with a small smile. "Deal."

Trey began to walk off but turned when a thought struck. "You need help moving your stuff in?"

"Uh, no. Not really. I don't have much at the motel but some clothes and a few things I managed to accumulate since the fire. I'm pretty much starting out fresh. I don't even have much left in the way of files." She shrugged, keeping up a brave front, but Trey figured Maddie was as broken up inside as that old border collie. "Guess I'm just going to have to improvise."

Trey nodded, recalling that Maddie had lived in a small apartment above her office in town and she'd lost almost everything. The insurance company came through with a small sum for the time being, but the rest of her claim was contingent upon an investigation into the cause of the fire.

He tipped his hat. "I'll be here, if you need me."

He was just being neighborly, doing the polite thing, he told himself, yet those words sent his body into small shock. He shuddered and turned to walk away before Maddie noticed. No sense worrying the girl. She had enough to worry over. But the fact remained that Trey didn't want to be needed. Ever and especially by a female. He'd been cursed in that regard. Both his father and grandfather had had a bad track record when it came to women. They'd done a great job of breaking hearts and wrecking lives. Trey had seen the destruction firsthand and it hadn't been pretty. From early on, after one failed engagement, Trey had vowed to keep his own life simple. And women close only when both agreed on temporary. Trey didn't do permanent. Nothing was going to change that.

And now that pretty little filly Maddie Brooks would be sharing bath towels with him under his roof. An image instantly flashed—Maddie's petite body wrapped in a two-by-nothing towel and bumping into him in the hallway. He paused, letting the image sink in of soft ripe curves and healthy tanned skin all tucked into a tight little package. He caught himself and cursed up a blue streak then kicked up his heels so fast that his boots cut a straight arrow path back to the corral.

Sometimes, being neighborly came with too high a price.

Maddie slowed her Dodge Ram truck to a stop by the rubble that was once her home, her office and her very existence in Hope Wells. The small place on the edge of town she had proudly called home for the past year and a half was gone. She sucked up enough courage to glance once again at the devastation. Through the truck's window she noted large cinders still radiating heat. Everything was black, charred beyond recognition.

Maddie stepped down from the truck and the scent of destruction, as that deadly combination of burnt belongings and wafting smoke billowed up and nearly choked her lungs. Only a small broken-down remnant of her storefront sign remained. The sign that had once said, The Animal Place, *T.A.P. Gently,* Madeline M. Brooks, D.V.M., now only touted the first three letters of her first name, Mad. How appropriate. A little irony of life, she thought sadly. Tears welled in her eyes as she stared at the loss.

Goodness, she still didn't understand how the fire started exactly. Faulty wiring, one firefighter guessed. He'd known old Dr. Benning for years, the man who had sold Maddie his veterinary practice before moving to Dallas to be closer to his grandchildren. He'd been a mainstay in the community, a man who cared for animals until his eyesight had just about given way. Maddie, fresh out of an internship in northern California, had been overjoyed at the prospect of buying a small but fully established practice and had just enough funds to cover a down payment on the asking price.

Doc Benning had stayed on for one month after the sale, guiding Maddie, introducing her to his clients, acting much as a mentor would tutor a new student. Maddie had been grateful for the help, but she'd been eager to get started on her own. She'd studied hard, learned fast and her love of animals came easily. She'd been graced with the "touch" from a young age, a special way she had of communicating with animals on a plane that went beyond description. Her well-honed instincts served her as well as all of her schooled learning and Maddie was extremely proud of the combination of talent.

She reached into the truck, grabbing a beat-up pair of leather work gloves and tiptoed her way through the charred remains. Heat curled her toes from inside her boots, but it wasn't unbearable, so she ventured forth, searching. This would be the last chance she'd have to find something, anything left partially intact, before a crew would come in to clear away what remained. She'd been through the place once already, right after the fire but she figured she'd been too distraught to really see anything beyond the damage.

Maddie tiptoed carefully through the wreckage, her gaze traveling along slowly, eyeing each inch of ground carefully in hopes of finding something she might recognize, but nothing appeared salvageable. With a heavy sigh, Maddie turned to leave. She shouldn't have come. It was as fruitless a venture as it was painful. Everything was gone.

But then a glint of something shiny caught her eye. Afternoon sunlight beamed down and at first Maddie thought it was just light reflecting on burnt metal. She stepped closer and bent to make a better inspection, putting on her gloves. With nimble fingers, she parted the ashes that partially covered her discovery. The Appaloosa emerged, a sterling silver necklace given to her by her Grandma Mae when Maddie had graduated high school. Maddie lifted the piece, picking it up by the chain, dangling the necklace before her eyes. She gasped her relief then chuckled with glee. "Hello, Aphrodite. I should've known nothing would keep you down."

The charm appeared undamaged, except for a layer of ash that Maddie quickly blew away with a forceful gush of air. Then with a gentle rub of her gloved thumb the sterling horse winked back with luster, appearing unscathed and good as new. Maddie clutched the charm to her chest. Tears stung her eyes—tears of relief, of happiness and of gratitude.

If there were one thing Maddie would have chosen to salvage from all this destruction, it would have been Aphrodite. Maddie believed that small miracles happened every day, and today she'd been graced with one tiny precious miracle.

Grandma Mae's sage words flashed through her mind as she recalled that cloudless spring day when she'd been given the family heirloom. "Love who you are, child. Love what you do. Love your family and friends and God's creatures, and then love will also find you."

"I'm glad I found you."

Maddie whirled around suddenly, the deep resonating sound of Trey Walker's voice startling her out of her thoughts. With her heart in her throat, Maddie peered at him as he stood with arms folded, leaning against the cab of her truck. Trey's voice did things to her. His impossible good looks knotted her stomach. His long lean stature, that cowboy stance, the hypnotic way a tic worked at his jaw, all conspired to throw Maddie's once nicely orchestrated world upside down.

At one time, she had thought to be in love with him. She'd hoped to gain his attention since the first time she'd laid eyes on him, out in his barn at 2 Hope.

Trey had called Doc Benning out to see to an aging mare. The old girl had been failing for quite some time and Doc had brought Maddie along with him to give her the experience.

She doubted she'd ever forget the image of Trey Walker bent over that old roan, whispering soft soothing words in her ear. Strong, work-roughened hands slid gently and with masterful grace over the horse's muzzle. He worked his hands along her mane, each stroke careful, calculated to give the old girl peace.

There wasn't anything she or Doc Benning could do, but give the horse a shot to put her down. But Trey disagreed. He wanted her to go as God intended, *when* He intended. And Maddie knew, without a doubt, that Trey had made the right choice. The horse had eased out of the world with Trey's loving hands caressing her softly, spilling words from his heart and speaking a final farewell to a longtime friend.

Maddie had fallen in love with Trey Walker that day—instantly and without a doubt in her mind.

But she'd been clearly disappointed when Trey Walker ignored her every attempt to gain his affection. Oh, he'd been polite, sweet as peach pie when she'd come out to check on his livestock. But he'd also been distant and at times, indifferent. Maddie had even tried a supreme makeover once—highlighting her hair, learning to do her makeup without smearing herself all up and wearing the most revealing, cleavage-spilling clothes a woman dared to wear. Nothing had worked. He hadn't given her the slightest glimmer of hope. Clearly he wanted no part of her. And seeing him around town making easy conversation with women at times surely broke her heart.

Heck, you don't have to hit Maddie Brooks over the head with a sledgehammer. She'd finally gotten the message. She'd given up. Wholly and completely.

But darn if the man standing right in front of her still didn't make her legs go wobbly. Only now, Maddie was smarter. She armed herself with steely resolve. She didn't have a clue about enticing a man like Trey. She wasn't the sort of woman to catch Trey Walker's attention. She understood that now. "Trey, are you looking for me?"

Trey glanced at her tear-smudged face but Maddie refused to let it bother her. She wasn't out to impress Trey Walker anymore. She wouldn't rub her cheeks dry, but they burned hot as Trey's deep blue eyes studied her.

He pushed away from the truck and stood at the edge of the ashes, his gaze holding hers. "Ah, Maddie, you're crying."

Maddie stiffened her shoulders against Trey's knowing eyes. She lifted the necklace and swung it out, catching his attention. "Happy tears. I found something…something that wasn't destroyed. Something…precious."

Trey glanced at the necklace then arched a brow, but nodded in understanding.

"My grandmother gave this to me when I graduated high school. I wore it every day in college. It has special meaning."

Trey stepped into the rubble, coming up close for a

better look. He reached for the necklace, his fingers brushing over her gloved hand. Even through thick leather, Maddie felt the shock of his slight touch. The careful way he'd lifted the jewel from her as if he'd trusted that it was indeed precious, only magnified the sensation. She stared at the dark fringes of his eyelashes as he peered down and she noted a tiny quirk of a smile erupting. "It's nice. I'm glad you found it in all this mess."

Maddie glanced around. "Yes. It's about all I found." When she turned to him again, she'd wondered if he'd purposely sought her out. "What are you doing here? Do you want me for something?"

Trey pursed his lips, disguising a devil-made grin. Hell, he'd never seen anything like it. Maddie Brooks, traipsing through these ruins, tearstains running a path down her cheeks and smudged with white ash with her red-gold hair a tangle around her face. She'd looked like a lost child—a vulnerable one at that, but he'd yet to find anyone prettier, or more appealing.

Did he want her for something?

A loaded question and one Trey would never answer.

"I was heading to town to buy feed for the horses, when I realized I hadn't given you the key to the house. But first," Trey said, placing his hands on her shoulders and turning her around so that her back was to him. He lifted her hair and slipped the necklace around her neck, letting the loose chain slide down her throat to fall into the soft valley between her breasts. He breathed in, a sharp intake of oxygen that left no room for doubt where his mind had drifted. The subtle scent of raspberries, sweet and pungent wafted up as her hair fell back into place. "There," he said and stepped away.

Maddie turned around, removing her gloves so she

could finger the charm. Joy lit her eyes, but she guarded her delight carefully, as if she were afraid to indulge in happiness for too long. Trey understood that, better than she might guess.

"Thank you," she said with a small smile.

He nodded, keeping his eyes focused on her face and not on the deep inviting cleavage that framed the necklace. He slipped a hand into his pocket, coming up with a key ring. He removed one and handed it to her. "Here you go. Come and go as you please on the ranch. I won't wait up."

"Oh, I won't be going out much, unless I have to make a late-night house call."

He nodded again, not happy with the notion of Maddie Brooks underfoot every night. "Sometimes, I get in late," he admitted, "but if you need anything when I'm not around, you know Kit, my foreman?"

"Yes, we've met. But I'm sure I'll be fine."

"Okay then. I'd better get that grain before the store closes."

She lifted the key to the ranch house. "Thanks again. I guess I'll get my things from the Cactus Inn now."

Trey reached into his back pocket and presented her with his red bandanna. "For your face."

"Oh." Color rose from under her smudge marks, brightening her face to a rosy hue. "Is it that bad?"

"Doesn't bother me a bit. But I figured you'd want to clean up before heading to the motel."

She began swiping her face for all she was worth. "Thanks. I must look like he…heck."

Trey turned his back on Maddie, released a reluctant sigh and headed for his truck, mumbling, "*Heck* never looked so danged cute."

Trey got into his truck, gunned the engine and took off, his wheels spitting up a cloud of dry Texas dust. He'd come into town to help Maddie move her things from the motel. It hadn't set right that she'd refused his offer. What kind of man would allow a woman, who was down on her luck, alone in the world, and who had lost most of her possessions, to face that task alone?

But one look at her today, standing there in the midst of her one-time home, and something powerful stabbed at him. It wasn't like anything he'd felt before, this protective, warm feeling he had for her. Trey didn't like it, not one bit. If he wasn't careful, he'd be under her spell, he'd have her under his sheets and then disaster would strike.

Maddie would come out the loser.

And Trey figured the woman had enough troubles. He didn't want to add to them. As much as he wanted to help her, going to the motel wouldn't have been wise. Trey shook his head. Spending time with Maddie Brooks would just be dang foolish. He'd have to nip this problem in the bud, before anything dared to blossom.

Tonight, he'd lay things out straight with Maddie.

But in truth, he'd be more comfortable wrestling half a dozen big, hungry grizzly bears.

Maddie had always wanted to see the inside of Trey's house at 2 Hope. The long sprawling adobe and mason ranch house, with true column pillars spoke of elegance and grace. Although weathered, beaten down from time and perhaps a bit of neglect, the house commanded certain respect.

Her heart squeezed tight as she entered the one-story structure, as undisguised warmth seemed to invite her in. She stood in the entry, gazing at a massive stone fireplace, complete with a heavy beamed mantel and a wide accommodating hearth. The only thing missing from this picture was the moose head above the fireplace. Instinct told her Trey wouldn't approve or indulge in the hunting of innocent animals, thank goodness.

A slightly worn, completely comfortable-looking leather sofa graced the wall facing the fireplace, and antique pieces from days gone by surrounded the room. Maddie couldn't help feel like an invader, intruding on Trey's privacy, the total masculine feel of the room alluding to Trey's lone-wolf demeanor. It was apparent that a woman had no place here. There were no lace curtains or hand-sewn pillows, nothing feminine at all, yet the house had a welcoming, solid, lived-in feel. A house built for and made for a man.

Maddie was certain Trey didn't want her here.

And she certainly didn't want to be here.

But she'd had no other option. She had responsibilities, clients who depended on her to keep their animals healthy. There was no one else in Hope Wells to look after the animals of the twenty-odd ranches in the county. And just the other day, she'd had to neuter Randolph Curry's rambunctious Irish setter, before the neighbors shot the dang dog for lewd acts of conduct on the main streets in town. Then there was young Bessie Mallery's cat Lucky, who'd surprised everyone with a litter of seven. Maddie had had to untangle that feline's umbilical cord before three of the kittens strangled themselves, getting all twisted up in the cord. Fortunately Lucky's name had held true, and she hadn't lost any of her offspring, much to Bessie's delight.

With a nod, Maddie concluded if she were to keep

her practice going, she would have to accept Trey's hospitality. But she'd made a solemn vow to stick to her business and stay out of his way, until the time came when she could rebuild her own office in town.

"All settled in," Trey said, coming to stand before her. "I put everything inside your room. Down the hall, third door on the left."

"Thank you," Maddie offered. When she'd pulled up just minutes ago with her oddball assortment of clothes, medical books, some veterinary equipment—the smaller tools of her trade she'd been able to salvage—Trey had been waiting on his front porch. He wouldn't allow her to lift a thing from the bed of her truck. He'd just reached in and grabbed everything, loading up his arms and telling her to make herself comfortable inside the house. "The house is nice, looks like it's been lived in some. I'll bet there's a batch of stories hidden in these old walls."

Maddie bit her lip and glanced away. She'd never been one to babble, but then she'd never felt this darn awkward before.

Trey grinned. "This house goes way back. It was one of the first ones built in Hope Wells back in the day when there was free range. I know a few stories, but they aren't fit for telling in polite company."

Maddie sighed, wondering what wonderfully sinful things had happened at 2 Hope years ago. "I'd love to hear them sometime."

Trey looked her over, and began shaking his head. With a dubious expression plastered on his face, he flat out refused. "No way, Maddie. You don't want to hear any of *those* stories."

Maddie fumed silently. She'd never shed her wholesome, good-girl image. The one time she'd tried transforming into a sexy siren, she'd failed miserably. Trey hadn't paid her any notice at all. She was over it, and him, but she wished that he would treat her the way he treated other women. She wasn't a child who needed protecting from vile stories. She wasn't a frail dove that needed rescuing. She was a strong woman who knew when to give up on a hopeless cause. Maddie had given up on Trey Walker.

"I think I'll put my things away now. Thanks, again." She moved past him, heading down the hallway.

"Dinner's at eight."

She swirled around. "Oh, I don't expect you to feed me."

"You have to eat."

"I…I guess I didn't think—"

"Kit and the guys are off tonight, so you're stuck with my cooking. With any luck, I'll manage not to poison the both of us."

Now that's encouraging, she thought. "What's for dinner?"

"Stew?"

"I'll help and don't even dream of refusing the offer. It's the least I can do. After all, you're putting me up and allowing me to keep my practice running on your property. I certainly don't expect to be waited on. I want to pull my weight around here. Besides, I don't have a kitchen anymore and I sort of miss cooking."

Hands on hips, Trey stared at her. "Are you through?"

Maddie's mouth dropped open. "Uh, yeah."

"Meet me in the kitchen in an hour."

She gulped then nodded. She couldn't tell if Trey was amused or annoyed at her little outburst. She had to remind herself that he was a man who wasn't accustomed to having a woman around and he was probably already sorry he'd agreed to their deal.

"This is hardly poison, Trey." Trey watched Maddie polish off her second bowl of son-of-a-gun stew. "And I never figured you for a liar."

He arched a brow. "Liar?"

"You can cook. I mean *really* cook. You had the meat marinating in this wonderfully delicious sauce and then, you did this amazing thing with the spices. I've never had better stew."

"You helped," Trey said, standing to take his plate to the sink.

Maddie immediately rose and gently grabbed the plate from his hand. "All I did was cut up potatoes and carrots. Essentially, you made the meal, so I'm going to do all the cleanup. It's the least—"

"I know, it's the least you can do."

"Yes, so please sit down and I'll pour your coffee. It'll take me only a minute to have this kitchen back in order."

Maddie brought him a mug of steaming hot coffee— cream, no sugar, just the way he liked it. Trey decided to sit, rather than argue. He sipped from his coffee and watched her bustle about his kitchen. Wasn't too often a woman graced his kitchen. In fact, the last time he could recall was when his father had married wife number four and they'd held the wedding here at the ranch. Then, there'd been a wagonload of women in the kitchen, cater-ers and servers alike, cooking up the wedding feast.

The marriage had lasted all of ten months. Hell, Trey couldn't even remember the gal's name exactly. Elisa, Elena, something with an E.

"How's the coffee?" Maddie asked as she bent down to load the dishwasher.

Trey's gaze fastened on the derriere pointing in his direction. He couldn't quite help watching the wiggle as she shifted to make room for more plates. He had a tantalizing view of her backside, and petite as Maddie was, everything she had was perfectly proportioned. Her tank top pulled up as she bent and a slice of skin appeared in the gap at the small of her back. The combination of her wiggling behind and that particular delicate area, newly exposed, caused Trey a moment of grief and that grief was growing harder by the second.

"Coffee's fine," he managed.

She closed the dishwasher door and lifted up, thankfully. Trey gulped down the rest of his coffee, landing his mug down on the table with a thud.

Maddie appeared before him with the coffeepot in hand. "Another cup?"

Before he could answer, she leaned over to begin pouring. That damn silver horse she wore around her neck caught his eye as it swung out. He followed the glint until the charm settled right smack in the deep hollow between her breasts.

His grief intensified.

He wasn't used to having a pretty woman around, helping with the meals, serving him in his kitchen as though she really belonged here. This cozy domestic scene would give him hives if he weren't careful. And the last thing he needed was to walk around stiff between the legs all day.

He reached out and took hold of Maddie's wrist. "Sit down, Maddie. We need to talk."

Maddie's eyes grew wide, probably from the sharpness of his tone. She sat in a chair across from him and suddenly Trey felt older than his thirty-one years. He opened his mouth to begin, but a commotion coming from the corral had him clamping his mouth down. He listened in, certain now it was his stallion whinnying and snorting, kicking up a fuss. Trey bounded up from his seat. "Storm's fixing to have a tirade. I'd better go check on him."

Trey headed to the corral quickly, knowing what damage his feisty stallion could do. He reached the fence just as Storm lifted his front legs up in a flurry, snorting loudly, disturbing the quiet of the night. "Hey, boy. Simmer down," he cooed, trying to soothe the stallion's ire. Storm took note of him, pranced around the perimeter of the corral then stomped, sifting dirt with his front hooves, communicating to Trey the only way he knew how. "I know how you feel, boy. But I can't let you out. Not with the way you're all tangled up inside."

Trey whistled softly, an old cowboy tune he'd learned as a child, the melody something Storm recognized. The horse snorted again and pranced against the wind, his ink-black mane catching the moonlight.

He was a thing of beauty, Storm. Trey understood his restless nature. He was wild at heart, an animal that didn't hold much trust. Trey understood that horse better than he did most people.

"He's a free spirit." The gentle voice came from behind.

Trey turned, noting Maddie standing in the shadows. She stepped closer, carefully, with one eye on Storm. Trey trusted her not to spook the horse. Leaning against the fence, he rested his arms on the top rail. "We understand each other."

Maddie smiled. "I guess I know what you mean."

Trey nodded. "I guess you do."

Storm had pretty much settled down, his tirade all but over. He pranced a bit more, showing off his beautiful grace and agility for Maddie's sake, Trey figured. He didn't blame the horse for trying to impress the lady.

"Do you ride him?" Maddie ventured closer, taking up space next to him by the fence.

Trey chuckled. "He doesn't care much for riders."

"Have you had him long?"

"Less than a month. I went to a cattle auction, took one look at the stallion and that was that. I had to have him. His previous owner said he'll never be *all* yours. It was what I liked best about him."

What he didn't add was Storm's owner had practically given the horse to Trey, having had his fill of the wild, unruly stallion.

Maddie smiled then called softly to the horse. "Hey, Storm. Here, boy." She put out her hand, reaching beyond the fence.

Much to Trey's amazement, Storm wandered over, coming to stand before her. "Careful, he doesn't know you."

Maddie placed her boots on the lower rung of the fence rail and lifted up, coming eye to eye with the stallion. She reached out gingerly, smart enough not to touch the feisty animal, and the horse snorted, as if taking in her scent, each one completely aware of the other. "There, boy. You just need some attention, don't you? All alone out here in this corral."

Maddie's voice, her calm demeanor, her confidence with the now sedate animal, impressed the hell out of Trey. He'd seen her work with animals before and it never ceased to amaze him. She had special qualities.

Trey swallowed hard, watching her speak softly, her delicate hands reaching out in a nonthreatening way, until Storm allowed her a touch. She slid her hands slowly, carefully, but without hesitation over Storm's mane. The stallion snorted, stomped, but didn't back off. He allowed her a brief stroke, one time, before racing off.

Maddie smiled warmly, her heart-shaped mouth turning up with genuine affection. "He knows me now. I think I've made a new friend."

Trey's groin tightened. His mouth went bone-dry. Maddie cuddling with his wild stallion was a sight to behold. The last thing he wanted was to have lusty thoughts about Maddie Brooks. She had a gentle nature, one he couldn't destroy. "About that talk…"

Maddie's smile evaporated as she glanced one last time at Storm. She jumped down from the fence, but the heel of her boot caught on the fence rung just as a gust of wind blew by and she lost her balance. Trey caught her just before she tumbled, his hand brushing the swell of her breast. He wrapped her tight against him, relishing her small, delicate body against his big frame. "Whoa. The wind nearly blew you over. You okay?"

Trey forced himself to release her and step back. She stared up at him, her eyes gleaming, her face lifting up to his and that perfect mouth trembling slightly. "I'm… okay. You wanted to have a talk?"

Yeah, he needed to talk to her. He needed to lay things on the line, leaving no room for doubt that this was strictly a business arrangement. He needed to protect her from the "Walker Curse." In the long run, she'd be better off. And so would he. Maddie wasn't a woman to fool with. But the words that had played out in his mind a dozen times wouldn't come. They stuck in his throat like a mouthful of dry cotton. He opened his mouth then clamped down.

His fingers still tingled from where he'd touched the soft small slope of her breasts and his body shook with powerful need. He couldn't tear his gaze away from that lovely upturned face. He simply stared, swallowing hard, a colossal debate warring in his head. He didn't get it—this unwelcome need he had for her. Maddie in the moonlight was a beautiful thing, but it was something else, something more powerful that drew him to her. He wanted to hold her again. To feel her softness crushed against him. The need inside him was great and all of his hard won mental rules slipped away instantly.

Maddie Brooks was the last woman on earth he should touch.

But he wanted her. Just once.

He leaned in, bending to cup the back of her head with his hand. Her silky hair fell against his palm as he gently tilted her up, toward him.

"Trey, what are you doing?" she asked, her voice a breathless whisper against his lips.

"Being a damn fool."

Then he brushed his mouth over hers.

TWO

Nothing could have shocked Maddie more. Trey pulled her up against him and brought his lips down, taking her in a dreamy kiss that belied every single fantasy she'd ever had about the elusive cowboy. Their bodies brushed intimately as Trey made his claim. Confusing and wonderful, mystifying and breathtaking thoughts rushed into Maddie's head.

She fell into his kiss like a thirsty woman given a tall, cool drink. She imbibed heartily, kissing him back, pressing her lips against his with equal passion and desire. She'd dreamed of this too many times to count. Feeling his heat, the gentle yet commanding way he possessed her, went beyond anything Maddie might have imagined. In her heart of hearts, she'd always known Trey Walker could turn her inside out.

If he was a damn fool as he'd claimed, then Maddie was easily out of her mind.

Trey toyed with Maddie's hair, stroking the strands and then taking a fistful. The playful tug then release triggered rippling waves of electricity to course throughout her body and a soft moan tumbled from her lips.

Trey wedged his body closer, tightening the gap, meshing fully against her as he continued to kiss her. He coaxed her lips open, and when their tongues mated she braced herself against the onslaught of his passion, the erotic joining being almost too much to bear. A completely male sound escaped his throat and Maddie too was lost.

Moonlight beamed down in soft rays, and in the background, Maddie heard Storm whinny and stomp his front legs before taking off in a fast run around the corral. The stallion had a spirit all its own. Wild and untamed and one with the land, so much like Trey Walker.

Maddie lifted her arms up grazing Trey's shoulder, her fingers dipping into dark wavy locks of hair at the base of his neck. He smiled into her mouth, obviously pleased with her display, and slanted his mouth once again over hers, taking her in another long deep, sexy kiss.

Maddie breathed in his scent, leather and earth—so raw, so masculine, so completely Trey. He was a man's man, a special breed and a man who knew how to please a woman. As his lips claimed hers once more, Maddie realized that she could easily fall under his spell again.

Too soon, Trey pulled away and cool Texas air replaced his body's heat. They stood there, facing each other, eyes locked, hearts beating.

Trey blinked.

Maddie tried for a smile, but his expression wouldn't allow it. He appeared shaken, taken completely unaware. So many expressions crossed his features that Maddie didn't know what to think. She didn't know what to say, either. Moments ticked by and then Trey finally broke the silence. He stood with his head bent, scratching his neck in the same spot where Maddie's fingers had explored just seconds ago. "That was entirely my fault. A big mistake."

Maddie crossed her arms over her middle and stood her ground. In the past, she may not have had an abundance of experience with men but she had excellent female intuition and Trey Walker wasn't getting away with this. He'd *wanted* her. And he wasn't so much of a fool not to see that she'd *wanted* him back. Finally, after all this time, Trey had come around. She didn't know why exactly, because for the past year he hadn't given her the time of day but suddenly Trey had taken notice.

What they'd shared tonight was something short of heaven. Maddie hadn't felt anything like this before. And she wasn't about to allow Trey to deny it. "It didn't *feel* like a mistake."

Trey's head snapped up. "Well, it was."

"Are you saying you didn't want to kiss me?"

"No…I mean…yes. What I'm saying is that it shouldn't have happened."

"But it did, Trey. It happened."

He sighed. "Maddie."

Maddie took one step forward, keeping her eyes on Trey. She spoke softly. "*I* liked it, in case you didn't notice."

He swallowed, his gaze locking onto her lips. "I noticed."

Trey Walker had turned her life upside down this past year. She needed to know how he felt inside. She needed to hear the words. She smiled and spoke softly again, taking a brief glance below his belt buckle. "And I noticed how much *you* liked it."

Trey's brows shot up. She might have shocked him.

"Okay, damn it. It was hot. Probably the hottest kiss I've ever…it doesn't matter, Maddie. We're business partners and I shouldn't have taken such liberties. That's what I wanted to talk to you about before Storm acted up."

Hurt and disappointed, Maddie's voice rose. "*That* was what you wanted to talk about. You and me, kissing?"

What was Trey trying to do, add insult to injury? He'd just kissed her senseless, probably ruining her for any other man, and now after he'd given her a small taste of heaven, he wanted to tuck her safely away and pretend nothing had happened. He wanted to make sure that nothing like that would ever happen again.

"Not exactly. I wanted us to sit down and have a logical, *reasonable* discussion about our living arrangements. I've never had a woman live out here with me and well, I suppose it's a fact of nature that in a weak moment…" He paused, taking a breath of air, before continuing. "What I mean to say is that the only way this is going to work is if we keep our distance. I wanted to make sure you saw it the same way."

With chin held high, Maddie stepped closer until she stood boot to boot with him. "You call kissing a girl until her knees buckle, keeping your distance?"

Trey focused on her mouth. "I'm taking all the blame." And those incredible intense eyes softened. "It was a great kiss, Maddie. But wrong."

"If you knew it was wrong then why'd you do it?"

Trey looked away. And they were immersed in silence. Only Storm's occasional quiet snort could be heard. Patiently, Maddie waited.

Trey turned and his dark eyes pierced hers. This time she knew she'd have the truth. "I've wanted to kiss you for a long time."

Maddie's heart lurched. She hadn't expected to hear him admit anything of the sort. All of this time, he'd been aloof and detached, giving her no reason to hope. He'd spoken about having a weak moment, but now Maddie knew it wasn't just that. He'd been thinking about her, just as she'd been thinking about him. "You have?"

He nodded and spoke with firm conviction. "But it isn't right."

"Why, Trey? Why isn't it right?" she asked, trying to puzzle through Trey's admission.

Trey shook his head, his expression filled with regret. He softened his tone, but his words cut straight through her heart. "Because wanting you and doing right by you are two different things. It's best you understand that. I'm not the man for you, Maddie. I never could be."

Trey stalked off and headed to the older barn, leaving Maddie standing there in the moonlight. He'd made a world-class mess out of things and he'd hurt Maddie in the process. Nothing about this night had turned out as he'd hoped. Why couldn't he have left well enough alone? Why'd he have to kiss her? His body still hummed from the impact of that kiss, the soft sweet way Maddie had given herself to him. The way she told him with every movement, every little moan, that it could only get better.

That kiss blew his mind.

Trey's well-honed control had been tested to the limit and had failed. Miserably. One petite little redhead had thrown him off-kilter. She'd made him hard. She'd made him want.

It had been a long time since Trey had taken up with a woman. He'd made a pact long ago that "temporary" involvement was all he could manage. One-night stands were even better. Not that he'd indulged lately, but he knew that sticking to his plan, especially with Maddie, would benefit everyone and hurt no one. Trey's vow to keep his distance couldn't be sharper or laid out more clearly because now he knew what kissing her was like; now he knew that he wasn't immune to her whole-some charm.

Trey walked to the stall that housed one of Maddie's patients. "Hey there, Maggie. How're you doing, girl?"

The fair-haired dog looked up with big sad eyes. She'd been accidentally shot with a round of birdshot by Willy McGill, a young boy who'd been playing with his daddy's gun. "Feeling any better tonight?"

Trey bent to scratch the old girl behind the ears, gently stroking her coat. "The doc fixed you up real good. You'll be going home soon."

Trey stood and checked on all of the other animals, making note of how well cared for they all appeared. After the fire that had claimed Maddie's office Trey had worked like a demon to get this place ready for the animals, mucking out the stalls, cleaning them the best he could. He'd laid down blankets for the larger animals and had gathered up cages he'd had on the grounds for the smaller ones. Of the eight stalls, more than half were filled with animals on the mend.

The tack room in the back served as Maddie's office and examining room all in one. She'd brought in what few supplies she'd salvaged, others she'd purchased including a makeshift examining table made of heavy aluminum. She had all that she needed to start up her practice again.

Trey shouldn't lose sight of that. He shouldn't forget the good Maddie coming to 2 Hope Ranch would serve. The animals needed her expert care. The deal he and Maddie had made insured the animals would receive it.

In the year since Doc Benning had left Hope Wells, Maddie's practice had grown. She'd gained a reputation as a compassionate, intelligent veterinarian who loved all animals, seeming to have special talents communicating with them. She'd been young, coming straight out of college, but it hadn't taken her long to earn the town's trust. And for the time being, she'd be working here, treating the animals.

And living with him.

Trey would just learn to adjust.

Maddie entered the kitchen through the back door and glanced at the coffee cups that had been left on the table. All of this had started by Storm's sudden outburst. The stallion had interrupted what would have been Trey's attempt at setting up their "business" arrangement. What he'd really wanted to do was lay down the rules. Rules, according to Trey Walker, not to be compromised or challenged. Rules that left no doubt in Maddie's mind that the cowboy simply was not interested.

She cleared the coffee cups from the table and loaded them in the dishwasher. Then she refilled the sugar bowl and creamer and put them away, straightening up the kitchen the best she could, keeping her vow to pitch in and share in fifty percent of the daily chores. She owed Trey that much. He'd been kind and generous, coming to her aid when she'd needed help the most.

Her mind still raced at one hundred miles per hour.

She doubted she'd be able to concentrate on one single thing tonight, other than Trey's incredible kiss. Maddie would never forget that earth-moving, heart-stopping experience, but it seemed that for Trey, it hadn't been enough. It hadn't been what he wanted. Maddie would have to respect his wishes. She was here at 2 Hope living off his hospitality, with a roof over her head and, more importantly, a place to treat the animals.

That mattered to her above all else.

With the kitchen clean, Maddie headed for her bedroom, taking one last peek out the window. Storm pranced and snorted, making his way around the perimeter of the corral, his shiny, sleek mane catching starlight.

"He'll never be *all* yours," Trey had been told.

How well Maddie understood that. The stallion's instinct, his spirit, the very heart of the animal, wouldn't allow it. Stallions could be trained, but they could never be fully trusted. Just when you believed them tame, their wild side would emerge, creating havoc and fear. An untamed spirit exposed their true temperament—one that thrived solely on strength, independence and freedom. Storm belonged to no one but himself.

And Maddie realized now what Trey had seen in Storm. He'd seen himself.

Maddie woke early the next morning after a restless night. She'd never been one for change, and sleeping in a strange bed in someone else's home hadn't been as easy as she'd hoped. She missed her small apartment in town. She missed her things. Unfortunately most everything she owned had gone up in smoke. She had few worldly possessions now—not the fancy rhinestone hairclip that had seen her through her teen years, not her favorite pair of worked-in jogging shoes or her tattered but extremely cozy chenille bathrobe. She'd loved to surround herself with books and they'd come in all varieties from pleasure reading to heavy-duty research books. To her sad chagrin, she realized she missed her old college books, too, even the ones she knew she'd never use again.

Instinctively Maddie fingered the silver charm around her neck. She still had Aphrodite. The precious heirloom brought her a good measure of comfort and Maddie's cheerless mood instantly changed. She had plenty to be thankful for.

She glanced around the large bedroom that would now be her home. There was space enough to move around in this room. She'd slept in a good-size bed, a thick hand-quilted comforter keeping her warm throughout the night. Her meager belongings were housed in a lovely carved oak armoire that stood against the opposing wall. The armoire's intricate workmanship spoke of decades past giving this room a sense of history, but it was the fresh flowers placed in a cut glass vase on top of the armoire that tugged at Maddie's heart the most.

Trey must have put them there sometime yesterday as a gesture of welcome. He must have known how hard this was for her, coming to live at 2 Hope Ranch, invading his territory so to speak, while attempting to start up her life again.

In so many ways, Trey Walker was a mystery to her—an unreadable man who rarely let his guard down, who rarely allowed anyone inside. He'd given her a taste of that last night by pulling her into a deep passionate kiss, then closing up tight, not allowing her even a glimpse of his true feelings. He'd pushed her away. She'd gotten the message. She'd have to forget the wonderful kiss they'd shared and the way it felt to be tucked into Trey's strong embrace. She'd have to put him out of her mind and try to establish a cordial, but business-like relationship with him from now on.

Sunlight beamed in bright and warm through the shuttered window, and Maddie was reminded that she had better get a move on. Today would be her first official day on the job since the fire. She had to set up her office and see to the animals. She couldn't wait to get started. Maddie tossed off the covers, donned her robe and headed straight for the bathroom. With thoughts of a refreshing shower, Maddie pushed open the door and stopped dead in her tracks.

Shirtless, Trey stood facing the mirror with razor in hand, the unshaven half of his face still lathered up with white foam. Fresh lime permeated the air, the soapy clean scent appealing to all of her female senses. "Oh, sorry."

Trey glanced her way for one second then faced the mirror again, taking a swipe at his beard and examining his progress. "Nothing to be sorry for. I should've been up and out early this morning. Would have been if the pipe hadn't busted in the other bathroom. Now, it looks like we'll be sharing this one until I get the plumbing fixed."

"Oh," Maddie said numbly. When she'd made this bargain with Trey he'd offered her this bathroom, closest to the bedrooms, while he had opted to use the one nearest the kitchen during her stay. "I hope it isn't too serious."

But as she looked at him, Maddie knew it was *serious*. She fought to direct her gaze away from the wide expanse of Trey's solid chest. She struggled to seriously adjust her focus from the tiny hairs curling around his nipples, leading down his torso in a narrow path that flowed into a tight pair of unbuttoned jeans. Tall, tanned, muscular and about as sexy as a man could get, Trey seriously took her breath away.

"Don't know. My uncle Monty's the expert. He can fix just about anything." Trey took another swipe at his beard then rinsed the razor in the sink. "I gave him a call, but he can't get out here until next week." He stopped shaving to turn to her. "If it's a problem, I'll call in a plumber today."

Struck by the full force of Trey's appeal, Maddie tried for nonchalance. After all, he'd set down the rules last night. Maddie would learn to ignore Trey Walker, even if it killed her. She shrugged. "Not a problem at all. I'll shower later."

The last thing she wanted was to be a burden. Or cost Trey any money. She knew from their deal that Trey wasn't in good financial shape right now and hiring a plumber could get expensive. If need be, she'd share the bathroom but she'd make darn sure not to barge in on him again.

Maddie turned to leave, but Trey stopped her. "Maddie?"

She looked up. "Yes?"

Trey leaned both hands on the tiled counter and bent his head, staring into the sink. Half-shaven, half-naked and more tempting than Maddie wanted to admit, he spoke softly, "About last night—"

With a tilt of her head, Maddie finished his thought. "It was a mistake."

His head snapped up and his dark eyes studied her for a moment. "Right."

"And it'll never happen again."

He hesitated. "Right."

"Anything else?" She asked on tiptoes, ready to turn and make a quick retreat.

Trey glanced at her lips then let out a breath. "Just that I think it's best that we move forward and forget about—"

"Already done, Trey. It's forgotten."

"That easy?"

The question seemed to have slipped from his tongue and if he could have pulled the words back, Maddie was certain he would have.

She lifted her lips in a quick smile. "Easy as peach pie," she said and headed back to her bedroom.

She heard the shower door open then close, the sound of water raining down. Maddie couldn't block out the image of one naked cowboy soaping up in a hot steamy shower.

Heart pounding, she shut her bedroom door then leaned heavily against it, closing her eyes. "Easy as peach pie," she repeated on a whisper. "Maddie Brooks, you are such a terrible liar."

Three

"It's Dr. Maddie! Mommy, Dr. Maddie is here!"

Annabelle Portman raced straight into Maddie's legs as she stepped down from her truck. The four-year-old clung on and hugged tight.

Maddie patted Annabelle's head. "Hey there, sweetie. How's my favorite helper?"

Annabelle beamed. "I groomed-ed Dumpling, and Mommy said I did a good job." And then the child's expression fell. "But now her leg is broke. Mommy said you can fix her."

Maddie bent down to the child's level, looking her straight in the eyes. "I'm going to do the best I can, Annabelle. Dumpling's a healthy horse and she probably just pulled up lame."

"That's what I think, Maddie. At least it's what I'm hoping," Caroline Portman said as she approached the truck.

Maddie straightened and smiled at her good friend. She and Caroline had met on the first day Maddie arrived in Hope Wells. They'd nearly collided on the main street in town, their cars missing each other by mere inches and both women had instantly realized how lucky they'd been, not winding up in a hospital that day. They'd gone to lunch after that and had been close friends ever since.

"Hi," Maddie said, wrapping her arms around Caroline in a warm embrace. "It's good to see you."

And Maddie meant it with her whole heart. There weren't too many constants in Maddie's life right now, with the fire, losing nearly everything she owned, then coming to live with Trey, a man who would surely cause her more than one sleepless night. A visit with a good friend was just what Maddie needed today.

"It's great to see you, too. I've been planning on having you out for dinner, but dear sweet Dumpling beat me to it. She's in the barn and I've got her iced, using one of my old pant legs sewn up, just like you said. The ice pack seems to be working fine."

Annabelle giggled. "Dumpling looks funny wearing Mommy's pants."

"I bet she does," Maddie agreed with a grin, "but it's the best way to make her leg feel better."

"I'm hoping it's a sprain. It seemed warm to the touch," Caroline responded.

"Did she flinch when you applied pressure?" Maddie asked.

Caroline nodded. "And she gave me a sour look to boot."

Maddie reached for Annabelle's hand. "Well then, let's go take a look."

As they headed for the barn, Caroline said, "I wasn't sure you'd be ready for business yet. How are things at 2 Hope?"

"I set up my office this morning." She explained with a wry smile, "Of course, that took all of ten minutes, since I'm pretty much starting from scratch. There isn't too much going into my file cabinet just yet. But I've got a barn full of animals that need my attention."

With a tilt of her head, Caroline asked, "And are they the only ones getting your attention?"

Maddie knew what her friend hinted at. She'd shared with Caroline a little of her previous fascination with Trey. She couldn't blame Caroline for her curiosity and she wondered if small-town tongues were wagging over the situation. After all, she'd moved in with Trey Walker, the most eligible bachelor in three counties. "I hate to disappoint, but there's not much happening there."

"Hmmm. We'll have lunch after you take a look at Dumpling and you can tell me all about it."

An hour later, Maddie sat in the Portman kitchen relieved that Dumpling hadn't broken any bones. "Dumpling should be fine in a few days. Just use the heating liniment I gave you. Massage it in really good and it'll improve her circulation."

"I'm glad it wasn't more serious," Caroline said, setting two plates of fried chicken salad down on the table. "And thanks for including Annabelle. Letting her help out makes her feel kind of special. And Lord knows that child needs to feel special, after her father up and left us both last year."

"Yeah, that's got to be hard on her. Do you ever hear from Gil?"

Caroline glanced out the kitchen window, watching her daughter skip rope. She twisted her mouth and lowered her voice. "He calls to speak with Annabelle every month or so but he hasn't seen her since he left. Guess I wasn't such a good judge of character, was I?"

"It wasn't your fault, Caroline."

Caroline set the napkins and utensils down along with two glasses of iced tea then took a seat to face Maddie. "I think it was. He wasn't ready to settle down. And maybe I pushed him a little too hard."

"He's a grown man, responsible for his own actions. You can't deny that. A real man should know what's in his own heart. He shouldn't play games."

She laughed and cast Maddie a direct look. "Are we still speaking about Gil?"

Maddie blushed. "Maybe." She smiled as she sipped her tea. "Maybe not."

Caroline leaned in, bracing her elbows on the table. "You know I'm dying of curiosity. What's it like living with Trey?"

"I've only been there one night."

"Sometimes, that's all it takes," her friend said with a twinkle in her blue eyes.

Maddie gulped down. At times, it seemed Caroline could read her mind. Or maybe she was capable of reading Maddie's guilty expression. She really wasn't good at hiding things. "Okay, something happened last night, but it's not worth talking about."

"Let me decide what's not worth talking about. I'm knee deep in Talking Elmo and Candyland. I love my daughter dearly, but a girl's got to have an adult conversation once in a while. So, what happened?"

"He kissed me," Maddie confessed.

Caroline's blond brows drew up. "Already? I thought that might take a week or two."

"*A week or two? Are you serious?* It was the last thing in the world I ever expected from Trey Walker. It really threw me. He admitted that he'd wanted to kiss me for a long time, but after he did, well, he backed way off. He says it was a big mistake and that we need to keep things strictly business."

"Really? Doesn't sound that way to me. Unless…the kiss wasn't any good."

Heat crawled up Maddie's neck. She'd been thinking about that kiss all morning. "Oh, it was good."

"How good?"

"Better than cool summer rain. Better than hot chocolate by the fire. Better than…anything," Maddie admitted on a whisper. Then she straightened in her seat and said with certainty, "But it's over and done with. We've come to an understanding."

"For as long as that lasts. I've known Trey a long time, Maddie, and if he kissed you, he's interested. That man isn't into playing games. He's about as serious as they come. He doesn't let women get too close, but then, he's probably never met anyone quite like you before."

"Yeah, the wholesome girl-next-door."

"Correction, the girl-in-the-next-bedroom. Be careful, honey. You're probably scaring the stuffing out of him. I wouldn't want to see you with a broken heart."

"That's exactly what I'm doing. I'm being very careful."

With a sunburst of orange gold setting low on the horizon, Maddie pulled up to the barn at 2 Hope and parked the truck. After her lunch with Caroline, she'd spent the rest of the afternoon making house calls to neighboring ranches, checking on her more recent cases and making sure everyone knew how to reach her in the event of an emergency. She'd given out her cell phone number, making certain to always have her phone on hand now. Also, Trey had given her permission to use his house number if necessary. The barn hadn't a phone line and both had decided that it wasn't worth the expense to install one, since Maddie's stay here was temporary.

Maddie hopped down from the truck and slammed the door shut, glad to have had a successful day. She felt much better about her situation now, confident that everything would work out. She should be hearing soon about the insurance claim she filed and hopefully the money would come through for her to rebuild her office in town. With that thought in mind, she headed quickly toward the barn door, anxious to check on Maggie and the other animals one last time before she closed up for the night.

As she rounded the corner of the barn, she collided right smack into Trey. The impact took her completely by surprise. He knocked her off balance and she rocketed backward, sprawling onto the ground. Her head hit a small mound of straw, a slight cushion against the solid packed dirt underneath.

Stung by embarrassment, Maddie tried to lift her head, hoping to make a quick getaway, but Trey was immediately by her side, gently pressing her head back down. "Don't try to get up," he said with quiet authority, bending on one knee. "Lie still a minute and let me see if you've got a bump."

With nimble fingers, Trey worked his way through her hair, searching her head. She closed her eyes, both mortified at this awkward position and fascinated by the soft gentle way he moved his hands through her hair. "I'm sorry, Maddie. I didn't see you coming."

She opened her eyes and stared at him. She saw so much in those deep dark eyes—emotions that he held back, concern that he'd tried to hide as he continued to probe for injuries. "I thought I was the doctor here," she said, trying for humor.

Trey sighed, shaking his head.

"I'm fine, Trey. Really. My mama used to say I'd be two days early for my own wedding, 'cause I'm always on the go, always rushing around. I've got to learn to slow down."

"And I've got to pay more attention."

Trey paid attention then, perusing her body, his gaze traveling slowly over her, lingering in places that made Maddie's heart race. "Are you hurt anywhere?"

"Just my pride. You pack a wallop, Trey Walker."

Trey grinned then, a sudden quick beautiful smile that left Maddie wanting more. "So I've been told. But I usually don't knock over petite females. Especially, not when I've come searching to ask a favor."

Maddie lifted up then, but none too quickly. Trey had a hand on her shoulder, guiding her up to a sitting position at a slow pace. "A favor?"

"Yep," he said, standing and then lending a hand to help her up. Maddie wasn't too prideful to accept his help. She still felt a little shaky, her head swimming from the fall. Trey held her firm, making sure she felt secure on both legs, before releasing her hand. "I found a young heifer on the south pasture tangled up in barbed wire. I released her the best I could but there's a deep wound. It'll wait. You're in no shape to work right now. I'll go back and check on her later."

"I'll be fine in a minute," Maddie said, as a wave of dizziness struck. Her legs nearly buckled then and Trey grabbed for her.

"Whoa," he said, holding her steady. Then in a quick move, Trey lifted her up into his arms.

"What are you doing?" she asked, hazy from the fall, but even more hazy from being in Trey's strong arms once again. That heady mix of leather and earth wafted down to her, the scent being Trey's alone. She felt safe and secure and silly all at the same time.

"Making sure you sit down and rest." He carried her to the front porch and planted her gently into a wicker love seat that had seen better days. A fleeting thought crossed Maddie's mind that the bench seat could use a woman's touch, some soft material and a bit of lace. She thought the same of Trey—he too could use a woman's touch. Although he held her with such care, such tenderness, he was a hard man who thrived on his solitude. She envied the woman who might eventually soften him.

To her surprise, Trey took the seat next to her. His long legs spread out, he leaned back with his arm resting on the back of the love seat. A minute passed in silence, then he faced her. "I'm not used to having a woman around here, Maddie. It'll take some getting used to. I might've guessed you'd be around the barn, but I barreled around it like—"

"Like you owned the place," Maddie said with a smile.

Trey laughed, his dark eyes gleaming through fading sunlight. "Well, yeah."

"No need to apologize, Trey. It was an accident."

"How's the head now?" he asked, his gaze locked onto hers.

"Better," she said truthfully. "I'm not dizzy anymore."

"That's good," he said and leaned in, his gaze studying her face, but his focus moved down to her mouth and lingered. Maddie's heart pumped in double time. She thought he meant to kiss her and, fool that she was, she wanted that, too. The anticipation nearly killing her, she held her breath and waited. Trey came closer and reached up, his hand going into her hair.

A rush of heat coursed through her body.

Trey pulled a strand of straw from her head.

He stared at it. "Looks like I drew the short straw, Maddie."

"Does that mean you lose?"

Trey glanced at her mouth one last time. He nodded and stood to leave. "Yeah, it means I lose."

Maddie Brooks was the damnedest, most stubborn woman Trey had come across in years. Not one hour after he'd nearly squashed the tiny woman like a bug, she'd insisted on seeing to that wounded heifer. With him or without him, she'd threatened, she was heading for the south pasture.

With him, he'd decided without question. The sun had set and the road wasn't easy to navigate. They drove in his Chevy truck over rough terrain, Trey taking cursory glances at Maddie, making certain she was up to the bumpy drive. One thing he noticed about the redhead, she was determined and no amount of dissuading on his part would work. He worried each time she lifted a hand to her head, if even to brush hair from her face.

He recalled probing for bumps earlier, the soft silky strands of red ginger flowing through his hands. The sensation had wrapped around him, and he found himself wanting again.

He'd wanted to kiss her. He'd wanted to lift her up into his arms and instead of depositing her in that love seat, he'd wanted to see how she looked out of her blue jeans and tiny T-shirt, lying on his bed. To see those soft silky strands of hair flow over his pillow.

But Trey had drawn the short straw when it came to women like Maddie Brooks, and what she didn't know was that if he acted on his impulses both of them would come out the loser. Trey wouldn't forget that.

"Are we close?" she asked, her eyes probing through the darkness for signs of the injured animal.

He pulled to a stop and searched the area where the barbed-wire fence needed repair. "It's right here," he said, getting out of the truck and coming around to the passenger door to help Maddie down. She handed him her medical bag and then jumped down unaided.

Stubborn.

Trey held a butane lamp and guided Maddie to where the heifer lay wounded in the ground.

"Hey there, little one," Maddie said softly as she bent to see the extent of the injury. Trey sat down cross-legged and placed the Hereford's head in his lap while Maddie opened her medical bag. "Looks like you have a deep gash here." She stroked the heifer's withers softly as seconds became minutes. Under Maddie's patient loving touch, the frightened animal soon relaxed, and Trey sensed a bond of trust developing, as crazy as that might seem.

Maddie glanced up at Trey. "Most of the time the cuts heal on their own, but this is a three-corner tear and needs clipping or it won't heal properly."

Trey watched as Maddie worked diligently, cutting away the flap of skin hanging as well as the surrounding hairs. She cleaned the area with a solution and applied an antiseptic with tender care. "There now," she said, finishing up. "We need to keep the wound clean and dry. The antiseptic is a fly repellent as well, but I'd feel better keeping an eye on her for at least a week. Do you think we can get her into the back of the truck?"

Trey nodded. "Let me get a blanket and lay it down in the bed."

Maddie stayed with the animal, soothing her with kind words and stroking her head while Trey prepared the bed of his truck. When he returned, he found the heifer standing upright, nudging her nose into Maddie's leg. He chuckled. "How did you do that?"

"Do what?" she replied with an innocent expression.

"I didn't think she'd be able to stand. I couldn't get her up when I found her out here earlier."

"Oh, she and I have come to an understanding," Maddie said with a smile. She moved toward the back of the truck and the wounded heifer followed. Maddie climbed up first and Trey had no trouble, heavy as the heifer was, lifting her up and placing her inside the bed. She immediately walked to Maddie's side and lied down next to her on the blanket.

Trey shook his head and closed the tailgate. "Damn amazing."

He drove slowly back to the ranch, trying to avoid as many ditches and bumps as possible, for Maddie's sake. He still hadn't gotten over knocking her down and almost out. Trey had never hurt a woman in his life. Not physically, anyway.

But he'd hurt one or two emotionally and he was dead set against allowing that to ever happen again. He'd been engaged once, and they'd almost married, which would have been a bigger mistake. But then Trey had been ten years younger, less experienced and a bit naive regarding the "Walker Curse." He'd let everyone close convince him marriage was what he'd wanted. What had ensued afterward had been a disaster. He'd hurt his fiancée and nearly alienated everyone he cared about in the process.

Trey glanced through the back window of the cab noting Maddie sitting with head bent, speaking to the heifer. "Damn amazing woman," he said, with a shake of his head.

Amazing with animals.

Amazing to look at.

Amazing to touch.

Lord only knew what other amazing things Maddie could do.

And then his father's dying words rushed into his head in haunting fashion. "Don't make the same mistakes I made, son."

Trey was immediately reminded of his solemn vow to steer clear and keep their arrangement strictly business.

And no matter how amazing he found Maddie to be, Trey would honor that vow.

Four

Maddie immersed herself in her work, having little time to do much else but fall into bed at night. She'd been on the ranch for five solid days now and things were finally settling into a routine. She and Trey had a polite, but distant relationship. She believed Trey admired her talent as a competent veterinarian, and she knew him to be an expert rancher. They had mutual respect for one another, but they made sure not to let things get too personal. Over their brief dinners at night, they'd speak about their work, his livestock and her cases, the weather, the newest reality show. But they shied away from any private subjects.

Trey employed four ranch hands, all of whom lived off the ranch with their own families. On occasion, the foreman named Kit would stay to fix supper and chew the fat with his boss. Maddie had come to know Kit

Carver from her visits to 2 Hope in the past and considered him more friend than acquaintance now.

But tonight Trey and his foreman had taken off after the evening meal. Maddie had offered to clean the kitchen, and now she found herself alone, enveloped in the silence of this big sprawling house. Most nights she found solace in the quiet, but tonight she wandered around in restless disarray, not quite ready to turn in, not quite sure what she wanted to do.

When Maddie heard Storm causing a ruckus outside, she decided to investigate. She exited the back door and headed to the corral.

Storm kicked up a big fuss. The stallion rounded the corral's perimeter at breakneck speed, snorting, his breaths loud and labored. When he caught sight of Maddie approaching the fence—his fence—he stopped up short and stared at her.

"Hey Storm," she called out. "Are you restless, too?"

Storm continued to stare at her, edging up closer to the fence one careful step at a time. Maddie too edged closer, keeping her eyes trained on Storm. "Don't be afraid."

Storm came closer still, until he stood three feet from the fence. "Thata, boy."

Maddie hummed a slow easy tune, the melody catchy enough to gain the stallion's attention. She knew better than to force the situation. She stood her ground, not daring to move any further. Patience worked hand in hand with trust.

Low lying clouds and dim moonlight cast Storm in ominous shadows making the noble horse seem somewhat sinister, but Maddie knew that not to be the case at all. Storm wasn't what she'd call tame, but he had a

good heart. He was prideful and intelligent and in time
he would come around. "I know you," she said softly.
"You think you're fooling me, but I know you."

Maddie headed back to the kitchen and grabbed a
handful of sugar cubes. It was the oldest trick in the
book, but the method was tried and true, working successfully for years. It wasn't so much a treat she was offering, but a way to gain Storm's trust.

She set the cubes on top of the fence post, leaving
Storm to wonder what she had done. "See you tomorrow, boy."

After entering the kitchen, Maddie stood by the window and waited. She stared at the obstinate horse for fifteen minutes, until finally, he approached the fence post
and licked it clean.

"Thata boy," she whispered and Maddie knew she
had a challenge on her hands.

She might not be able to get through to Trey Walker,
but Storm was a different matter. Determined now, Maddie made herself a promise not to give up on the feisty
stallion.

One way or another, she would gain Storm's trust.

Trey entered the house by the back door, Kit having
dropped him off minutes ago. They'd gone into town tonight to have a few beers and listen to honky-tonk music
at Tie-One-On, the local bar. Recently married, Kit
missed his wife, who was visiting her relatives in Hous-
ton. He'd needed a diversion, a way to pass the time, so
the two had headed into town.

They'd sat at the bar having drinks, Kit fending off
the advances made by hopeful females. Trey envied
Kit's commitment to his wife. He envied the man his fu-

ture, one filled with the love of a good woman and the promise of a family. Those things seemed so far out of Trey's reach that he'd put them completely out of his mind. He resigned himself to his life at 2 Hope, having been happy for most of his time here. That is, until one perky redhead came to live with him.

Tie-One-On was a place to help a man forget, a place to loosen up and have a good time. Half a dozen women had approached Trey. He'd danced with a few, held them in his arms, but his mind kept going back to Maddie. Thoughts of her filled his head and he found himself sitting at the bar with his friend, amid a crowd of fun-loving people, feeling lonelier than he could ever remember.

Trey grabbed a beer from the refrigerator and headed to the parlor. He plopped down on the sofa, kicked up his boots on the table and clicked on the television set. He finally settled in when he found an old John Wayne movie.

The scent of raspberries drifted by and as he turned his head around, he saw Maddie making an about face. "Maddie?"

"Oh, hi," she said, tightening her white robe around her. "I didn't know you were out here. Don't let me disturb you."

"Can't sleep?"

"Not really. Guess I'm a little restless tonight."

Trey studied her appearance. Her face was washed clean of the little makeup she wore, her hair fell in waves around her shoulders as if she'd just brushed through it and her bright green eyes held a certain shyness. Of all the women Trey had spoken with tonight, of all the women he'd danced with and had briefly considered going home with, only Maddie Brooks appealed to him.

Both of them were restless tonight.

Both needed companionship.

He knew better than to ask, but he asked anyway. "Do you like John Wayne?"

Maddie smiled. "Love him."

Trey patted the sofa next to him. "Pull up a seat."

A short while later after sharing a movie, a bowl of popcorn and a few lingering looks, Trey stretched out and continued to listen to Maddie's soft, soothing voice. "And so after my folks passed, my Grandma Mae and I moved to this little apartment in the heart of New York City. I knew immediately that I wouldn't do well in a big city. I needed space and freedom and animals. For one, you don't see too many animals in New York, unless you go to the zoo."

"So you knew early on that you wanted to work with animals?"

With a subtle tilt of her head, Maddie responded, "I know this sounds corny, but it wasn't so much what I knew inside. I was drawn to it, like a magnetic pull. I know what it means now when people say that they met their life's calling. Being a veterinarian was my calling. It's as if I had no choice in the matter." She smiled softly. "Does that make any sense?"

"More than you know," he agreed. Trey knew there were greater forces out there, working either for or against you. At this very moment there were forces working against him ever being with Maddie. It was something Trey just plain understood. "Sometimes, choices are taken from you." He scrubbed his jaw a moment. "It worked out for you, though. You're doing exactly what you were meant to do."

"And what about you, Trey? Are you doing what you're meant to do?"

Trey shrugged. "Ranching's in my blood, I suppose—2 Hope has been around a long, long time. We've had some rough patches, but we're hanging on."

"I'd love to know how 2 Hope got its name," she said. "Or is that one of the stories not fit for polite company?"

Maddie wiggled closer on the sofa, her robe parting slightly. Trey caught a glimpse of thin silky pajamas underneath. Her exposed skin shone like polished porcelain and that necklace she wore caught his eye. The damn thing dangled right smack in between her breasts.

Trey drew in oxygen and glanced back up to her face. He wasn't immune to her wholesome charm, not in the least. He figured he was better off looking into pretty green eyes than lusting over soft creamy skin.

"Now that's a story I *can* tell you," he said. "Legend has it that my great-great-granddaddy was down on his luck when he arrived in Hope Wells. Didn't take him long to figure out what he wanted. A ranch and my great-great-grandmother. Only problem was, my grandmother was Rachel Hope, the daughter of the richest man in town. And Will Walker didn't have two nickels to rub together. But he found a way. He won the ranch in a poker game and shortly after," Trey said, with a smile he couldn't hide, "he won Rachel. Seems my grandfather's opponent in that famous poker game had drawn a full house. He made no bones about it. He'd told everyone what he held in his hand. Poor old Will thought he was done for, all he had was a pair of two's. Was too much to hope for—another pair of two's, but dang it all, if he didn't draw them. He won the hand with four of a kind—four two's."

Maddie smiled, a distant winsome expression on her face. "Two Hope. That's a lovely story, Trey. It must be nice knowing about your ancestors. You have such a deep foundation here, a sense of belonging."

"When things get rough around here, and I think I'm ready to chuck it all, I recall the way the ranch got started."

"That's admirable, Trey."

"There's nothing admirable about it."

"What do you mean?"

Trey shook his head. He hadn't meant to blurt that out, yet he felt he didn't deserve her compliment. He wasn't that noble. Lately he'd been feeling resentful—hating the traits he'd inherited that made him lack a sense of commitment. If Maddie only knew how many times he'd been tempted to sell off the ranch, to rid himself of the headaches and make a fresh start somewhere. If she only knew how much he'd wanted to be more solid, more stable. He'd messed up enough in one lifetime. He had bad genes to thank for that. His father, and his father before him, hadn't set the best example. Neither of those men were anything like Will Walker. Will had had staying power. Will Walker had had the guts to see things through.

"Nothing. Forget it, Maddie."

"But—"

Loud howling coming from the barn interrupted Maddie's thoughts. She stopped speaking to listen. "Sounds like Maggie and Toby."

Trey sat upright and listened carefully to the dogs' barking. "Something's got them upset. I'd best go check."

Maddie rose quickly. "I'm coming, too."

They raced outside toward the barn, Trey searching the area with sharp probing eyes. He wished he'd thought to grab his rifle as he yanked the barn door open. The dogs' barking simmered some. Maddie swooped down next to Toby, the black and white border collie she'd been nursing from a car accident.

"Oh no. Toby's ripped open his stitches. He's bleeding, Trey."

"What can I do?"

"Stay with him while I get the supplies I need."

Maddie rose but Trey grabbed her arm. "Be careful. It might have been a coyote scratching to get inside. He's probably long gone by now, but I'm not sure."

"I'll be careful."

Trey stood and watched Maddie enter her office space, keeping a vigilant eye out for whatever culprit caused the animals to get into such a ruckus. He only relaxed when he saw her running back toward him, her arms filled with the supplies she needed.

"Okay, Toby," she said softly to the injured collie. "Looks like you're not going home tomorrow, after all."

An hour later, Trey escorted an exhausted Maddie to her bedroom door. Together, they'd worked on Toby, Trey holding the dog while Maddie administered to the freshly opened wound. Maddie wouldn't leave until the dog finally calmed and had fallen back asleep.

"Hazards of the barn," Trey offered by way of apology. "We get all sorts of wild animals out here."

Maddie shrugged. "I think Toby will heal just fine. And using the barn to practice is a far cry better than having no place at all."

"True enough," Trey said. "But maybe we should change the name from 2 Hope to Last Chance Ranch."

"After that wonderful story you told me, don't you dare." Maddie reached for Trey's arm, her subtle touch searing his skin under his shirt. She'd shed her bathrobe in the barn, and both had been too caught up with their task to notice, but now, Trey noticed. The soft silky tank top left little to the imagination; her perfect breasts stretched the material in ways that made his mouth go dry. And her cotton drawers, decorated with blue and white clouds, hugged her hips below her navel, accentuating her delicate curves. "I really do appreciate being able to practice here, Trey. I know it isn't the perfect situation, but I'm grateful for everything. Including your help tonight."

Trey wasn't sure who'd received the most benefit tonight. His evening had livened up the moment Maddie had entered the parlor. He'd been unsettled and lonely and as soon as he'd seen Maddie, everything had changed. In truth, Trey couldn't remember having a more satisfying and enjoyable evening.

"I'm glad to help out."

"Thank you," she said, staring into his eyes.

He stared back, captivated by this pretty, petite woman. She was warm and kind and sweet, and Trey realized he wanted more than a bed partner in Maddie, he wanted to be her friend.

He bent down and touched his lips to hers softly. "Good night, Dr. Maddie."

"Good night, Trey," she whispered, leaning her head against the door.

Trey backed up quickly, and turned away from the longing he witnessed in her eyes, the surprised smile on her face. He turned away from the tempting woman, turning away from every single instinct calling him back.

"Damn it all, Uncle Monty."

Trey cursed so darn loud, Maddie nearly spilled her

morning coffee. She sat in the kitchen, reading the newspaper, trying to fully awaken after getting in so late last night. It had been worth the lack of sleep, spending one of the best evenings of her life. With Trey. And then, contrary to what he'd preached, he'd kissed her again.

The kiss seemed different this time, less passionate, but somehow more intimate. As if they'd somehow created a bond. Maddie knew Trey wasn't playing with her heart. The way he'd kissed her had been innocent and spontaneous, as unplanned as Texas heat, making it all the more special.

"Turn the water *off,* Uncle Monty." She heard him shout from the bathroom, clearly irritated.

Her curiosity heightened, Maddie headed into the smaller bathroom where all the noise was coming from. She found Trey facing a broken out wall, holding together a galvanized pipe with both hands, trying to keep the leak from sprouting again. *"Off,"* he shouted out the window.

Maddie giggled.

Trey turned in surprise, releasing his hands slightly.

Water rained out, spurting him in the face and shoulders. Within seconds, Trey Walker was drenched, the leaky pipe gushing out until finally and apparently, his Uncle Monty had turned the water *off.*

Trey's hair hung in wet clumps around his head. Water plastered his T-shirt to his chest and the top half of his blue jeans were saturated.

Maddie couldn't hold back any longer. She laughed heartily at the sight of Trey looking like a soaked scruffy pup. "Having trouble?" she asked, with a grin.

"You might say that," Trey growled. "My uncle

doesn't seem to know the difference between 'on' and 'off' and why the heck are you laughing?"

Maddie turned to the cabinet to get Trey a towel. "Because you look like—"

But when Maddie turned back around, she found Trey removing his T-shirt, the material stretching over his smooth wet skin in one quick movement. He tossed the shirt into the bathtub and ran a hand through his hair, slicking back the dark strands until he looked better than a *GQ* model in blue jeans.

Maddie swallowed, trying to keep her expression from faltering. She'd seen Trey shirtless before and admittedly it had been glorious, but he hadn't been wet, with droplets falling from his hair onto his shoulders, with water licking at the scattering of hairs on his chest until a puddle developed in his navel.

Goodness. Maddie was certain there wasn't a more appealing man on the face of the earth.

"Like what?" he asked, his growl simmering, a curious expression taking over.

Maddie balled up the towel and approached him. "Like a mangy old mutt I once treated," she fibbed, holding her breath as she dabbed at his powerfully built, solid chest.

He stared at her, his voice holding a hint of disbelief. "An old mutt?"

She nodded, continuing to dab at him. "Uh-huh. Poor thing had fallen into the river."

Maddie couldn't bear it another second. Touching Trey this intimately had just about done her in. She'd held up well, she thought, considering that she was mere minutes from jumping the man's bones. "All finished," she said, thrusting the towel into his arms. She took a step to back away but Trey let the towel drop to the ground and grabbed her wrists, tugging her gently closer.

He grinned mischievously, "Not quite."

Before Maddie knew what had happened, Trey reached down into the rain bucket used to catch the leak, and splashed her with handful after handful of water. "Trey!"

Maddie backed away and stared down at her clothes, which were fully and completely drenched.

This time, he laughed. "The mangy mutt wanted a companion." Then he came closer, grabbing a dry towel. "Here," he said, approaching her. "Fair is fair." He dabbed at her face, taking care to dry her cheeks, mouth and chin. Then he sent a searing look down past her shoulders. "If you toss off your blouse, I'll do your chest," he offered softly. "Just like you did mine."

Fleeting forbidden thoughts of Trey patting her naked body dry flashed in her head and she realized she'd never had a better offer in her life. She grabbed the towel out of his hands, "Not a chance, cowboy."

Trey threw his head back and laughed even more, stepping back and away from her.

"Well, what have we here?" Monty Walker asked, catching the two of them red-handed. Guilt washed over Maddie in waves. She glanced at the floor. "Hi there, Monty."

Trey still had laughter in his voice when he volunteered, "Maddie was teaching me the finer points of plumbing."

Monty glanced from Trey to Maddie. "That so?" Then he added, "Well, somebody's got to." He winked at Maddie. "The man's an expert horseman, but doesn't know diddly about fixing a leak."

Trey stood next to Monty, putting an arm around his shoulder. "At least I know which way is…off."

"Oh, that. I was just funning with you."

Trey's expression went bleak the second he realized what the older man had done.

Maddie giggled again.

"The woman loves to laugh at me," Trey said to Monty. "But I'll get back at her when I cook dinner tonight."

"Oh," Maddie said, realizing she'd forgotten to tell Trey she wouldn't be home tonight. "Guess I'm getting off easy then. I won't be home for dinner."

Trey nodded. "A late-night house call?"

Maddie shook her head. "Not tonight. I have a date."

Five

Trey sat in a booth at the Hungry Wrangler Café with his uncle Monty and his cousin, Jack. He and Jack were about the same age and had been more like brothers than cousins while growing up. Trey pushed around his food on the plate, while the other two ate with gusto.

"Ain't you hungry, boy?" Uncle Monty asked, eyeing Trey's half-eaten steak. The retired sheriff of Hope Wells pulled no punches. He spoke his mind. Most of the time, Trey enjoyed his uncle's antics, but tonight he wasn't in the mood. Common courtesy and a true measure of gratefulness had Trey offering to treat his uncle to dinner. He'd worked most of the morning and half the afternoon fixing that doggone leak.

"Have at it," he said, sliding the plate his way. "Guess I'm not that hungry after all."

Jack glanced up from his meal and cast him an inquisitive look. "You sick or something?"

Jack Walker wore his uniform proudly. He'd just been reelected as sheriff of Hope Wells. First Monty, then Jack—between the two they had five decades of law enforcement under their belts.

"No, I'm not sick, just not very hungry." He sipped his iced tea.

Uncle Monty grunted as he stabbed at Trey's steak. "The man's lovesick, if you ask me."

Jack's brows rose, his expression none too subtle. "That pretty little Dr. Maddie getting under your skin?"

Uncle Monty didn't give him time to answer. He chimed in, "Under his skin? The boy wants her under his *sheets*. Should have seen his face when she told him she had a date tonight."

"Turned green, did he?" Jack jested.

Trey slammed down his glass. They were having too much fun at his expense. "Enough!"

Monty and Jack looked at one another then burst out laughing. Trey waited until their laughter died down. "You through now?"

Both men nodded. "Good, because I'll say this only once. Nothing's going on between Maddie and me. We made a business deal and we're sticking to it."

Uncle Monty lifted his fork and pointed it his way. "Yeah, monkey business. Looked like you two were having a wet T-shirt contest when I walked in this morning."

Trey ground his teeth. "That wouldn't have happened if you had turned the water *off*."

Monty scratched behind his ear. "She sure is cute."

Jack nodded. "Is she seeing anyone in particular?"

Trey shook his head. "I don't know. We don't discuss things like that." But he had to admit he was dying to know where she was tonight and with whom.

"Maybe I should give her a call," Jack said, his expression thoughtful.

"You don't own any animals," Trey reminded.

Jack smiled. "Maybe it's time I get one."

Trey glared at his cousin, but wouldn't give an inch. He and Jack had had a friendly competition going ever since they were young boys. Trey hated to admit the sensations washing over him. He wouldn't put a name to them and he wouldn't get caught up in his cousin's game. He shrugged. "Fine by me."

"It really cost you to say that, didn't it?" Jack asked with a big grin. But before Trey could make a denial, Jack added, all manner of jesting aside, "Look, I'm not going to call her, but if you're interested, I wouldn't hesitate. Maddie's got a lot going for her and some lucky guy is bound to discover that soon."

"She deserves to be happy," Trey said truthfully.

"Dang it, Trey. You're holding on to that 'Walker Curse' thing, aren't you?"

Trey stared at his cousin. Jack had no idea how many women had been hurt by the Walker men in his family. His cousin had no idea how bad Trey was at commitment. He had no idea how strongly he felt about this subject. Trey's mind was made up. He spoke with slow deliberation. "You come from a family who uphold the law. Your heritage is different than mine, cousin. I come from a long line of men who break hearts. True, we have the same grandfather, but his traits didn't seem to rub off on you."

"We don't know that yet."

Jack was true blue. Jack wouldn't ever let down anyone he loved. Trey was sure of his cousin. "I know you. You're as loyal as they come. And besides, you both have it all wrong. Yes, I'm in a sour mood tonight, but not because of anything having to do with Maddie."

"Then why?" Jack asked.

Trey frowned. "Because your father told me this afternoon that eventually, sooner more than later, I'm going to have to replace all the old galvanized pipes at the house with copper. Seems my plumbing is somewhat out of date."

Monty grinned, his gray-blue eyes twinkling. "Hell boy, that's what we've been trying to tell you."

Maddie stood by Storm's corral, eyeing the stallion in the moonlight. She'd noticed once again that Trey wasn't home, giving her the perfect chance to work with the feisty horse. She'd been sneaking out here for the past four nights, ever since her dinner date with Caroline and little Annabelle last Saturday night. And during those nights, Storm had been guarded but every so often Maddie would see a spark of change, a subtle softening in Storm's demeanor that had encouraged Maddie to continue to gain the horse's trust.

Maddie had used treats, but she also depended on her innate ability to read an animal and she sensed that Storm was getting ready to accept her. Each night, Maddie approached with caution. Storm, too, approached warily. Last night, Storm had actually taken the sugar cubes from her hand.

Tonight, she merely stood by the fence and watched as Storm pranced, snorted and then raced around the perimeter of the corral, all the while communicating with Maddie in a language she truly did understand.

When he'd finished his exercise, he stopped and stared. Then ever so slowly, he approached the fence where Maddie stood. "Are you glad to see me again?" she asked softly. "Well, I'm sure glad to see you."

He came right up to the fence and Maddie stepped upon the bottom rung in order to reach him. "Hey, boy," she whispered into the still night and reached her hand out to stroke his ink black mane. Then bravely, and only because she sensed he was ready, she ran her hand smoothly down his snout.

The horse lifted his head in a quick movement, but he didn't back away. Maddie stroked him once more, continuing to speak to him in a soft soothing tone.

When Maddie heard Trey's truck in the distance, she jumped down from the fence and said farewell to Storm. "See you tomorrow night." Unable to make her escape into the house without seeming obvious, she stood by the front porch as the truck came to a stop a short distance away. To her surprise, a pretty young woman who was at least six months pregnant exited the driver's seat. Trey got out of the passenger's side, and the woman strolled over to him and reached for his hand. They stood there speaking quietly for a few minutes.

Maddie's heart took an elevator ride down to her toes. Her gut clenched involuntarily and feelings she thought she had under control emerged with raw clarity. Seeing Trey with another woman, one he might have an involvement with, knocked her for a giant-size loop. All sorts of images popped into her head, and none of the scenarios she came up with helped to ease her mind. She didn't know who this woman was and she decided she couldn't bear to know. Not tonight. Not with the realization that Trey hadn't come home for dinner in the past four nights.

Maddie made a move to enter the house, but the woman caught sight of her and called out, "Hi there."

Maddie turned to find the woman heading her way, with Trey beside her. "Hello."

The woman was even prettier up close, a young Texas lady through and through, with deep blue eyes and long blond hair. "I've been meaning to get out here to say hello. Sorry to hear about your office burning down. My name is Brittany Fuller. I'm a friend of Trey's."

"Nice to meet you, Brittany. I'm Maddie Brooks."

"I know. Trey's always talking about you. He says you're a real good veterinarian."

Maddie glanced at Trey who appeared darn uncomfortable, his tanned face taking on color. She shrugged. "I love working with animals."

"I had to drive Trey home," the pregnant woman offered, smiling at him. "No offense, Trey. But you're one stubborn man." Then she explained to Maddie, "He hurt his hand working on my baby's new room. A beam of wood fell down and when Trey tried to catch it he got splintered up."

For the first time since he'd walked up, Maddie took a really good look at Trey. And suddenly she understood the expression on his face. Pain. She peered down at his right hand. "Oh! That doesn't look good at all."

Gently she reached for his hand to get a better look. Holding his hand in her palm, she noted where five or six long splinters had been hastily removed, the hand puffy, swollen and red.

"Paul and I wouldn't let Trey drive home. Though he did argue some."

Maddie glanced up. "Paul?"

"My husband. He'll be here in a minute. Paul and Trey have been friends just about forever, I guess. And when Paul hurt his back a few days ago, Trey came over first thing to help finish up the room." She patted her rounded belly. "Our baby will be here before you know it."

"Oh," Maddie said, dumbfounded. This was almost too much information to digest all at once. All of her initial suspicions about Trey and this woman were unfounded. She'd let jealousy rule out over reason. This woman and her husband were his friends. Trey had been doing a good deed and Brittany had driven him home because he'd gotten hurt. "Well, congratulations on the baby. Do you know what you're having?"

She shook her head. "We want to be surprised."

"That's nice. I wouldn't want to know, either," she said, realizing this was the first time she'd really given any thought to having a child. Suddenly it was clear that she did want children. And she too wanted to be surprised. "I hope your husband's back injury isn't too serious."

"The doctor told him to rest up a bit, but Paul's a stubborn one, too, and wouldn't stop, so Trey decided to come over and do the heavy work. Wouldn't take no for an answer. Even my thrown-together suppers didn't scare him away."

"Your suppers are delicious, Brit," Trey said with sincerity.

She smiled softly. "But now *you're* hurt, too."

"It's not that bad."

Maddie disagreed, "It looks kind of bad, Trey. Maybe you should see a doctor."

He twisted his mouth, lifting his hand up. "For this? No way."

"I was hoping…" Brittany said to Maddie, a look of concern on her face.

"Of course," Maddie said instantly, fully comprehending. "I'll patch him up."

Trey shook his head. "There's nothing to patch up."

"Yes, there is," both women chorused.

And before Trey could argue, Brittany's husband pulled up in a white Ford Explorer. "Looks like my ride's here," she said, and after Maddie had been introduced to Paul, Brittany got into the car and waved farewell.

Maddie turned back to Trey.

"There's nothing to patch up," he said stubbornly.

"Sit down, Trey, and don't be a baby," Maddie said softly, pointing to the kitchen chair. She'd gathered up her medical supplies and was ready.

"I don't need any doctoring, Maddie," he said again, but the woman wouldn't take no for an answer.

She stared at him with expectant eyes, so pretty, so dewy-grass-green, so *determined*. She'd accused him of packing a wallop the other day, but she was guilty of the same. One look at her sweetly concerned face had him sitting, obeying like a small puppy at obedience school.

Trey didn't want her to doctor him. He didn't want her anywhere near him. She was too much of a temptation, too much of a distraction. He'd been trying to keep his distance, but living under the same roof with her made it damn difficult. Every time he got close to Maddie, he would do something stupid, like taking her into his arms and kissing her.

Maddie set a bowl of warm water down on the table then took a seat close to him and the subtle scent of raspberries wafted by. She lifted his hand and set it into the water. "We'll let it soak for a while."

She opened his hand carefully and with delicate care massaged his fingers. She stroked gently, easing soreness and bringing back circulation. It felt good, damn good. Trey closed his eyes and let the sensations run through his body. Maddie had a great touch. Maybe too great, he thought, because circulation began to build in another area of his body as well. He cursed under his breath.

"Does it hurt?" she asked immediately, lifting her head from the task.

"No."

"I thought I heard you groan."

Trey kept silent.

"I'm going to dry your hand, put on an antiseptic and wrap it."

"I can't work with it wrapped."

Maddie smiled. "So you'll take the day off tomorrow."

"I don't take days off, Maddie. Not when I'm running the ranch on a shoestring."

Maddie shook her head, her doctoring instincts taking hold. She spoke in a stern voice, one Trey had never heard before. "You're lucky you don't need stitches, Trey. Those wood bits ripped your hand up real good going in, and whoever yanked them out ripped your hand up again."

Again, Trey was silent.

Maddie read straight through his poker face.

"Let me guess, you're the one who pulled out those splinters."

"Good guess."

She sighed. "Trey."

Trey leaned back in the chair, crossing his leg over his knee and watched as Maddie administered to his hand. With her head bent to the task, Trey stared at her coppery hair falling in soft waves onto her shoulders. She held him so carefully, mindful when the antiseptic stung and lifting apologetic eyes his way. She took gauze out of her medical bag, placing it over the wound then wrapped his hand with surgical tape, taking her time, using her skills as a healer.

Whenever he looked at Maddie, he saw his future. But the vision was false, a deception of the mind, because Trey wasn't the man for her. She deserved someone she could trust not to wound her gentle soul. He chalked up these unwelcome sentiments to being around Paul and Brittany all week. With the new baby coming, their excitement had rubbed off on him. He found himself longing for the same, a wife and family. And being with Kit wasn't much help, either. That man was so doggone smitten with his new wife he barely spoke a sentence without mentioning her name.

Trey knew people with successful relationships. That's all it was—this *wanting* he'd been experiencing lately. But his father's words haunted him daily. And Trey had vowed not to make those same mistakes. Trey was smart enough to realize that *wanting* and *having* were two different things. He wasn't cut out for family life. He'd tried that once and had failed miserably.

"Promise me something, Trey," Maddie said when she was all through with the bandaging. "You won't go busting up this hand I worked so hard on tonight. You won't injure yourself again." She held his wrapped hand in both of hers and stared at him with softness in her eyes.

"Hell, Maddie," he whispered, leaning close, beckoned by her caring nature and her sweet, tentative smile. "When you ask me like that, there isn't anything I wouldn't promise you."

Maddie leaned in also, coming dangerously close, their eyes meeting. "There isn't?" she asked breathlessly.

Raspberry sweet and red-haired sexy, Trey had a mind to kiss her again, the need so strong that he couldn't pull away. He stared at her heart-shaped mouth, glossy and full, parting slightly. He wanted to lift her out of the chair, put her onto his lap and brush his lips over hers until kissing wasn't enough.

Hell, who was he kidding? He wanted to lay her down on the kitchen table and…

And then the phone rang.

Trey jerked back in his chair and into reality. He'd almost made another mistake and although it would take his body a moment to adjust, he was glad for the interruption. He bounded up and answered the wall phone by the refrigerator. "Hello."

A few seconds later, he brought the receiver over to Maddie, stretching out the long cord. "Do you know a Nick Spencer?"

Maddie's face beamed with joy. She stood up, practically standing on her toes. "It's Nick? Really?"

"That's what he said," Trey answered, handing her the phone.

"Nick, I can't believe it's you." Maddie twirled the cord around her fingers. "How did you find me?"

Trey walked out the back door and into the night air, giving Maddie some privacy and him a place to cool off. He told himself over and over he was glad he hadn't kissed her again. He told himself he was glad Maddie had a personal life outside of her work. He told himself he was glad this guy Nick had called, interrupting the wild fantasy Trey had entertained.

He glanced down at his bandaged hand, flexing his fingers and feeling no pain. He took a deep crisp breath, realizing that most of all, he was glad he hadn't made any promises to Maddie.

Promises that he couldn't keep.

Six

The next day, Maddie knocked on the hotel room door at the Cactus Inn, anticipation growing in her stomach. She hadn't seen her dear friend Nick for more than a year, since she'd moved to Hope Wells. They'd gone to UC Davis together, Nick receiving his DVM two years before she'd graduated. But she and Nick had stayed in touch while he'd worked as an intern in Fresno, California. He'd made quite a name for himself in the field of veterinary medicine, having saved the life of a K-9 from the *Faithful Partner* program. That particular police dog had taken a bullet for his human partner and Nick had worked relentlessly to save the dog's life.

He'd become something of a local hero then, but that hadn't slowed him down. Nick went on to join an international symposium on bioterrorism among other worthy animal-related endeavors. In short, Nick was brilliant and Maddie considered herself lucky to be his good friend.

Maddie smiled when he opened the door. "Hi, Nick."

Nick grinned that winning handsome smile of his and took her into his arms in a warm embrace. "Maddie."

Maddie pulled away to look into his sky-blue eyes. "You look wonderful. I can't believe you're here."

He had blond good looks and charm enough to spare. He was as clean-cut as they come, always wearing button-down shirts and pleated trousers, today being no exception. "I'm here to see my best friend."

"*Best* friend? We haven't spoken in months. I was beginning to think you'd forgotten about me way out here in Texas."

"Nope, I couldn't forget you. I've been busy, Maddie. That's why I'm here. We have to talk. I have a proposition for you."

"You came way out to Hope Wells to proposition me?"

He took hold of her hand. "Yes, I did. Listen, I know you don't have more than an hour or so with me this morning before you have to get back to work and I'd like to see something of the town. Show me around, and we'll talk tonight, over dinner?"

"A proposition *and* a dinner invitation? How can a girl refuse?"

"You can't and you won't, I hope. But I don't want to get ahead of myself here." He stopped smiling and squeezed her hand. "I'd like to see where your office was, Maddie. I came as soon as I heard the news. Thank God you and the animals weren't hurt."

"Yes, we were fortunate. And I have Trey Walker to thank for taking us all in."

"He's the man you're living with?" There was nothing suspect in his tone of voice, yet Maddie felt the need to clarify.

"Yes. It's a business arrangement until my office can be rebuilt. I'm renting out a room at the ranch and I'm practicing out of his old barn."

Nick nodded. "You always were enterprising, Maddie. Good for you."

Nick had been Maddie's biggest fan while in school. He'd always admired her dedication to her work and her special talent with animals. They'd gotten along great at the university and she was glad to see that their camaraderie hadn't faded. "Thanks, Nick."

"Are you ready to show me Hope Wells?"

Maddie nodded and they walked hand in hand into the streets of town.

Trey held a pair of aces in his left hand, the best you can draw in Texas Hold 'Em. He glanced at his opponents, Kit, Jack, Monty and two of his ranch hands, keeping his poker face. None of his opponents looked too happy.

"I'm all in," he said, pushing all of his chips into the center of the kitchen table, taking care with his bandaged hand. He'd abided Maddie's request and hadn't done any manual labor today.

The men grumbled and only one player decided to call the bet. Jack tallied up Trey's stack and pushed an equal amount of chips into the pot. All in all, the pot size equaled less than ten dollars—playing with nickel and dime chips doesn't allow for too much loss. Which was good, since Trey's funds were meant for essentials such as hay and feed and household expenses. But the Walker clan had been playing poker since Will Walker's days.

That family tradition would never die as long as Trey had something to say about it.

Both Jack and Trey turned over their two cards. Jack held a pair of sevens. Trey's aces had him beat so far.

The dealer flopped three of the five community cards onto the table, each player being able to use those cards to make up the best possible hand. With Trey being all in, Jack couldn't raise the bet, so the fourth community card was dealt. So far neither of the cards drawn helped either player, keeping Trey in the lead and once the fifth and final card, known as the "river" card, was dealt a winner would be named. Trey's chances of winning the pot were good, the percentages greatly in his favor. He'd waited a long time for a hand like this.

But before the dealer dealt the last card, Maddie's voice stole into the room. "Hi guys. Just wanted to say good night and have fun."

All of the players' eyes darted toward the doorway, beckoned by Maddie's sweet voice.

"C'mon in here, girl, and let us see you properlike," Uncle Monty encouraged.

"I don't want to interrupt."

"Ah hell, it's just our usual monthly poker game. You're not interrupting."

Trey took his eyes off of his cards to look up at Maddie as she stepped into the room and his breath hitched in his throat. Beautiful came to mind, right after sexy, sinful and seductive. Trey felt a headache coming on, just as another ache developed below his waist.

Maddie was dressed to destroy, with her coppery hair all fluffed up, wearing a tight light-green dress that matched the color of her eyes, with cleavage spilling and her shapely legs exposed. She wore three-inch black strappy heels. Hell, a man could fantasize for days about those shoes alone, but the whole package was enough to turn Trey's poker-faced cool into steamy hot sizzle.

"Wow, you look great," Jack said, his eyes nearly bulging out of his head.

"You can interrupt any time," Kit said with a wink.

The others added their compliments as well, one man letting loose a long, low wolf whistle.

"Got a hot date?" Uncle Monty asked, a bit too gleefully for Trey's way of thinking.

"No, just dinner with an old friend," Maddie replied, her face flushed with color. Trey wondered what had caused her to blush, the all-around compliments tonight or the idea of her date with that Nick Spencer guy? "Nick and I go way back. We went to college together. He was passing through town and stopped to say hello."

"Hell, no one just passes through Hope Wells," Uncle Monty advised. "That man did some zigzagging to get to you."

Maddie chuckled.

Trey frowned. This morning, he'd driven past her burned-down office on his way to the grocery and had seen the two of them, hand in hand, peering at what was left of Maddie's veterinary office. She'd had her head on his shoulder and it certainly didn't appear that they were just friends. Hell, the image of the two of them like that had put him in a sour mood all day.

"Trey, don't you think Maddie looks pretty tonight?" Uncle Monty prodded.

Trey ground his teeth. He knew what Uncle Monty was up to, but he'd call his bluff; this was, after all, *poker* night. Trey pulled out his chair and stood up. He walked over to Maddie and stared deep into her eyes. "I hope your date appreciates how beautiful you are, inside and out," he said, taking her hand. "C'mon, I'll walk you out."

"Okay," Maddie agreed. "Good night everyone."

"Have a great time," Uncle Monty said.

The others also bid her farewell and Trey guided her toward the front door with her hand clasped in his. It felt so natural, so right, as if this should be their date, as if she'd dressed up special just for him, as if they had a wonderful evening to look forward to. And if things were different, Trey would take her hand and steal her away so no other man could hold her, no other man could touch her.

But Trey knew he had to let her go.

He released her hand. "Enjoy your evening out, Maddie. Have fun tonight."

"Thank you. I always enjoy being with Nick."

That comment slashed through his gut. Trey nodded and Maddie took a step toward her truck.

But she spun back around and stared into his eyes. "Trey, do you really mean it?"

Trey stood ramrod still. He couldn't believe Maddie had called him on this. But she had, and her expression held something akin to hope. He couldn't breathe, couldn't think. Emotions washed over him, fast and furiously, and he could only hear what his heart told him. Did he mean it? Did he want her to enjoy her evening with another man? Hell, no. But he couldn't admit that to Maddie and, right now, he couldn't lie to her, either. They stared into each other's eyes for a long drawn-out moment, his poker face hopefully back in place.

Uncle Monty called out, "Trey, boy, you playing poker or courting the lady?"

Trey lifted his lips in a wry smile. "I'd better get back to the game."

"Go," she said, "they're waiting. And Trey," she added, just as he was about to head back to the game, "I'm glad you took care with your hand today."

She turned her back and walked away.

Trey watched her climb into her truck and pull away, an ache gnawing through his stomach. He walked back into the kitchen and stood over his poker hand. "Let's see that last card," he said to the dealer.

The dealer turned over a seven of hearts.

Jack hit three of a kind, his three sevens beating out Trey's two aces.

Trey slumped into his seat. "Boy, I didn't see that coming."

"Sorry, Trey," Jack said, hauling in all of his chips. "Looks like you're through."

"That's poker for you," Uncle Monty said bluntly. "It's a lot like life. You don't see it coming, until it's too late."

A short time later, after the game had ended, Trey grabbed empty beer bottles from the table and tossed them in the trash. Only Jack and Uncle Monty remained, the others leaving just minutes ago. Jack had battled Kit in the final hand and had won the evening.

"Too bad you came out the loser tonight, cousin," Jack stated, putting poker chips back in their holder.

Trey shrugged. He didn't take poker too seriously. It was a game meant to uphold the Walker tradition. It was a way to get together with friends, have a few beers and shoot the breeze. "I'll get you next month."

Jack's mouth twisted. "I wasn't talking about the game, Trey."

Monty sidled up next to Trey and laid a hand on his shoulder. "You didn't see that hand coming, cause you weren't looking, boy. The same holds true in life. You think you're holding a winning hand and then someone comes along with one better. Before you know it, the game's lost. That's what Jack's talking about."

Trey took a sharp breath. "You're talking about Maddie."

Monty looked him straight in the eyes. "You took a risk tonight. You went 'all in' on a hand you believed would win. Sometimes you've got to do that right here." He pressed a finger into Trey's chest, just above his heart. "Go *all in,* boy. Don't lose that girl."

"Lose her?"

"Yeah. You've got to ask yourself, what would be worse, winning that girl or losing her forever?"

"You're forgetting that I took a risk on that last hand and came out the loser anyway."

"Ah, but at least you gave it your best shot." Monty smiled, his eyes crinkling and his voice elevating. "Remember, if you don't play, you can't possibly win. Get in the game, Trey. Play the percentages. Judging by the way that little lady looks at you, I'd say you're the odds-on favorite. She's worth the risk."

But Maddie would be the one taking the biggest risk, because sure as the sun sets in the west, Trey knew he would break her heart. And that was a chance he wasn't willing to take.

Later that night, Maddie pulled into the gate at 2 Hope Ranch, her mind spinning from her dinner with Nick. He'd really thrown her off balance with his proposition, giving her a whole lot to think about. It had been all she *could* think about tonight and as she'd traveled the road toward 2 Hope and Trey, she tossed around all of her options. She'd wondered about her future here in

Hope Wells comparing it to the marvelous opportunity awaiting her with Nick.

A fleeting sense of belonging assailed her as she parked the truck by Trey's ranch house. She'd come to think of this place as home. She'd settled in quite nicely here, enjoying the peace of ranch life, surrounded by green pastures and solid earth with animals in abundance. And Trey. *He* was here.

She liked the thought of coming home to him.

He'd looked at her differently tonight, as though he'd really *seen* the woman that she was, his gaze raking her body over with appreciation and desire. Maddie's heart had raced the moment she'd stepped inside the kitchen and when he'd taken her hand to walk her outside, her insides had quaked. She'd wished the date had been with him, that he'd been the one to ask her out.

But mentally, Maddie scolded herself for allowing such thoughts when she knew darn well that 2 Hope wasn't really her home. And Trey Walker wasn't the man waiting for her. This was a temporary business arrangement that served both she and Trey well. No use holding on to sentimental thoughts.

Maddie climbed down from the truck and glanced at Storm's corral. Once the stallion had seen her, he'd trotted right up to the fence and waited.

Progress.

Maddie smiled and called softly to the horse, "I'll be right back."

She tiptoed into the darkened house through the back door and proceeded to her bedroom. All was quiet, Trey having probably turned in hours ago. Still, Maddie made little noise as she undressed, taking off her dress and slipping out of her heels silently. She couldn't pass up this chance to work with Storm. He'd been on her mind quite a bit lately. Maddie enjoyed the private time she spent with the stallion. She found getting to know the intricacies of the animal's spirit as rewarding as the act of healing itself.

Once dressed in her regular work clothes—jeans and a denim shirt—she headed outside, mindful not to wake Trey. There was a part of her that wanted to surprise him with Storm's progress, but she also worried that Trey wouldn't approve of these late-night tests of will.

One look at Storm and Maddie knew the horse was nearly ready. Without qualms, she opened the corral gate and entered Storm's territory. They had a staring bout for a few seconds before Storm allowed her approach. "Hey there," she cooed softly. "It's just me."

Maddie stroked the horse's mane, then moved her hand to his snout. Fearlessly she came around to face him and looked up into his eyes as she continued to stroke him. "You're beginning to trust me, Storm. That's a good thing, boy." She reached inside her jeans and handed the stallion half a dozen sugar cubes. "Or are you charming me just for these treats?"

The stallion gobbled them down without hesitation. "One hundred percent male," Maddie said on a soft chuckle. "But let's see if you really trust me."

And Maddie headed to the barn for a lead rope.

Trey slammed the door to his Chevy Silverado and entered the house, realizing he hadn't shared a meal with Maddie all week. He'd been working late in the evenings helping Paul and Brittany with their baby's new room addition. He had Maddie to thank for that, her ministrations had helped his hand heal real fast and he'd started working at their place again the night after the poker game. Now, the nursery was officially finished.

Trey grabbed a beer from the refrigerator, twisted the cap and took a swig as a great sense of accomplishment washed over him. He'd been happy to help, the reward being a pretty new room for Paul and Brittany's baby...

Brittany had insisted on throwing a small party for all of the people who'd pitched in on the project and she had included Maddie. She'd given Trey direct instructions to give Maddie the hand-written invitation this evening. Trey knew better than to argue with a pregnant lady, especially one determined to make a new friend. So Trey finished his beer and strode to Maddie's bedroom, reaching into his breast pocket for the invitation. When he found her door open, he stood just outside the threshold and called out, "Maddie?"

She didn't answer so he peeked inside the darkened room. "Maddie, you in here?"

A ray of hallway light and one quick glance told him she wasn't. Trey knew she wasn't out on a late night call because he'd seen her truck parked by the house when he'd pulled up and she couldn't be out with her "friend" Nick. He'd left Hope Wells days ago. She had to be working late inside the barn, maybe making her last rounds, checking on the animals. Trey headed that way, deciding to give her the invitation and call it a night.

Once outside, Trey sensed something wrong. A howling in the distance disturbed him while his immediate surroundings remained still and quiet. There were no lights on in the barn and as he surveyed the grounds, his gaze taking everything in, he stopped dead in his tracks, realizing what had been niggling at him.

Storm's corral was empty.

Trey tried to remain calm, weighing the possibilities, but his heart raced anyway. Images flashed in his head as he recalled Maddie's fascination with the stallion. There wasn't a day that went by, where he hadn't caught her communicating with the horse, detouring her way around the ranch just to make eye contact with him, and Trey certainly had noticed the stash of sugar cubes in the cupboard had gone down lately. He also knew Maddie didn't take sugar in her coffee, but darn it all, she sure as hell had found another use for it.

Storm.

And just as he'd made that assessment Storm appeared, a black vision dashing out of the darkness, clearly agitated, with fury in his eyes. He snorted, blowing air loudly from his nose as he raced around the outside of the corral. He stopped, coming just five feet from Trey, lifted up his front legs, rearing back, trying to shake the saddle from his back.

Trey's body quaked with fear. He'd never seen his stallion this frenzied.

Storm wore a *saddle*.

And his rider was missing.

Seven

Trey held Maddie in his arms, shielding her with his body from the dust swirling around in gusts. He'd been lucky to find her so quickly, relying on his instincts as to where she would be and grateful his hunch had been right. He'd driven his truck like a demon through the dust storm, fearing the worst, and praying for a miracle.

On the drive up here, Uncle Monty's words kept repeating in his head. "Don't lose that girl, boy."

Trey had never known such fear. The thought of losing Maddie had eaten away at him, corroding his insides. He didn't know if he'd find her in time. He didn't know the extent of her would-be injuries. When he'd seen a saddled Storm with no rider, he'd immediately realized the dangers Maddie could have encountered. He also realized what he should have guessed the minute he'd heard the howling sounds at the ranch. An unmerciful dust storm had moved through the territory. The stallion must have startled, throwing Maddie. Fortunately she'd landed on soft grass.

He gazed down at her slightly bruised face. She smiled and relief poured through him like a rushing river. He smiled back and another realization struck him hard, right between the eyes.

He had fallen for her.

If he'd doubted that at all an hour ago, he knew it for certain now. He'd never known he could feel so intensely, never known he could fall so hard.

"Maddie." He stroked her face, gently, careful not to touch the bruise on her cheek. She had a small gash across her forehead also but it had already stopped bleeding.

She looked up at him as if surprised. "Trey, you found me."

Wild wind howled and dust continued to swirl. Trey's shirt billowed, making flapping noises against his chest. "I've got to get you inside the truck," he said. "Can I lift you?"

"I'm s-sore," she said, "but nothing's broken."

Trey held her carefully, hunkering down, using his body to block the wind and lifted her into his arms. He strode to the passenger side, setting her onto the seat, then ran around to his side and climbed in, locking them both inside. Blasts of air struck the truck, shaking it up, but Trey was sure they were safe enough. He'd weathered more than a fair share of these storms in this truck.

He glanced at Maddie sitting there, tousled and roughed up a bit, but apparently not injured.

"Are you angry with me?"

Trey ran a hand through his hair and sighed. "More

like scared spitless, honey. I didn't know what I'd find when I got up here."

Maddie closed her eyes. "I'm sorry."

Trey grabbed his first aid kit from behind the seat and sidled up next to her. "I should be rightfully pissed, but I'm too doggone relieved right now. Hold still," he said, ripping open an antiseptic wipe and dabbing at the cut on her forehead then the bruise on her face.

She didn't flinch, taking her medicine like a good patient.

"What happened to Storm?"

"He's back at the ranch. I didn't stick around long enough to see to him, though."

"We were doing fine, really, Trey. He'd progressed so far, but it was his first time out with a rider and…"

"And he wasn't ready, Maddie. Don't make me think about that right now." Trey knew his anger would settle in later, after he got back to the ranch. Maddie had taken a stupid chance with Storm. She could have been killed, or seriously injured. He might not have found her in time. But Trey shoved aside those worries for now, grateful that he *had* found her quickly and that she was safe. "I don't want to get riled up."

Maddie's green eyes rounded and she whispered softly, "You don't?"

Trey shook his head. "No," he said, spreading his legs out wide and reaching for her. "Come rest against me. Looks like we'll have to wait out the storm."

Without hesitation, Maddie moved into his arms, resting her head just under his chin. He tucked her small frame into his, wrapping his arms around her.

"Are you cold?"

Maddie shook her head.

"Scared?"

"Not anymore," she answered.

Trey began stroking her back, slowly massaging the muscles that must surely ache. "How does this feel?"

Maddie crooned, "Better than a hot fudge sundae."

Trey smiled. "That good?"

Maddie nodded, laying her hand over his heart. If only she knew how fast his heart beat at the moment. If only she knew how much holding and protecting her meant to him.

"Yeah, that good."

After a few brief seconds of silence, Maddie lifted her head and kissed him sweetly on the cheek. "Thank you for coming to my rescue."

Trey spread his hand through her hair, coppery waves spilling over his fingertips, soft and smooth and silky. "You nearly gave me a heart attack, Maddie," he whispered. "I'm gonna need a better thank-you."

Maddie slipped her hand inside an opened button on his shirt, stroking his flesh until his skin fairly sizzled. Then she lifted up and gave him the best thank-you of his life, an openmouthed, long, hot, sexy kiss that knocked the breath out of him.

"Was that better, Trey?"

"Better," he croaked, barely catching his breath.

Maddie stared deeply into his eyes and every shred of willpower he could muster wasn't enough for the intoxicating look of desire she cast him. His manhood rose to the occasion, pressing against his jeans uncomfortably, and Trey was at a complete loss, helpless to hold back. "Ah hell, Maddie," he whispered, brushing his lips to her ear, "how am I supposed to keep my hands off you now?"

A sweet triumphant smile emerged on her face. She spoke softly, "Maybe you're not supposed to, Trey. Maybe we were meant to be here together, trapped inside the truck, but trapped more by what our hearts are telling us."

"Yeah, maybe," Trey admitted, closing his eyes briefly and allowing her words to sink in. He ached for her physically, but his heart was involved, too, and no matter how much he denied his feelings, he wanted Maddie with powerful gut-wrenching need.

The storm raged outside. The truck trembled as wind gusts rocked them back and forth. Small particles of earth spiraled up to strike the windshield encasing them in darkness.

Trey *was* trapped by the storm, but he was also trapped by something stronger. His desire for Maddie. He knew if he touched her again, there would be no going back. Yet, he had to touch her. He had to feel her sleek skin under his palms, to slide his hands along her body and bring them both immeasurable pleasures. He'd fought the battle in his head long enough.

Trey stretched out, using the full "king" of the cab and pulled Maddie down with him, so that her petite frame lay across his. She fit him perfectly, the feel of her slight weight upon his an intoxicating elixir. He wove his fingers in her hair and claimed her lips, taking her in a slow, deliberate there's-no-going-back-now kiss. Maddie moaned with pleasure and kissed him just as slowly, just as deliberately, moving on him to adjust her position and rubbing his body enough to destroy him.

He ached for her, his erection stretching the material of his jeans to its limit. He'd never been so turned on in his life. He'd never *wanted* so much. He kissed her forehead, her cheeks, her nose, then stroked his tongue over her mouth. She opened for him and they kissed again, openmouthed and frenzied, with heat building and all semblance of grace disappearing. She was as hot for him as he was for her. He tore his mouth away long enough to whisper, "We have too many clothes on."

Without hesitation, Maddie sat up, pressing her derriere to his manhood, and unbuttoned her blouse. She took her time removing it, allowing him time to enjoy the view. The ache below his waist intensified, growing harder each second. Trey's body pulsated with need, and when she unhooked her soft white cotton bra and her breasts spilled out, he went hot all over. "You're beautiful, honey."

"Thank you." She smiled and leaned forward. "Now it's your turn," she said softly and began unbuttoning his shirt. Trey helped her. He couldn't get the damn thing off fast enough. And once done, he pulled her down again, crushing her breasts to his chest, molding her soft full flesh to his. Raw and powerful need assailed him. He took her in a wild erotic kiss, then moved his mouth to her throat, kissing her, loving her, cupping her breasts in his hands, flicking his thumb over two erect pink peaks.

Maddie moaned.

Trey cursed, the need in him strong.

They were both lost.

He took her in his mouth then, his tongue stroking over one breast, laving the rosy pebble hard nipple until Maddie sighed with pleasure. She wove her hand in his hair and guided him, showing him with each move, each little sound, what she enjoyed, what brought her satisfaction.

Trey wanted to please her. He wanted to bring her every ounce of enjoyment he possibly could. This was no one-night stand, where his mind wasn't attached to his body. He cared too much for Maddie not to make it good for her. And he wanted to make it damn good.

"Baby," she pleaded ever so softly.

One plea, one softly spoken word from Maddie turned him inside out.

Baby.

Trey's heart slammed against his chest. Powerful sensations ran a track race throughout his body. An overwhelming need to possess this woman, body and soul, struck him hard, like a staggering car crash. "Hold on, honey."

He reached down to unzip her jeans and slipped his hand inside, meeting with soft silk and lace. He played with the thin strap, amazed that this sensible, level-headed doctor wore sexy panties.

"A thong?" he asked, hooking his finger under the strap.

She chuckled. "I'm afraid so."

"Damn." He was done for. He knew that from this moment on whenever he'd see her on the ranch wearing her clinical lab coat, an erotic image would instantly flash in his head. Maddie Brooks and her mind-blowing thong.

Trey kissed her again as he spread his hand flat against her belly and stroked her slowly. She whimpered, a little throaty sound that made his erection granite hard. He moved his fingers over her petal flesh, sliding back and forth, slowly, and erotically, bringing her pleasure and feeling her sweet heat. She rocked with him now, both lost in the rhythm as their bodies ground together in unison.

"I hope to God I have a condom," he muttered.

Maddie wove her fingers in his hair and gazed at him with half-lidded dewy eyes, her lips full and love-bruised, her sexy little body damp and slick. Trey no longer hoped; he *prayed* he had a rubber in his wallet.

She pressed her mouth against his chest, laving his nipples with her tongue until he ached so much he had to lift her off him. "Let's get naked."

Pants and boots were tossed off in a hurry. Trey fumbled around in his jeans, opened his wallet and pulled out a wrinkled foil packet. Instant relief washed over him. He didn't know what he'd have done…

Maddie took the packet from his hand and arched a brow. "Should I be glad you carry this around in your wallet?" she asked, and Trey understood she wasn't exactly teasing.

"It's old, Maddie. Ancient. This brand is nearly obsolete."

Maddie smiled and ripped open the packet. "Old is good, Trey."

"It's the truth."

"I know."

Then she fitted the condom over his erection and lifted up, positioning herself over him. He slipped inside her, causing a little moan to escape her lips and sensation after sensation rocked him to the core. He'd never experienced anything so powerful in his life.

The storm had ended and a sliver of moonlight lit the cab, shining upon Maddie as she rode him up and down, her movements graceful and slow and as heady a sight as Trey had ever seen. Trey took the pleasure she offered, fascinated by the beautiful woman making love to him, stunned by the woman creating her own kind of storm.

Watching her face change with each stroke, each undulation, her eyes closed, her head thrown back, Trey's heart raced, his body shook and his soul—she'd touched that as well. "You're amazing."

"Trey, I've never…" But she didn't finish her thought. She didn't have to. Trey knew. He felt the same way.

He cupped her bottom and guided her, helping her drive harder, faster, her breasts heaving, her hair flying, her body moist and ready.

"Hold on, honey," he said, wanting to make this last as long as possible for reasons he held in the back of his mind, reasons he couldn't deal with at the moment. For now, he wanted to prolong the night, prolong the pleasure.

Maddie's only response was a slight little encouraging sound.

Trey lifted her and together they rolled, bumping heads into the steering wheel and dashboard, until finally, she was under him. He kissed her again and again, touching her all over, breathing in the sexy scent of an aroused woman. Trey was more aroused than he'd ever been before.

The confinement of the cab worked to their advantage. They couldn't get far from each other. Maddie rested her back against the window, held on to the steering wheel for support and Trey too grabbed the steering wheel, entering her with one thrust that shook him violently. "Ah, Maddie," he groaned, the pleasured pain almost too much to bear.

"Baby," she cooed, her expression one of pure joy.

Trey's erection swelled and he was lost from then on. He moved like lightning, driving deep into her, watching pure lust and potent need cross her features. She moved with him, rocking when he rocked, rising when he rose, trembling when he trembled.

He took her lips in one final deep kiss and released with everything he had, climbing the highest hill and taking her with him. She groaned aloud and both came down hard, trembling, quivering, their bodies spent and satisfied.

Trey kissed Maddie softly then maneuvered her so that she sat next to him on the seat. He'd almost forgotten what she'd been through tonight. And he hoped like hell he hadn't hurt her. "Are you okay?"

Maddie nodded. "A bit overwhelmed. That was…"

"Incredible?"

She looked deeply into his eyes as soft light glimmered into the cab. "More than that, Trey. It was much more than incredible."

Trey's breathing began to slow and his brain finally kicked into gear. A slow uneasy tremor coursed through his body.

He'd given in to his desire.

He'd made love to Maddie.

Now, she cast him a look filled with hope and expectation.

The two things Trey didn't have to offer.

Maddie sat in the passenger side of the truck in front of the ranch house, watching Trey shut down the engine. After they'd made love, they'd dressed quickly, quietly and rode home in silence, Trey's expression growing dimmer each second.

Maddie's emotions had been on a rollercoaster ride for much of the evening. First the fright with Storm, being tossed off the stallion and left alone in bad weather and then experiencing great relief at having Trey rescue her. Confined in the truck and filled with strong desire, they'd made love. For Maddie, there weren't sufficient words to describe making love to Trey—a dream come true, her fantasy in the flesh. She'd ridden a high she'd never known, discovered sensations she never knew existed and now this—Trey's silent withdrawal, his distant body language.

"Trey?" she asked finally. He hadn't made a move to get out of the truck. He just sat there, running a hand down his face, seeming to do battle with something going on in his head. "I need to know where we go from here?"

Trey turned to face her, a look of deep regret and anguish crossing his features. The look alone frightened her and she almost couldn't bear to hear what he had to say. But Maddie had never been a wilting willow—she fought her battles head on.

"That's just it, honey. There's nowhere to go from here."

Stunned, Maddie sat there silently for a moment, letting his words sink in. He couldn't possibly mean that it was over before it began. He couldn't possibly mean that tonight meant nothing to him. Nothing but…sex. Maddie tried not to spit the words out bitterly, "So that's it? A one-night stand?"

"No," he said adamantly. "You could never be a one-night stand."

"Then, what are you saying?" Maddie fought tears, barely keeping her emotions in check and waiting patiently for Trey's explanation.

Trey sighed deeply and peered out the truck's windshield. "I never meant for any of this to happen, Maddie. I tried keeping to our business agreement. Things got out of control."

Maddie held her chin high. "We made love and it was wonderful, Trey. But apparently, it didn't mean anything to you."

"It meant something to me," he rushed out. "That much is more than true."

"Just great sex?"

"The best sex of my life, Maddie. I won't deny that. But it was more."

Maddie closed her eyes. She believed him and should have been elated at Trey's admission but instead she experienced great anguish. She knew a brush-off when she encountered one. She feared what was coming, but didn't understand why.

He scrubbed his jaw and took a deep breath. "I don't want to hurt you."

"Then don't."

He cast her a solemn look. "I'm trying not to, Maddie. I'm trying damn hard to protect you."

"Protect me? From who? From…you?"

"Well, yeah."

Trey paused and Maddie waited.

"I'm no good with commitment," he said finally. "I've failed too many times in the past. I have a bad track record with women. And the trait goes back generations. It's like a curse."

"Trey, I don't recall asking you for a commitment."

Trey shook his head fiercely. "No way, Maddie. I may not know a whole lot about women, but I do know one thing. You are definitely not a one-night, one-week or one-month stand. You're a keeper. You're the kind of woman that settles a man. I wish I was the settling kind, but I know I'm not. I don't commit. I tried that once. Did you know I was once engaged?"

Maddie shook her head. She whispered, "No."

His lips curled up in a self-deprecating smile. "Yeah. I left my fiancée just before the wedding. I ran off like a stupid fool and hurt her real bad. Left her to make all the explanations, left her to deal with a broken heart. It really tore her up. I knew then that my fate was sealed. I'm just like my father and his father before him. They took what they wanted with no regard for the women who would get hurt. My father wasn't a bad man. He just didn't come to recognize his faults, until it was too late—five wives too late. The days of Will Walker are long gone. My great-great-grandfather was loyal. He had clarity. He knew what he wanted and went after it. He toughed it out and didn't give up. He had what I lack, Maddie. *Staying power.*"

Maddie's heart ached, yet she found herself wanting to know more. Maybe it was the healer in her, or maybe it was just morbid curiosity, but she wanted to learn about Trey's one-time engagement. "How long ago were you engaged?"

"I was twenty-one. Ten years ago, give or take."

"You were young, Trey. You weren't ready."

She thought about her good friend, Caroline, and what she'd been through because of a man who hadn't been ready. He'd abandoned his wife and child, yet Maddie had a hard time comparing the two men. Trey was too good a man to abandon his family, but it was clear that he believed he would, and right now, that's all that mattered—what Trey believed about himself.

"I was ready enough to ask her to marry me. I was ready enough to set a wedding date. I was ready enough to make plans for a future. Only thing I wasn't ready for was following through on my promises. Like I said, no staying power."

"And you think you'll break my heart?"

Trey closed his eyes briefly, letting go a long sigh then he stared deeply into her eyes. "Yeah, I'll break your heart."

She threw caution and all good sense to the wind. Her pride flew out as well. "Maybe I'm willing to take that chance."

Trey shook his head. "I can't let you do that. You deserve better than me. You deserve someone who has everything to offer you. Someone steady."

"Like Nick Spencer?" Maddie didn't know exactly why she'd brought Nick's name up, but she had and now she wanted to see Trey's reaction. She and Nick were friends, period. But somehow she doubted Trey believed that and a small part of her had rejoiced when she'd thought he'd been jealous of Nick.

Trey became quiet and long moments ticked by. Then he finally nodded, "Yeah, if he makes you happy."

Maddie wanted to scream. Trey was the one who made her happy. He's the one she'd wanted since the day she stepped foot in Hope Wells. He's the one who had just made earth-shattering, mind-blowing, heart-stopping love to her.

She decided to lay it all on the line, to let him know the truth about Nick's proposal. If Trey cared for her at all, she'd find out right now. "Nick's part of a new clinic being developed in Denver and he wants me to work alongside him there. The clinic will have all the latest state-of-the-art equipment and we'd be on the ground floor of many new techniques in veterinary medicine. It would mean leaving my practice. It would mean saying goodbye to Hope Wells for good."

Trey's expression faltered for a moment, and she

witnessed deep regret in his eyes. He spoke so quietly that Maddie had a hard time hearing him. "Maybe you should go."

A sharp slap in the face couldn't have stung more. Tonight, they'd shared something powerful, something special, something *beautiful*. They'd made love like there was no tomorrow, like their lives depended on it. And now, Trey had dismissed her. Easily. Without much debate or thought. He'd simply decided what was best for her. He wouldn't even give them a chance. He didn't care enough to try.

The pain went deep. Tears flowed then, a few drops that she couldn't hold back any longer. She reached for the door handle and turned away from Trey. "Yeah, maybe I should."

Maddie pulled the door open and when her feet hit the ground, she strode quickly to the house. Once inside her bedroom, angry, bitter tears spilled out and she sobbed silently.

Her heart had never ached like this before. She'd never known so much anguish. But Maddie allowed her tears for only a few minutes, before inhaling deeply and trying to come to terms with the events of the evening. She realized while her tears would subside, the sadness she felt tonight would linger for a long time.

She stood by her bedroom window and peered out into the night. A shadow of a figure emerged through the darkness. She recognized Trey, pulling a lead rope, with Storm on the other end. Storm kicked up a fuss, but Trey held firm and instead of retiring the stallion in his corral, he led him to the stables. Trey would probably stay with Storm throughout the night, making sure the horse settled down, keeping a vigil until Storm calmed.

Maddie had always thought Trey was so like Storm.
Two wild spirits, two untamed souls who didn't know
how to trust. She'd been with both tonight, optimisti-
cally thinking the two had been ready and hoping the
bond she'd developed with each had been enough. Maddie had tested the waters and had nearly drowned. And
she'd come to realize one distinct difference between
Storm and his master. While Storm couldn't trust in
others, Trey couldn't trust in himself.

But Maddie saw Trey so differently than he saw
himself.

He claimed he had no staying power, but Maddie
knew better. She knew him to be a man of worth and
even if she decided to leave the ranch, Hope Wells and
Trey Walker, she hoped to help him learn the truth about
himself.

She figured she didn't have anything to lose.

Her heart was already broken.

Dawn forced its way through dark clouds, shedding
dismal light and bringing a frosty chill to the air. Maddie
showered quickly and dressed in her usual attire, jeans
and a button-down blouse, then quickly headed to the
barn where Storm was stabled. She had to make amends
with the stallion. She'd pushed him too far last night and
even though he'd responded to her more than any other
person on the ranch, he still had a long way to go.

She wrapped her arms around her middle and entered the damp barn, realizing that while Trey had the
means to heat the barn for the animals, he didn't have
the funds. Only extreme temperatures warranted going
to that expense.

Maddie recalled the first conversation she'd had with

her friend, Caroline regarding this unpredictable climate. "If you don't like the weather in Texas," she'd said with a grin, "just wait about five minutes."

This week had gone from warm sunny days to gusty dust storms and cold temperatures. She wondered about Denver and how well she would adjust to the climate there. In truth, she'd stayed up most of the night considering Nick's proposal, thinking about moving and wondering if leaving Hope Wells might be best for her.

Maddie put that thought out of her head as she walked up to Storm's stall. The horse rested on his side, lying down on a bed of wheat straw that was piled up high around the edges. With Storm's restless nature, a good bank of bedding against the walls insured the animal's safety. Trey had always put his animals first, whenever he could. It was probably the first trait that had attracted Maddie to him—his willingness to protect his livestock.

"Morning."

Maddie whirled around and stared into the dark eyes of a rumpled Trey. His morning appearance, including an unshaven face and disheveled hair, reminded her that if things had turned out differently last night, she would have been waking up to that look today.

"He's all right," he said, gesturing to Storm. "Took some time to get him settled, but we managed."

Maddie nodded. "You stayed with him all night?"

"Most of it. Didn't get much sleep."

Trey scratched his head, then ran a hand through his hair, attempting to straighten it, but only making stray strands stick up even more. His plaid shirt hung loosely over jeans that were smattered with dirt stains and sticky straw. Maddie wondered how a man could appear incredibly vulnerable and downright sexy, all at the same time.

She ached inside, seeing him and knowing that what they shared would never be again. The pain went deep and Maddie struggled to keep her composure.

"Actually, I'm glad you're here," he said quietly, and she wondered if his lack of sleep had anything to do with his dismissal of her last night. She wondered if he ached inside the way that she did. "I was planning on checking on you. How are you feeling this morning?"

Did he want to know her heart had broken?

"You took a fall and…well after, when we—"

"I'm fine, Trey." She couldn't bear to discuss their lovemaking from last night. She couldn't speak to him casually about something that had meant so much to her. He'd made his feelings clear, rejecting even the thought of a relationship with her. Yes, she'd been terribly hurt, but not from the fall.

Trey swallowed and looked away.

Maddie turned to leave. It seemed there wasn't much else to say. She came to check on Storm and the poor animal looked exhausted. Apparently it had been a tumultuous night for all three of them. She promised herself to return later to make amends with the stallion.

"Maddie?"

She turned around. "Yes?"

Trey's gaze held her immobile. "You might not believe this, but I don't regret last night."

She did believe him. Didn't he say he'd never had better sex. At least she had that to cling to on lonely nights. "Neither do I," she replied honestly.

She walked to the barn door and then turned once again to find Trey's dark captivating eyes on her. "You know, it was a lucky day for Storm when you brought him to 2 Hope. You've stuck by him all along, believing in that feisty headstrong stallion, even when others gave up on him. There aren't too many men who would have spent half the night in a cold dreary barn worrying over him. He *does* belong to you, Trey. Just like you belong to him."

Trey's brows rose in surprise and his thoughtful expression left Maddie with a gladdened heart. She walked away with a smile.

Eight

Under ordinary circumstances, Maddie would have looked forward to an evening with new friends. But tonight, her heart simply wasn't up for it. She stared in her bedroom mirror to find a woeful reflection looking back. Her bleak mood matched the gloomy rain they'd been experiencing for days now. How was she going to put herself together enough to share a dinner with Trey and his friends, Paul and Brittany tonight?

She held up the lovely handwritten invitation and re-read the beginning sentiment. *The pleasure of your company.*

Maddie had almost forgotten all about this invitation until Brittany had called yesterday specifically making sure Maddie would come. She'd been caught off guard and fumbled around in her head for an excuse, but Brittany's sweet demeanor and her hopeful tone caused her to change her mind. She didn't want to disappoint the woman, and Maddie had to face facts. She couldn't hide from Trey Walker. They lived in the same house.

She'd treaded carefully, trying not to purposely bump into him these past few days. That hadn't been too difficult a task, since she'd been working long hours, taking on appointments, making referrals when her limited ability to treat the animals hadn't been enough and going out on house calls. After the night when she'd taken off on Storm, she'd been swamped with work. She welcomed the distraction.

Trey hadn't been around the house much either. She'd see him on the cloudy mornings ride off on his horse with Kit or some of the other ranch hands, doing what cowboys do, but she didn't look for him at night. She'd retire to her bedroom in the evening with a good book, trying to put thoughts of him out of her head.

With a deep sigh, Maddie fingered the silver necklace around her neck. "I've got a big decision to make, Aphrodite," she said, thinking of Nick's proposal. He'd given her some much-needed time to make her decision, but she knew he couldn't wait indefinitely. He had a time frame and Maddie wouldn't take advantage of his good nature. She'd have to come to her decision soon.

From down the hall, the shower door opened, closed and water pelted down, reminding her that Trey also readied for the dinner party tonight. And as she moved about her room, shedding her work clothes, she heard his sounds, becoming familiar with the noises he made while getting dressed.

Maddie quickly donned a pair of tan slacks and a soft buttercream scoop-neck sweater. She dressed her outfit up with drop pearl earrings and a matching bracelet.

She'd debated whether to wear the pearl necklace that matched the set, but she didn't have the heart to remove Aphrodite. If ever she needed to feel a bond, that special closeness to Grandma Mae, it was now. Okay, so she wouldn't make the greatest fashion statement tonight, but she'd have something more important.

Maddie styled her hair, letting the waves fall where they may, gave it a quick spray and grabbed her purse. Taking one last look in the mirror, she pasted on a smile. The transition was complete. She inhaled, fully ready for the evening, and opened her door.

Trey stood at the threshold, his hand fisted as if he were about to knock.

"Trey?" she said, taking a step back. She hadn't expected to see him standing there, fully dressed and looking better than sin itself.

He wore dark trousers, a white dress shirt and a thin black bola tie decorated with a triangle of turquoise. His hair, pushed back from his face and still a little damp, exposed clean-shaven skin, high cheekbones and unreadable dark eyes. "Are you almost ready?" he asked.

Maddie swallowed. "Uh, ready?"

He nodded. "For dinner at Paul and Brit's?"

Maddie stared at him. "Yes, but I think I need to change. Maybe I should wear a dress," she said, mostly to herself. Trey looked drop-dead gorgeous. She'd never seen him in anything but jeans and a work shirt. The man cleaned up nicely. And suddenly Maddie felt underdressed for the occasion.

She made a move to shut her door. Trey put up his hand to hold the door ajar, halting her from retreating into her room. "You look beautiful, Maddie."

"But, I—"

He offered again, more firmly, "Look. Beautiful."

Her heart did a little flip. It wasn't often Trey offered up a compliment. Yet, Maddie thought that he was the one who looked beautiful and, as she gazed into his dark appealing eyes, she wondered if she'd be able to keep from staring at him all night.

With a quick smile, Maddie said, "Thanks. I guess I'll see you over there." She brushed by him, catching a whiff of his aftershave. The pure male scent with a heady mix of musk and lime did something pleasant to her insides.

"I figured we'd go together."

Maddie stopped in the hallway. "Why would you figure that?"

"Because the rain's only going to get worse. A T-storm is brewing and the roads might get washed out. It only makes sense, we're going to the same place and we'll be returning back here when it's over."

Maddie knew she was being unreasonable, but she didn't want to arrive at the dinner party with Trey. She didn't want to be drawn to him anymore than she already was. She didn't want to sit next to him in the truck and be reminded of the night they'd made love. She couldn't face any of those things right now. She spoke softly and directly into his eyes. "I think it's best if we go separately, Trey."

Trey stood firm, pursed his lips in displeasure then inhaled deeply. "If that's what you want."

None of this was what Maddie wanted. But Trey hadn't given her much of an option to her wants and desires. He hadn't given them a chance, but that wouldn't stop her from making him see his own potential. If she could leave him with one gift, it would be to make him trust in himself again.

Even though she'd been hurt, she wasn't angry at Trey any longer. She understood him and where he believed he had a weakness, she saw it only as a loss of faith. Once his faith was restored, Trey Walker could move on with his life.

She gave him a slow nod then walked to the kitchen. Opening the refrigerator, she removed a frosted lemon layer cake and carefully set it onto a large plate.

Trey followed her and now stood in the doorway. "What's that?"

"I baked a lemon cake this afternoon."

"You...baked?"

Maddie chuckled. "For what it's worth, I did."

"Lemon's my favorite."

Maddie glanced at Trey's puzzled expression. She'd learned a lot about Trey Walker lately, but she hadn't known his favorite...anything. "It was Brittany's suggestion."

"Oh."

"She and Paul think the world of you, Trey. You've been a good friend to them, working at their place nonstop, and even after you hurt your hand—"

"Hell, it was a scratch, Maddie."

"And even after that, you went back to finish the job you'd started. That new baby is going to have a wonderful nursery, thanks to you. Your friends want to show their appreciation."

Trey found the floor real interesting then, scratching the back of his head. "They don't have to do this."

"They *want* to. I imagine there'll be a lot of your favorites at dinner tonight."

Trey stepped closer to stare into her eyes. He tucked

a finger under her chin and cast her a heart-melting smile. "I imagine so."

"Trey?" Maddie's blood warmed considerably.

"You're one of my favorites, Maddie," he whispered and bent his head.

Maddie couldn't allow him to kiss her. She'd fall deeper and harder than ever, and that would prove disastrous. She took a step back, whispering, "Cross me off your list."

Trey's head popped up. He ran a hand down his jaw, staring at her lips with regret in his eyes. "I'm trying," he said solemnly, as if caring for her was the worst of all possible options. And sadly, Maddie knew that in his heart, Trey really believed his loving her would be her downfall. "Trouble is, I'm crazy about you."

Maddie wanted to shout the famous movie line, *"Snap out of it."* But instead, she grabbed the cake plate, headed to the front door, muttering under her breath, "Maybe, we're both just plain crazy."

A little bit of hurt was far better than a whole world of hurt, Trey rationalized, as he sat on a wing chair in the Fuller parlor, sipping beer. Trey knew that he'd hurt Maddie the other night. He hadn't meant to. He hadn't meant to touch her, much less make love to her. But he'd come to his senses far too late and even now he didn't regret that night. How could he, when everything had been so perfect? How could he regret the best night of his life?

He couldn't be more sorry about rejecting Maddie the way that he had, but it had been his only option because she deserved more. She deserved a fair chance in life. She deserved a man who would be there through thick or thin, a man who could weather any of life's storms, a man with staying power.

Trey would never forget the sober, nearly desperate look on his father's face, when he'd spoken those last bitter, haunting words. "Don't make the same mistakes I made, son." Trey hadn't told a soul, but today was the anniversary of his father's death. And today, more than ever, his father's plea had stuck in his mind with dawning clarity. That is, until he'd breathed in a delicious lemony aroma in his kitchen then witnessed Maddie lifting a two-layer cake from the refrigerator with pride in her eyes. That is, until he realized that Maddie Brooks had baked him his favorite cake.

He'd lost all sense of clarity then and nearly kissed her.

Stupid move.

She'd been right to step away. She'd been right to protect her heart. Trey had little willpower when it came to Maddie. But he wouldn't subject her to that whole world of hurt. Hooking up with Trey Walker meant disaster to any decent woman and she was the last person he wanted to injure.

Outside, the storm raged. Thunder boomed and lightning illuminated the night's sky, yet all seemed peaceful inside the parlor with licking flames crackling in the fireplace. Maddie sat on the sofa next to Paul and Jack. She'd been introduced to a few others as well and everyone held a tall glass of champagne in their hands. Everyone except Trey and Jack. Walker men didn't drink anything with bubbles.

"It's time for a toast," Paul said, standing and holding up his glass. Brittany stood beside him, her glass filled with sparkling cider. All the others stood as well. "To Trey," Paul began, "our good friend. We couldn't have finished the baby's room without you. You worked hard, my friend," Paul said sincerely, then winked, "and even after we tried to kill you with that wood beam, you came back to finish the job. That's friendship."

"Or stupidity," Jack interjected and everyone chuckled.

Brittany slugged him in the arm. Then she moved into the forefront and spoke softly. "And if we have a boy," she said, darting a quick loving glance at Paul, "we've decided that Trey would make a fine middle name for our son."

Overcome by Paul and Brittany's kind gesture, Trey stood and smiled with heartfelt gratitude at his friends.

"To Trey Walker," Paul repeated, clinking his glass to Trey's beer bottle then everyone else's glass met with his.

"Thank you," Trey said, surprised at the lump in his throat. He had trouble getting the words out. "I'm honored."

He glanced at Maddie. Her eyes had been on him, watching him with interest, bright green sparks touching him and conveying her innermost thoughts. She held that look of hope and expectation again, but those sentiments weren't for her this time. They were aimed at him.

"It's time for dinner," Brittany announced, breaking into his thoughts. "Follow me into the dining room everyone."

Trey waited as the others filed into the dining room, catching his breath, trying to absorb all the emotions whirling around inside him. He hadn't seen Maddie move close, but instead the scent of raspberries had alerted him that she stood beside him.

She reached up on tiptoes to whisper in his ear, "No staying power? You're a loyal friend, Trey. You wouldn't let your friends down. Paul and Brittany are naming their baby after you. They adore you and I can understand why."

Before Trey could respond, Maddie sashayed away, leaving him standing there amid her sweet scent, staring at her perfect backside as she walked into the dining room.

She looked beautiful tonight. It was hard to remember what his life had been like before she moved onto the ranch. And it'd be even more difficult imagining her gone. But Trey was certain she would leave Hope Wells now.

He'd messed up pretty badly, hurting her in the process. He'd witnessed the resignation in her eyes tonight, even though she tried covering it up. As much as he'd vowed not to get involved with her, he had, proving her wrong tonight. Helping out a friend was one thing but committing his life to a woman was quite another. Trey feared he couldn't do it and where would that leave Maddie?

Trey walked into the dining room with newfound determination. No matter how much pain her leaving would cause him, he knew he'd have to suffer it out. He and Maddie had no future together at 2 Hope Ranch.

"You're in love with her, Trey," Brittany said, wiping her hands on a dish towel in the kitchen.

"With who?" Trey glanced around the deserted kitchen. Hell, he'd only come in here to thank Brit privately for the wonderful meal. She had made all of his favorite things, chicken croquettes, sweet potato pie, creamed corn and fresh baked biscuits.

Brit cast him an irritated look. He knew she wasn't going to give in or give up until they had this conversation.

"With Maddie, and don't get cute."

"Me? I've never been accused of being cute."

"That's because you're drop-dead handsome, Trey. It seems as though Maddie thinks so, too. You two couldn't keep your eyes off each other tonight."

Trey shrugged.

"So, are you, or aren't you?"

Trey shut his eyes briefly and inhaled. "Nope. I can't be."

Brit leaned against the back of the counter, her belly protruding out. She looked as lovely as a pregnant woman could look in that state. And when she placed a protective hand on her abdomen, rubbing slightly, Trey wondered what it would be like fathering a child of his own. An image flashed instantly of Maddie, carrying his baby, her hand resting protectively on their child, smiling up at him.

"You *can't* be? What's that supposed to mean?"

"It means, I wouldn't do that to her."

Brit chuckled. "I think she'd want you to do that to her. Over and over again."

"Brit!"

"Well, I didn't get pregnant all by myself, Trey. I'm not that innocent. And I can see there's something strong between you. Are you denying it? And remember, Paul and I are your closest friends, so no fair fibbing."

Trey let out a deep sigh. "No, I'm not denying it. There's definitely something there. Maddie's pretty darn wonderful."

Brit reached for his hand, flipping it over to view his injured palm. "So are you, Trey. You deserve some happiness in your life. You've been alone too long."

Trey squeezed her hand and smiled. "At least this way, no one gets hurt."

"Or maybe both of you get hurt."

Jack busted into their conversation, striding into the kitchen at full speed. He spoke quietly, so the guests in the dining room wouldn't hear, but as forcefully as Trey had ever heard him. "Are you nuts or something?"

Trey shook his head. He seemed to be on the receiving end of one of his cousin's tirades. "What now, Jack?"

"Maddie told us that she's thinking of leaving Hope Wells. She's been offered a job in Denver."

"She has?" Brittany asked, both she and Jack staring at Trey.

"Yeah, I know."

"And you're not going to stop her?" Jack stood boot to boot with Trey now, his gaze penetrating.

"It's her decision."

Jack cursed then apologized to Brit. "You could ask her not to go. You could give her a reason to stay."

Trey hated being backed into a corner. He'd already made his decision regarding Maddie and was trying damn hard to abide by it. What right did anyone have to judge him? Anger simmered close to his breaking point. He stepped away from his cousin to avoid coming to blows. "Jeez, if you're so damn interested, maybe you should ask her to stay."

"Maybe I will!"

Trey ground out, "Good."

"Great. I backed off before because of you, but I like her a lot. What's not to like? She's smart and funny and pretty as a picture. Hell, if you're too much of a fool to see it, then I'm going to ask her out."

Trey's anger boiled over. He grabbed Jack's shirt and pulled him so they stood nose to nose. "You don't want to go there, cousin. Or you might have to arrest me for assaulting an officer."

Jack grinned and craned his neck to look at Brit. "He's in love with her."

Brit agreed. "You're in love with her."

Trey released Jack and they backed away from each other. He glanced at Brit then back to Jack. Both wore smug expressions. "Damn meddlers. That's what you are."

"Are you calm now?" Jack asked.

With a quick move, Trey shifted his shoulders, relieving tension. "Ticked off, but calm."

At that moment, Maddie walked in with Paul right behind her carrying dishes from the dining room. "Thought I could help you in here, Brittany," Maddie said, setting the dishes down on the kitchen counter.

"Oh, isn't that sweet."

"Looks like you've got plenty of help. What're you boys doing," Paul teased, "taking up with an old pregnant lady?"

Brittany swatted him with the dish towel then glanced at Maddie. "You know, I think I'll wait up a bit on doing the dishes. These boys need some of your lemon cake to settle them down."

Maddie glanced around the room taking in all of their guilty expressions. "I hope it came out okay."

Brittany smiled. "I'm sure it's just fine. Trey'll think so, no matter what."

"I know, but my lemon cake might not be—"

"It'll be delicious, Maddie," Trey offered honestly.

"Because you baked it special for him," Brittany said with wink.

"Hey Maddie," Jack started, darting a quick glance at Trey, "you ever treat a stubborn old mule?"

"Well, yes," she answered, her brows furrowing, clearly puzzled by Jack's question. "I've had some experience with stubborn mules. Why?"

Jack grinned again and Trey was about ready to slap that silly expression off his face. He shrugged. "I heard there's this mule in Hope Wells sorely in need of your attention."

Brittany chuckled, grabbing Maddie's hand and guiding her out of the kitchen. "Come on, we'll let those boys bring in the dessert. It'll give them something constructive to do."

Paul stepped between Trey and Jack, heading off trouble.

"Paul," Trey said through pursed lips. "Next time you have a party for me, I'd appreciate it if you didn't invite my cousin."

Jack picked up the lemon cake, and laughed his way into the dining room.

Maddie sat between Paul and a nice man named Burton, one of the Fuller's neighbors, facing Trey and Brittany. Jack sat at the head of the table, placed there specifically by the hostess. Maddie got the feeling Jack's new seating arrangement wasn't so much by choice, but rather in tune with a schoolteacher disciplining an unruly boy by placing him in the corner of the room. Jack didn't seem any worse for wear, he kept a smile on his face and every once in a while, she caught him watching her.

Paul poured coffee into delicate antique cups while Brittany reached over to cut the cake. Several times tonight Maddie had caught Brittany arching her back to rub that area, grimacing uncomfortably.

"It's so beautiful," Brittany said, staring at the lemon frosting swirls Maddie had designed with care, "I almost hate to cut into it."

"Then, let me," Maddie offered, wanting to take some of tonight's burden off her gracious hostess. "I'd love to serve the cake."

Brittany handed over the knife and cake server. "Be my guest." She plopped down, looking relieved.

Maddie cut several slices and had just finished sending the plates around the table, when her cell phone rang. "Uh, sorry about that," she said to Brittany and Paul, "but I have to get this."

"No problem. We'll wait for you," Paul said.

She exited the room quickly, and answered her phone. One minute later she stood at the dining room threshold making apologies. "I'm sorry, but I have an emergency call. I have to leave."

"Oh, sorry to hear that," Brittany said. "Is it urgent?"

"I'm afraid so. Darla Chester's dog is having a difficult birth. It's her first litter and Darla's beside herself with worry. I promised I'd come over right away."

Paul looked doubtful. "That's clear across the county, Maddie."

"And the storm's not letting up," Burton's wife, Tilly announced, looking out the window.

Jack volunteered, "I don't live far from there, I'd be happy to take—"

"I'll drive you." Trey pushed out his chair and stood.

Maddie glanced at the roomful of worried guests. "Oh, thank you all for your concern, but I'll be fine, really. I don't want to break up the party."

She felt really badly about this. Paul and Brittany had gone to a great deal of trouble tonight and Maddie hated being the one to spoil the rest of the evening. She'd learned early on in her profession that when duty calls, all else had to be forfeited. She didn't mind when her own plans were ruined, but she sorely disliked disrupting others' lives.

"I'm driving you, Maddie." Trey said, his tone brooking no argument.

"But you haven't taken a bite of your cake yet."

"I'll wrap up both of your pieces and send them along with you," Brittany offered, then added, "That's one nasty storm out there. I'd feel better knowing Trey was with you."

"So would I," Paul agreed, glancing out the window.

Brittany rose quickly taking both of their plates into the kitchen, while Trey strode over to her. "Do you have everything you need in your truck?"

"Yes, I keep it supplied in case of emergencies but, Trey, you really don't have to do this." Maddie glanced at the table of friends he would be leaving behind. "I'll manage. It's what I do."

Trey smiled warmly, turning on the Walker charm, something Maddie hadn't witnessed too often. "Honey," he whispered for her ears only, "if you don't let me drive you, I'm going to follow behind you all the way. You need to get there safely and I know exactly where Darla lives."

Maddie had a hard time resisting Trey's offer, not because she feared the thunder that boomed like a demon's wail, or the heavy rain teeming down, but because Trey spoke so sweetly, his dark gorgeous eyes troubled and concerned.

Her heart ached knowing that Trey cared for her, but wouldn't act upon his feelings. He wouldn't break down the wall that kept them from being together. But Maddie couldn't think about that right now. She had puppies to deliver, and now it appeared she had a chauffeur to deliver her to the laboring Labrador. "Thank you," she said. "We'd better get going."

Brittany handed Trey a small brown bag. "I wrapped your cake inside. " She reached up and kissed Trey on the cheek. "You're a wonderful friend, Trey. And our baby says thank you, too."

Trey leaned over to hug Brittany then shook Paul's hand. "You're welcome and dinner was great."

Trey said farewell to the others at the table and Maddie said her quick goodbyes as well, giving Brittany her special thanks for the evening.

"You two take it slow and easy now," Paul said, walking them to the front door. "And remember that Cody's Pass will be washed out by now."

Trey nodded. "I plan on avoiding the Pass. Don't worry. We'll get there just fine."

Paul opened the door and wind howled fiercely as cold air immediately chilled the warm room. A shiver ran down Maddie's spine. She hadn't seen weather like this in a decade or more.

"Hand me your keys, Maddie."

Maddie had no problem giving up her keys to Trey.

"You ready?" he asked, taking her hand and squeezing gently.

She nodded, hanging on to Trey's strong hand and they dashed outside.

Nine

After a slow laborious drive across the county, Trey delivered Maddie safely to the Chester house. Trey was steps behind her as she dashed inside dripping wet. To Maddie's chagrin, Darla greeted Trey with a bit of surprise and curiosity. "Trey? I didn't expect to see you. It's been a long time."

That charming smile of Trey's emerged as he looked at Darla, his gaze making a quick sweep of her body. "Hi, Darla. It has been a while. Maddie's not used to our T-storms, so I drove her here."

Darla glanced her way, finally making the connection. "That's right, you're practicing out of 2 Hope now, Dr. Brooks."

"Yes. Temporarily." Maddie cast her a small smile, but inside her heart took a tumble. She'd never felt "less" a woman than now, soaked through her clothes, her hair plastered to her head, and no doubt what had been left of her makeup smudged beyond repair, while Darla Chester stood tall and graceful with long waves of blonde hair falling nearly to her buttocks. Her thin frame only accentuated what Maddie would term a perfect namesake, *Chest*er. The woman was extremely well endowed.

Funny, but Maddie had met Darla a few times, treating her Lab at her office in town, but she hadn't felt this pang of envy, not until tonight, not until she saw Darla Chester in a whole new light, through Trey's eyes.

"I'm so darn worried about Candy. Thanks for coming out in this weather," Darla said, leading them into the kitchen. The yellow Labrador lay in her whelping box in the far corner, breathing heavily, trying as she might to deliver her pups.

Maddie instantly forgot about her bruised ego and got to work. "She's so tired already." She massaged the dog, stroking her gently, rubbing her belly. "She's probably got five or six in there." Maddie glanced up at Trey. "This might take a while."

Trey bent down next to her, smelling like fresh rain and looking sexy as sin soaked through his clothes. Maddie didn't know how Trey Walker did it, but she'd never met a more appealing man in her life. "I'm staying, for however long it takes, Maddie."

"Thanks."

"Put me to work," he said.

"Me, too, what can I do?" Darla asked, her amber eyes filled with concern.

"Well, first we have to get her up and moving. Normally I'd let her outside to stimulate her, but the weather's not cooperating. Does Candy have any favorite toys or anything she likes that might spark her interest?"

"Yes, she does," Darla answered.

"Good, because we're going to have to keep her busy."

They spent the next twenty minutes taking turns playing with the dog, trying to keep her mind off her tired uterus and stimulate her enough to allow nature to take its course. When Maddie thought she was ready, she guided her back down into her whelping box and the first pup eased out of her at half past midnight.

"That's a good girl, Candy," Maddie said, stroking her head gently.

The pup found her mama's teat easily and began suckling.

"Cute little thing," Trey said, his expression childlike, full of winsome interest. Maddie couldn't help but wonder how Trey would react to fatherhood. Though he would probably disagree, Maddie felt sure Trey would make a terrific father. He had all the qualities necessary, patience, kindness and a distinct affection for all beings, great and small.

"There's at least four more cuties like this in there," Maddie said, "but poor Candy's going to have to work hard through the night."

Darla walked up. "You folks must be cold and exhausted. I turned up the heat and made a pot of coffee. Forgive me. I should have offered it to you when you first arrived, but—"

"You were worried about Candy. That's only natural," Maddie responded.

Darla waved her over. "Come to the table. We can keep our eyes on Candy from here."

Maddie glanced at the laboring Labrador and shook

her head. "I think I'll stay by her side for now. She's a little unsure of things. You and Trey take a break. I'll be there in a few minutes."

"Are you sure?" Darla asked, biting her lip. "Is everything okay with her?"

"Everything's fine, really. It's just a precaution. Go on, you two and don't worry about us. We'll be fine."

Darla turned to Trey. "Coffee?"

"I'd love a cup."

"Cream, no sugar, right?" Darla asked.

Trey nodded. "You have a good memory."

Darla chuckled as they walked over to the table. "Sometimes I wish it wasn't so good."

Maddie concentrated on Candy, stroking her head and massaging her abdomen, but every once in a while she'd catch a bit of Darla and Trey's conversation. They'd laugh over something, then whisper softly. Maddie presumed by the way they spoke to each other that they'd known each other a long time, but she also got the impression something more had gone on between the two of them.

She told herself it was none of her business, but a niggling thought had stuck in her mind. Had Trey insisted he bring her here tonight so that he could see Darla?

She glanced up just in time to witness Darla lay her hand on Trey's cheek. She couldn't hear their words, but their soft quiet tone spoke volumes.

Candy made a whimpering noise and Maddie directed her attention back to the laboring dog. A minute later, the second pup was delivered.

"Hey, this one's a little bigger." Trey bent down and handed Maddie a cup of steaming hot coffee. "Here you go. I figured you could use this right about now."

Maddie leaned back against the wall, now that she was sure Candy and the pups were all right, and sipped the coffee. "Mmmm, this is good."

"Hits the spot, doesn't it?" Trey smiled.

"Yeah, it does."

"You know, just in case I haven't told you this before, you're darn good at what you do."

Maddie smiled. If there was one thing in her life that she could take pride in, it was her profession. She loved what she did, couldn't think of a time when she wouldn't be working with animals. "Thanks."

Trey nodded and studied her face. "Why don't you get up for a while, stretch out. I'll watch Candy for a few minutes. Besides, I think Darla needs some encouragement. She's acting like a worried mother hen over there, but she doesn't want to get in your way."

"She really adores this dog."

Trey slid a quick glance Darla's way. "She's got a good heart."

Maddie spoke ever so quietly, the whisper barely audible. "And did you break it, Trey?"

Trey looked into Maddie's eyes, hesitating with his answer. When he finally responded, his reply wasn't what she'd expected. "For years, I thought I had but that doesn't seem to be the case after all."

This wasn't the time or place to discuss his past loves, although Maddie couldn't deny that Trey's comment intrigued the heck out of her. Maddie rose and stretched, working the kinks out of her back, then walked over to Darla to reassure her that Candy was doing fine. She still had three or four more puppies to deliver.

If all went well, they'd be back at 2 Hope Ranch before sunup.

* * *

Trey stomped dirt off his boots, hung up his hat on a peg by the back door and entered the kitchen. Maddie stood waiting for him by the kitchen table, fidgeting with a linen napkin she was about to set down. She'd been halfway through cooking this meal, when she began to have second thoughts. Maybe Trey didn't like surprises. Maybe all he wanted to do was fall into bed after a hard day's work.

But Maddie owed him. He hadn't gotten a wink of sleep last night. It had been nearly dawn when they'd finally retired to their bedrooms this morning and just two hours later, Maddie heard Trey get up. And when she'd looked out the window, she'd seen his figure riding out on his horse, into the rain-soaked, dreary morning.

Even though he'd insisted on driving her to Darla's house, Maddie still felt a pang of guilt at keeping him up all night. Exhausted and beat, she'd thanked him again when they'd arrived home, but it hadn't been enough. And while her culinary talents weren't top-notch, Maddie knew how to make killer tamales and Spanish rice, a Texas staple and something she'd learned from her friend, Caroline. Maddie had been on the phone with her three times this afternoon, double-checking the recipe, making sure she hadn't forgotten anything.

"Hi." Maddie greeted Trey with trepidation and a big smile.

Trey glanced at the table she'd set with a pretty blue lace tablecloth she'd found in the linen closet along with mismatched napkins. Two tall tapered candles cast the room in mellow soothing light. "What's this?"

"Dinner and thank-you."

He lifted his nose in the air. "Smells delicious."

"Tamales and rice. Are you hungry?"

Trey grinned. "Is that a trick question?"

Maddie stumbled with her words. "Uh, well, I wasn't sure if you'd want to get right to bed, or, uh—"

Trey's eyes went wide and he stared at her then a playful smile emerged. "That's the best offer I've had all day."

Maddie tossed the napkin at him, but he caught it before it struck his grinning face.

"It's an offer for *dinner,* you dopey cowboy."

With a teasing light still in his eyes, Trey admitted, "I know, but a man can dream, can't he?"

Maddie shook her head, ignoring his teasing comment, because she knew there was no real substance there. She knew Trey wasn't dreaming about her, in or out of bed. "Dinner will be ready in ten minutes."

Trey walked up to her, coming extremely close and looked into her eyes. "You look real pretty tonight, Maddie."

Maddie blushed. She'd purposely dressed up, wanting to erase the horrible drowned-rat image from last night, when she'd gotten caught in the thunderstorm. Tonight, she wore a simple black dress, nothing too fancy, but a dress that made her feel womanly. "Thank you."

"Seems you're forever thanking me."

He slid the napkin back into her palm, and the slight brush of his hand was enough to warm her up all over. Then she stared deeply at him, really looking beyond his handsome features, noting that he didn't look tired at all. How can a man work and work and work, and not look like something the cat dragged in? "I thought you'd be exhausted by now. I felt bad all day, knowing you didn't get any sleep because of me."

"I slept."

"Yes, for about an hour early this morning."

Trey brushed his mouth to her ear, creating tingles Maddie struggled to conceal—tingles that made her knees go weak. He whispered his secret. "I slept today. Found me a nice dry patch of pasture and took a little nap. Didn't think I'd be able to keep my eyes open the rest of the day, otherwise."

"Oh."

Trey stepped back to gaze into her eyes. "Did you think I was Superman or something?"

"Maybe *or something*," she admitted.

The twinkle in his eyes, the smile on his lips did something wonderful to her. She'd never known anyone like Trey Walker before. She'd fallen in love with him almost from the first moment she'd met him, but she realized now, that she really hadn't loved Trey back then. She'd been fascinated by him and attracted by the gentle way he had with his animals. She'd been captivated by his good looks and intrigued by his polite yet distant demeanor. No, she hadn't loved him then, she knew that for fact.

Because she loved him now.

So much, so unnervingly much that she ached deep in her heart. This love was real. This love was clear. This love was pure. It struck her like a knife, sharp and swift.

She had come to know the real Trey Walker and had fallen head over heels.

Maddie turned away from Trey then, unwilling to show him the face of that realization. She couldn't let him see her devastation. She walked over to the kitchen table and set his napkin in place. "W-we have lemon cake for dessert," she said quietly.

"Maddie?" he asked, clearly puzzled by her sudden change in demeanor. "Honey, are you okay?"

His sweet tone tore at her heart. Maddie wasn't good at subterfuge. She'd always been the what-you-see-is-what-you-get kind of girl. Afraid her voice would tremble when she spoke, she bobbed her head up and down.

"Okay," he said with trepidation. "I'll catch a quick shower and be back in ten minutes."

She nodded again.

Once he exited the room, Maddie sighed with relief. She realized she had ten minutes to pull herself together. She couldn't let her feelings for Trey be known. It was imperative that, for however long she'd be living at 2 Hope Ranch, she maintain the budding friendship she'd developed with Trey and keep it that simple.

She'd fought a long hard battle and had lost.

She'd fallen in love with a man who couldn't love her back.

Trey forked the first bite of lemon cake and guided it into his mouth, savoring the pungent lemony flavor as it slid down his throat. He didn't know if it was the cake itself or the fact that Maddie had baked for him, but he'd never tasted better lemon cake.

The best he'd ever had.

Trey stared at Maddie across the table, taking a bite of cake, chewing thoughtfully and realized how much he'd enjoyed walking into his kitchen after a day's work to find her there, waiting for him. She'd cast him a small timid smile, looking apprehensive and so pretty in her black dress, with the table set and dinner cooking. Good

God, if he wasn't careful, he'd do something stupid, like ask her to stay on at Hope Wells, ask her to stay with him at the ranch.

An instant recollection came to mind of another "best" he'd ever had, the night they'd made love. He'd never wanted a woman more or experienced such intense lack of willpower. He'd lost all rational thought that night, allowing his natural instincts and raw desire to take over. He and Maddie had shared an incredible night, one he'd never forget.

Day in and day out, he fought his feelings for her, but still, he wanted her. Little Maddie Brooks, the animal doc, the petite wholesome redhead who had knocked his world off-kilter.

He figured once she left Hope Wells, he could forget all about her. He figured with miles distancing them, he'd move on and so would she. She'd settle in at the new clinic in Denver, dive into her work and most likely, hook up with that Nick character.

Trey frowned, his lips pulling down the corners of his mouth.

"Don't you like the cake?" Maddie asked.

She had misinterpreted his sour mood. Trey sent her a reassuring smile. "I was just thinking that you're spoiling me. Nobody's ever baked a better cake than this, Maddie."

"Really?" Her pensive mood lightened.

"It's the best I've—" he began, but halted immediately, noting Maddie's sharp gaze on him. He couldn't repeat the vow he'd spoken when they'd made love. The reminder would be too painful to both of them. "It's delicious."

He took another big bite, taking immense pleasure as he chewed.

Maddie played with a bit of frosting on her fork. "You could always ask Darla to bake you one."

Surprised, Trey nearly choked on a mouthful of food. "Darla?"

Maddie looked at him directly and nodded, her green eyes bright with curiosity. "Yes, Darla."

Trey laid his fork down and leaned back in his chair. "There's nothing between Darla and me anymore."

Maddie continued to look at him, waiting for more. Silently, Trey sighed, realizing that Maddie expected more of an explanation. He didn't like dredging up the past. Whenever he did, his recollections always proved what he knew in his heart to be true, that he wasn't cut out for relationships.

"We dated for a short time."

Maddie remained silent.

"Darla went through a pretty messy divorce. I think I was the first man she dated after her breakup. And well, in the beginning it was nice. We had a good time together. But then, Darla got serious about us and I started feeling closed in—like a vise grip crushing my neck. I felt lousy about doing so, but I broke it off."

"How did she take it?" Maddie asked.

"She wasn't happy and I'd hurt yet another woman. I'd made another mistake. For the longest time I felt guilty about that. But last night, she cleared all that up for me."

"How?"

"She told me, plain as day, she hadn't been ready for a relationship. She'd admitted that our breakup was the best thing that had happened to her. She'd needed time to straighten out her life. She's happier now than she's ever been. She has a long distance relationship with a man living in Corsicana, and that suits her just fine."

A small smile graced her lips. "And she's got five healthy pups and a new mama to keep her busy, too."

"Yeah, that, too."

"You must feel relieved. All this time you thought you'd hurt her and she came out better for it."

Trey couldn't agree. He'd entered into that relationship blindly, not realizing how vulnerable Darla would be after a terrible divorce. The potential for causing her pain had been there all along, but Darla had made her way through despite Trey's disregard for her feelings. "I bolted the minute things got too close for comfort, Maddie. There's no denying that."

Maddie's expression changed. She lost the beam in her eyes, the smile on her face. "Is that what happened between you and me? You got that closed-in feeling?"

"Hell, no." Trey shook his head and made a wide sweeping gesture with his arms. "With you, it was as if the whole world opened up and I was right smack in the middle of it."

Maddie blinked.

Trey cursed. He never wanted to admit that to her. He never wanted to give her reason to hope. Yet, something deep inside couldn't allow Maddie to think he'd used her that night. He couldn't allow her to think she'd suffocated him. Just the opposite was true. She'd made him feel alive and vital and open to all good things.

"I felt that way, too," she whispered.

Trey stood then and reached for her, guiding her up until she stood facing him. She looked so beautiful tonight, her sad green eyes catching the pale light. Trey couldn't resist holding her once more. He took her in his arms, splaying his hands around her tiny waist and spoke softly. "You're a dangerous woman, Maddie Brooks."

She stared at the collar of his shirt. "Do I scare you, Trey?"

Trey tipped her chin up with a finger and their eyes met. "More than you'll ever know." He bent down and kissed her on the lips. "So sweet."

"It's the frosting," she said softly.

He kissed her once again. "It's you, Maddie."

Maddie reached up and wrapped her arms around his neck, tugging him closer. The kiss went deeper this time and longer until the sugary sweet taste of Maddie was etched in his head for eternity.

In harmony, they both moaned, a quiet little plea that spoke of untold pleasure. Trey deepened the kiss further, driving his tongue in her mouth, mating with her in the most elemental way. Their bodies brushed once, then melded together perfectly as Maddie's soft supple form crushed against Trey's granite hard body.

Trey was at a loss to stop, his need for Maddie too great. He held her tight and kissed her passionately, igniting a spark that would surely burst into flames. He moved his hands to cup her bottom, molding her cheeks in his palms feeling the soft firm skin hidden under her dress, spurred on by her tiny little whimpers. Next he caressed the delicate small of her back, making small circles and gliding his hands over her. He slid them up to stroke her shoulders, until finally his hands found the back of her head. He wove his fingers into the silky copper strands, aching for all of her, wanting to take her to bed and make love to her throughout the night. And just as he began to speak those words, she pulled away, shaking her head, breaking off their intimate connection.

She closed her eyes briefly then opened them with regret and pain. "You're a better man than you think you

are, Trey. I wish you could see that you have more staying power than most men I know."

She walked out, leaving him bereft, not from the
aching hard-on in his pants, but from words spoken
straight from the heart.

Ten

"That's a good wild stallion," Maddie joked, holding a loose rope and walking with Storm along a path behind the ranch house. She'd finished work early and decided that a pleasant afternoon walk would do them both a world of good.

Maddie had made mistakes while living here at 2 Hope Ranch, but she planned to rectify what she could. And Storm had been high on her list. She'd never come up against an animal with so much resistance. Normally Maddie could coax a horse to do her bidding, but not Storm. He was definitely and infinitely a stallion with his own obstinate mind.

While she thought she'd gained the horse's trust, she really hadn't. She realized that she'd rushed him, thinking the little leeway he'd given her had been enough. So now, Maddie used a different tactic. She didn't want to destroy the animal's spirit, only settle him somewhat.

"You're not so different than Trey, you know," she said, speaking freely along the path, with no worry of being overheard. "You're both headstrong and feisty as all get out." Maddie let loose a quiet chuckle, a good release for her pent-up frustration. Last night, she'd wanted Trey as much as he'd wanted her. But Maddie was too much of a realist not to understand that until Trey came to grips with his heritage and his past, she'd only be letting herself in for more heartache.

As difficult as it was, she'd pushed Trey away last night for both of their sakes.

She moved along the path with Storm keeping her mind off Trey, speaking in a level voice with patience and care, hoping to create a special bond with Storm, hoping he would learn to accept her. "And afterward, if you keep up this good behavior, I'll give you a nice rub-down, a soothing little massage for your muscles." Maddie worked out a kink in her shoulder. "I only wish you could reciprocate," she said with a smile.

Maddie felt comfortable with this approach, taking small steps and bonding with the stallion as if he were hers. She understood Storm better now and realized he had a long way to go before he would relinquish his trust.

After thirty minutes, they headed back toward the ranch, Maddie feeling a great sense of accomplishment that Storm hadn't rejected the interaction between them. The stallion actually seemed content. She walked Storm into the barn, heading for his paddock, the largest in the building and Maddie's instincts took hold. As they by-passed a docile bay mare named Julip, one of Trey's cutting horses, she slowed her steps, careful and a bit wary of Storm's reaction.

Maddie had watched this particular mare during her

stay here, and she knew her to have the sweetest of natures. When Storm approached her stall, Julip sauntered over slowly until the two came face to face.

Storm bristled, breathing out nosily, stomping his feet. Maddie's heart pumped hard, hoping she hadn't made a big mistake. Normally, Storm stayed outside in his corral, too unruly and quite frankly, too lusty, to be thrown in with female horses.

But Julip merely stared at him, and if a horse could shrug and roll her eyes, Maddie was sure this mare had done just that. Julip turned her back on Storm and moved to the far end of her stall, clearly not impressed with the stallion.

To Maddie's amazement, Storm's little outburst nearly all but disappeared and she had to really tug on the rope she held to get Storm to move away from Julip's stall.

"Hmm. Interesting," Maddie said, as ideas stirred around in her head.

"What's interesting?" Trey's low voice from behind gave her a start.

Maddie turned slowly, both she and Trey behaving carefully, aware of Storm's unpredictable nature. She stared into the deep disapproving eyes of Trey Walker. "Oh, nothing. Storm and I just went for a walk."

Trey's brows furrowed and he winced. "You went for a walk *alone* with him? Not a good idea, Maddie. I thought you'd learned your lesson."

Maddie took her eyes off Trey. Looking at him standing there with hands on hips, wearing a black Stetson, dark shirt and leather-fringed chaps, the handsome cowboy stole all of her breath. Instead, she focused on the stallion, patting his neck gently. "Storm and I came to an understanding."

"Yeah? And what was that?"

Trey was not happy. He wouldn't take his eyes off of Storm, as if he fully expected the horse to bolt, or worse.

"We had a nice walk and now I'm going to give him a rubdown."

Trey blinked. He pointed at Storm and spoke with deadly calm. "You will not get in that stall with him, Maddie. To begin with, he's hardly ever in there. It's too confining for him. He won't like you invading his territory. You know well and good that he's more wild than tame."

"I think he's ready."

Trey folded his arms around his middle and dug in his boot heels. "No."

"No?"

"I forbid it." Trey grabbed the rope from Maddie's hands.

Shocked, Maddie repeated his words, "You forbid it?"

Trey nodded.

Maddie's eyes grew wide. Her face colored with heat and the hair at the nape of her neck stood on end. "You're forgetting that I'm an animal doctor, Trey. I know animals better than I know people. I can do this."

"He's not ready. He may never be ready, Maddie."

She planted her hands on her slight hips and spoke forcefully. "I disagree. He's pigheaded like you, but unlike you, he'll come around."

"Don't fight me on this, Maddie. I won't change my mind." Trey led Storm away, turning him around to head toward the opened barn door.

Maddie fumed silently. Normally she wouldn't be so bold. Trey owned Storm. He had the final say in his treatment and care. Maddie had no rights when it came to the stallion. But still, it irritated her that Trey wouldn't allow her this. He was as closed off as the first day she'd met him.

"Just who are you trying to protect?" Maddie muttered. And after Trey had left the barn entirely, she added, "Me or the stallion? Or maybe, yourself?"

Minutes later, Trey stood by the fence watching Storm race around the perimeter of the corral, his jet-black mane flying in the fading sunlight. The stallion was too spirited to tame, and though Trey had immense respect for Maddie's abilities with animals, he couldn't allow her to place herself in danger. Storm needed gentling over a long period of time—he couldn't be rushed. No doubt, Maddie had goodness in her heart. She was a positive thinker, believing that she could change things that were unchangeable. But Trey knew better, learning his lessons firsthand. He and Maddie probably would never see eye to eye on the subject.

He'd been harsh with her in the barn, perhaps overly so, to make his point. But the truth remained that he couldn't abide Maddie getting hurt again. She'd already made one bad judgment call with the stallion the night of the dust storm. She'd been fortunate in not sustaining life-threatening injuries. So he figured that while he couldn't do anything about the emotional hurt he'd caused her lately, he'd damn well see to it that she wouldn't get hurt physically while living on his ranch.

Trey presumed she'd be packing her suitcase soon anyway, anxious to leave 2 Hope, anxious to leave *him*. He'd made one mistake after another with her. With all the best intentions, he'd tried protecting her and wound up hurting her in the process. She'd be better off without him.

Much better off.

A car pulled up, kicking up dry dust and coming to a stop right next to him. Trey turned to find his cousin Jack exiting his patrol car wearing his tan sheriff's uniform and a big smile. "Howdy, Trey."

Trey wasn't in the mood for Jack's good humor. "Hey, Jack. What's up? Are you on duty or is this a social call?"

Jack glanced around, searching the property. "Maddie around?"

"You came out here to see Maddie?" Trey asked, masking his irritation the best he could. Jack didn't seem to notice, his gaze kept darting around the borders of the ranch.

"Nope. I came out here to see you." He grinned and Trey's irritation grew at Jack's mysterious behavior. "So, where is she?"

Trey shrugged. "She's probably in her office, working."

Jack glanced toward the old barn. "Good. I'm here on a mission. Caroline's throwing Maddie a surprise birthday party this Saturday night. She asked me to come over here to let you know about it. She didn't want to call the ranch, just in case Maddie picked up the phone."

"It's her birthday?"

"Not until next week. She'll be twenty-eight and Caroline is dead serious about keeping this a surprise. That's why she's doing it early. She has this idea to get her over to her place. She wants you to bring her."

"Me? How am I supposed to do that?"

Jack smiled. "She wants you to ask her out to dinner, so Maddie will dress up pretty and be ready. Caroline figured she'd call with a baby-sitting emergency asking Maddie to come over to watch Annabelle for half an hour before your date. The rest of us will be there waiting."

Trey began shaking his head. "No. I can't do that."

"Sure you can."

"No, I can't."

"You can't?" Jack wore his stubborn Walker expression. Trey recognized the tightening of his mouth, the set of his jaw. He'd worn that same expression more than a few times himself. "Well, why the hell not?"

Trey confessed, "Because I doubt Maddie would go anywhere with me."

Jack pursed his lips and eyed him with doubt. "I don't believe it. You two have been hot for each other since she moved in with you."

"Believe it," Trey said firmly.

Jack sighed aloud. "What happened?"

Trey refused Jack the details. He didn't need to know how Maddie's coming to live with him had been the best and worst time in his life. He didn't need to know that they'd lived in turmoil, Trey making one mistake after another with her. He didn't need to know how much Trey cared about her, willing to do whatever it took to keep her safe and protected. Hell, Trey had just come to that conclusion himself. "Doesn't matter. Maddie's not speaking to me."

Jack's expression changed to a full out grin. "She's not?"

Trey cursed. "You don't have to be so damn happy about it."

"I'm not," Jack said, adjusting his expression accordingly. "But I'm sure if you turned on the Walker charm, you could get her to go out with you."

Trey shrugged a shoulder. "Even if that were true, I'm not going to do it. It's best this way. Caroline is just going to have to figure another way to get Maddie over there."

"The party's in five days, Trey. That doesn't give her much time. And why is it best that you don't ask her out?"

Trey shrugged again. "She'll be leaving soon. I'm sure of it. Moving to Denver is a great opportunity for her." And he wouldn't be around to hurt her any longer. He wouldn't have to yearn for a woman he couldn't have.

"So, you're refusing?"

Trey nodded. "It's for the best. Trust me."

Jack removed his hat and rubbed the back of his neck, contemplating. "I'm going to have to ask her myself then. Caroline trusted me with this and I'm not going to let her down." Jack's mouth pulled down in a frown. "You think she's mad enough at you to agree to go out with me?"

Trey searched Jack's eyes. He could see his cousin's reluctance, but Trey had put him in a bad position. All in all, Trey realized Jack wanted what was best for him and as much as his cousin had teased and tormented, he wasn't eager to ask Maddie out. "If you ask her today, she'd probably join you on a trip to the moon."

"All right," Jack said on a sigh, before turning toward Maddie's office. "Hell, Trey. Sometimes, you are your own worst enemy."

Maddie exited the barn leading Julip out, all saddled up and ready for a ride. Maddie needed the distraction and this little outing would help take her mind off the Walker men. They had confounded and confused her enough for an entire lifetime. She was barely speaking to Trey, and just minutes ago, Jack had asked her out. She'd been quite stunned by his invitation to the Sheriff Department's Annual Benefit dinner, but he'd been so sweet and sincere, promising they'd not call it a date, but merely dinner with a friend. Maddie couldn't see any harm in going, so she had agreed.

"That's a girl," she said, stroking the horse's forelock and patting her neck before mounting, determined to ignore her frustration and concentrate on the ride. Once in the saddle, she leaned down and gave Julip one last gentle stroke. "You're the sweetest little lady at 2 Hope."

She rode toward the corral, keeping a safe distance from Storm and watched the stallion's reaction. She'd had a hunch about Storm and this experiment would prove whether she'd been right or not. The stallion raced to the fence, snorting air loudly, digging in and sifting dirt with his hooves, until he received what he wanted, the mare's attention. Julip glanced his way, seeming neither intimated nor interested.

Maddie missed working with Storm and had stayed away for two days, keeping busy with her own work and trying to forget about her heated conversation with Trey the other day. She kept telling herself he'd been within his rights. He owned the stallion and she had to respect his wishes.

But Maddie didn't have to like it. Seems that she and Trey butted heads more than got along these days. But she knew she could get through to Storm. She knew she could get him to trust, without breaking his spirit. And the sweet-natured Julip would be the one to help her.

She guided the mare slowly around the perimeter of the corral, several yards away from the fence. Julip seemed to enjoy the exercise and paid Storm and his initial tirade little mind. They made the turn once, then twice as Storm watched on from his stance inside the corral.

Maddie continued to keep the mare to a slow pace and the third time they'd circled the corral, Storm approached them, and to Maddie's delight, he began to move along with them from inside the corral, slowly, but taking a slight lead as any dominant stallion would. "That's it, boy," Maddie said softly. They continued on this way until Maddie felt it safe enough to guide Julip closer to the fence, so that now, it seemed the two horses rode beside each other, but for the separating fence. She picked up the pace and galloped around with Storm by her side.

"That's a different approach," Kit said, minutes later as Maddie dismounted Julip in front of the barn. "I gotta hand it to you, you don't give up. Nobody around here ever thought that stallion was worth the money Trey paid for it. We all sorta thought the boss made himself a bull-size mistake. But now," Kit remarked, taking off his hat to scratch his head, "seeing the progress you're making, maybe it wasn't but a little bitty mistake."

Maddie chuckled and patted the mare's backside. "I can't take all the credit. Julip is just what Storm needs."

Kit glanced at Storm, kicking up another ruckus inside the corral. "Maybe so. Maybe what you're doing is a good thing. Seems the right female will tame the wild in any male."

Just then, Trey pulled through the gate in his truck, the sound of the engine causing both to turn in his direction. He parked on the side of the house and got out, glancing their way.

Kit waved at his boss then yanked his hat low onto his head. "Maybe you just might have what it takes to settle him."

"I hope so," Maddie said, still reeling from the success of her little experiment.

"And I wasn't exactly talking about the stallion," Kit said, with a tip of his hat and playful wink.

Maddie's mouth dropped open but Kit had walked off before she could utter a word.

"Tell me why you feel the need to shop, again?" Maddie asked, needing convincing that she should have taken the afternoon off to carouse the shops in San Angelo. She and Caroline entered a trendy boutique and began perusing a rack of summertime dresses.

"Because you have a hot date with Jack Walker, that's why," Caroline answered. "We need to find you a special outfit."

When Maddie frowned, Caroline added, "And I need a day away from sandboxes and playgroups. I need a girl's day out."

"Just to set the record straight, it's not a hot date, Caroline," Maddie insisted. She'd never have agreed to go out with him, if she'd thought he wanted more than friendship. "Jack asked me to this benefit dinner for the sheriff's department. He made it clear that we'd go as friends."

Caroline shot her a knowing smile. "The old 'just friends' line. Tell me, how is it that you've got both of the Walker men lining up. First Trey, now Jack."

Maddie glanced at a pretty yellow and black two-piece silky suit, before addressing her friend. "First of all, Trey and I are barely speaking. And Jack, well, he's a sweetheart, but we really are just friends."

"Hmm." Caroline's blond brows rose in doubt.

"Really. I could never…I mean Jack is Trey's cousin and—"

"I know. It's always been Trey for you. Too bad, he's so hung up on his past."

Maddie lifted a flowery sundress off the rack and placed it under her chin, glancing at the mirror. "It isn't just *his* past he's fighting, but generations of Walker men."

Caroline shook her head at Maddie's choice. She set the dress back on the rack, agreeing with her friend's opinion.

"I'm hoping that maybe one day Trey will wake up and see that he's not the man his father was."

"And I'm hoping you're still around when he finally does wake up. Have you made up your mind about Nick's job offer?"

"I'm still thinking it through. He's been so patient with me. I spoke with him yesterday and promised he'd have my answer by next week."

"Don't go," Caroline blurted, then covered her mouth with her hand. "Sorry. I shouldn't have said that."

Maddie smiled sadly. This decision would change her entire life. She'd just settled in Hope Wells, having made some truly wonderful friends. Her practice was growing and if she decided to rebuild her office here, she wouldn't have a problem making ends meet. She truly liked living in Hope Wells, but she often wondered how difficult it would be to live in a small town and bump into Trey from time to time. How difficult would it be to see him move on with his life—to see him with another woman?

Sometimes, accepting Nick's proposal and moving to Denver made all the sense in the world, and at other times, like right now, as she stared into the sweet caring eyes of her best friend, moving away wasn't even a possibility.

"Caroline, you don't have to be sorry. I understand. I'd miss you and Annabelle so much if I left but—"

"You have much more to consider. You're talented and intelligent and that Denver clinic would be lucky to have you. Tell me, what does that stubborn cowboy have to say about you leaving?"

Maddie stared at her latest selection, deciding the dress wasn't right and hung it back on the rack. With a deep sigh, she turned to her friend as heartfelt emotions caught her by surprise. She hadn't intended to get misty-eyed, but darn if tears didn't pool up. She held them back and spoke quietly. "Let me put it this way. I think it'd be easier on both of us if I left."

"Oh, Maddie."

Maddie shrugged and Caroline put her arm around her as they exited the shop.

"I know what you need," Caroline said after a minute of silence, her voice light, filled with whimsy. "We'll worry about a new dress later. What you need is sexy lingerie!"

Maddie stared at her friend for a moment, then a bubble of laughter escaped. "What?"

"Trust me. When I was going through my heartache with Gil, nothing perked me up more than buying something soft and feminine and...*sinful*."

Maddie's mood changed immediately and she grinned. The idea began growing on her. "I feel better already."

"There. You see what I mean. Just wait until we find you something sensational. You'll feel so glamorous, you won't have a care in the world."

"Sounds good to me. But where do we find this sensational something?"

"Leave it to me. I know this place…"

With sunlight fading on the horizon Trey walked into the house and hung his hat upon a peg in the kitchen. He let out a long weary sigh, grateful he'd been able to catch up on chores that seemed to accumulate far too rapidly for a small ranch. His barn roof leaked, for one, a discovery he'd made during that last T-storm they'd had. Fences were down on the south pasture and he'd had to check on several cows heavy with calf, one being nearly ready. He'd moved her into a barn stall just minutes ago and he'd have to check on her every hour or so, a precaution he'd instituted after losing both cow and calf out in the pasture during calving last year.

Trey opened the refrigerator, grabbed a Coors and took one long cooling swig. The beer refreshed his parched throat and lent him some measure of comfort. Though he thought it best to avoid Maddie whenever possible, he had to admit that he missed being with her. He missed seeing her bright eyes alight when something surprised her. He missed seeing her sweet smile when something delighted her. He missed her energy and that way she had of making everyone around her feel good.

She'd been a breath of fresh air, a sweet-natured, strong-willed woman who had brought his mundane ranch to vibrant life. And as he tipped his bottle and took another tall drink, thinking up more of Maddie's virtues, out of the corner of his eye, he spotted a pastel pink shopping bag tipped over on the entry table, its contents spilled out in one big frilly heap on the plank wood floor.

Curious, Trey strode over to the antique table and set his beer down next to the pink shopping bag that read in delicate black letters, *Double-Dare*. He bent on one knee and lifted a garment up. Black Fishnet Boyshort, the tag claimed along with the Double-Dare logo. He ran his fingers along the panties, tracing a black stitched rose strategically placed on the garment obviously designed to tease and torment. He placed it carefully in the bag and lifted up the next two items attached by a tiny transparent cord. Embroidered Demi-Bra and Bikini Panties. Red/Nude said the fancy tag. The bra and panties were sheer except for the etching of crimson embroidery meant to barely cover a female's most private assets.

Trey swallowed hard, and though he'd just finished a beer, his mouth suddenly dried up like desert tumbleweed. His mind wandered to secret places he normally didn't visit, imagining Maddie wearing this set, her soft creamy skin encased in tantalizing red. She was a woman who enjoyed wearing sexy lingerie and the contrast from her day-to-day clinical demeanor to her nighttime hot-blooded nature turned him on. Big-time. Trey took one last look at the matching bra and panties, then shoved them into the bag.

The last item he picked up was labeled Lace Baby doll/Vintage Look. The mauve-colored nightie plunged at the neckline and dipped down so deep that Trey wondered why they even bothered. He inhaled sharply touching the soft lace, noting that the short hem would hardly cover what needed covering, but then, that wasn't quite the intent, he thought wryly. And then he saw the matching thong, a skimpy piece of lace attached by mere thread.

Trey stared at the nightie, his heart in his throat, his groin growing tight. He couldn't help but to imagine Maddie wearing this, looking the picture of innocence and sin all at the same time, flowing into his arms, her body pressed against his until neither of them could take a complete breath. He visualized running his palms over the soft lace, caressing her breasts, then moving his hands lower, testing the thong with his fingers, creating sizzling shivers until both of them were ready to combust.

He remembered Maddie so well, the heat of her body, the smell of her skin, the flaming burn of their lovemaking. So when the front door opened and Maddie entered, Trey couldn't mask the lust on his face. He wouldn't even try.

"T-Trey?"

She stood over him in mild shock, her hair in coppery disarray, her face smudged with dirt, her jeans coated with straw and grass stains. She looked a wreck, so much so that Trey had to smile. He had to because he loved her so damn much, that he saw past all of that to the beautiful, sexy, perfect woman underneath. He loved her so damn much that his heart burned clear through his chest. She was the woman he wanted beyond life itself. The woman he wouldn't hurt and could never have.

"What are you doing with my...things?"

Trey lifted the babydoll up. "You mean these? I found them on the floor when I walked in. The bag had tipped over."

"And you were nice enough to pick them up?"

Trey shook his head and stood, still holding the nightie. "Honey, there was nothing *nice* about what I was thinking."

Even through the dirt on her face, Trey noticed her blush. He placed that last garment into the bag. "Did you leave them for me to see?"

Maddie's face colored again, this time with anger. She grabbed the bag from his hand. "I had an emergency call the minute I walked through the door. I must have set the bag down there without realizing it."

Trey scrubbed his jaw, contemplating. "Makes sense. So, did you buy them for your date with Jack?"

Maddie closed her eyes and cursed. Trey had never heard her use such language and when she opened her eyes, staring deeply into his, she spoke quietly. "I *bought them* for no one in particular. And it's not a date, just dinner with a friend."

"Are you sure about that?"

Maddie shook her head and ran a hand through her wayward hair. She cast him a look of frustration and despair. "Trey, what do you want from me?"

Everything. "Nothing, Maddie."

"When I walked in here a minute ago, it didn't look like you wanted nothing. It looked as though you had something *definite* on your mind."

"What do you want me to say?" he rushed out. "That even dirt-stained and muddied up, you're prettier than any woman I've ever laid eyes on? That I held those sexy clothes in my hands and envisioned you wearing them for me? That I want you, with or without that fancy lingerie, regardless of how much you'd end up being hurt in the end. All that's true, Maddie. But I'm not going to do it. I told you once before, wanting you and doing right by you are two different things."

Maddie bit down on her lip, but the green in her eyes lit with full vital force. And she aimed all that potent energy in his direction. "Maybe the wanting and doing right by me are one and the same, Trey. Maybe you're all wrong about us. Have you ever considered that?"

Trey shook his head. "No. I'm not wrong."

The Walker Curse still plagued him. He'd never get out from under the genetic scar that deprived him of faith and trust. Maddie was a keeper. He'd known that from the very start. She deserved more than the heartache he'd send her way one day.

"Are you sure about that?" She tossed that question back in his face.

Damn it. No, he wasn't sure of anything anymore. Maddie had hinted, she'd cajoled and she'd insinuated that Trey was a better man than he thought he was. And all of her sweet-talking had worked its way into his head, making him wonder. Giving him, hope.

"Think about it, Trey." She said, as she walked out of the room, her hand clasped around the shopping bag filled with sexy lingerie that Trey would never see again.

Eleven

"Maybe I should cancel my plans with Jack," Maddie said, as she glanced at the laboring cow heavy with calf. She stood with Trey in the maternity stall they'd concocted of sand and sawdust to help the cow deliver safely.

"That's not necessary," Trey said, shaking his head. "I've delivered more than my fair share of calves. This one isn't going to be as difficult as we'd thought. You said so yourself. She's doing a great job on her own."

Maddie took another glance at the cow straining to deliver her young one. By all means, Trey was right. The cow would probably do fine, but part of Maddie's deal with Trey was to oversee his livestock and silly as it seemed, she felt guilty leaving Trey to deal with the cow while she went out for dinner. She felt guilty, even through her anger at him. It had taken her days to re cover from Trey's obstinate behavior regarding Storm. And finally, she'd decided it did them both no good to be at odds. Besides, Maddie wasn't one for holding grudges. "I know you're right, but—"

"No, buts, Maddie. I'm right."

Trey had enough confidence for twenty men when it came to ranching dilemmas. Sadly, he just didn't have much confidence in himself. So instead of Maddie spending Saturday night enjoying his company, she'd agreed to spend the evening with his cousin.

"Won't Jack be picking you up soon?" he asked.

"Yes, in less than an hour. How come you know so much about my plans?" Maddie asked, baffled by Trey's obvious nonchalance over her date with Jack. She expected him to be more…something. Yet he didn't seem annoyed or upset or jealous. In the past, Maddie's ego had been bruised, but never more than her time here at 2 Hope Ranch, never more than her dealings with Trey.

There were times when Trey would look at her like she was the only woman on the planet and her heart would soar with anticipation. His hot looks spoke of steamy nights ahead, but Trey never acted upon those looks. His actions always belied the heated glances and alluring stares he cast her. She knew he fought an inner battle. She knew he struggled with demons that had existed before they'd ever met. Yet, Maddie had hoped she'd broken through his defenses. She had hoped she'd made a difference in his life.

"Jack squared it with me."

Maddie's voice escalated. "He asked *your* permission?"

Trey let out a wry chuckle. "Hardly. More like he told me his plans, point-blank." He frowned and added, "Whether I liked it or not."

It meant something to Maddie that Trey didn't sound happy about her date with Jack, but she wouldn't explain her reasons for going. She liked Jack and he seemed so sincere when he'd asked her to go to this benefit with him as a friend. "Well, I'd better get dressed. But if the cow—"

"I'll come get you if there's a problem."

"Promise?"

Trey nodded. "Promise."

Maddie headed for the shower and once done she dried and curled her hair. She'd decided on a soft peach summertime dress with a frilly flounce at the hem. The dress wasn't overly fancy, something she'd picked up at a local shop, but a new pair of earrings and matching necklace brought the whole outfit together quite nicely.

She put on a pair of lacy sandals, grabbed her purse and exited the room, dressing in record time so she could take a moment to check on the laboring cow, but the knock came just as Maddie had reached the front door. She opened it to find Jack standing on the porch, wearing a chocolate brown western suit, the exact color of his eyes. Clean-shaven and well groomed, Jack cast her a winning smile. There was nothing ordinary about Walker men—every last one she'd met was as handsome as the devil himself.

"Wow," he said, his eyes twinkling. "You look great."

Maddie smiled graciously, returning the compliment. "So do you, Jack. You're handsome in your uniform, but even more so out of it."

Jack's brows rose and he chuckled.

"Oh, I didn't mean it that way. You know wh—"

But her cell phone rang just at that awkward moment, and Maddie glanced at the name that popped up.

on the screen. "It's Caroline," she told Jack, leaving the door open so he could come inside. "Excuse me for one second."

She answered the call privately and when she returned, she had a favor to ask of Jack. "Since we're early and Caroline needs help with Annabelle, do you think we could stop over there for half an hour? The baby-sitter has to leave and Caroline doesn't think she can make it back from town in time. I know it's a huge favor and I certainly don't want to make us late for the benefit, but Caroline sounded pretty desperate."

"Not a problem." Jack glanced at his watch. "The actual dinner doesn't start until eight. We have more than enough time."

Maddie beamed him a smile, wondering why she hadn't fallen for Jack. Everything seemed simple with him. He was easy to talk to, easy to be with and he certainly didn't entertain any thoughts of the Walker Curse. "Thank you," she said, closing the door behind them. "You're a saint."

Jack opened the car door for her. "That isn't the way most people would describe me."

Maddie smiled and took her seat. "How do people describe you?" she asked, enjoying the conversation and the company.

Jack slid into the driver's seat and turned to her. "Pretty much a big pain in the ass, but with a good sense of humor and a deep sense of loyalty. That's why my family puts up with me."

"Because you're loyal?"

"Nah, because I make them laugh."

And Maddie laughed.

Jack put the key in the ignition and started the engine

just as Maddie caught sight of Trey exiting the barn. She met with his eyes over the distance of the yard and he cast her a long look then gave her a reassuring nod. Maddie immediately understood all went well with the calf's delivery. Relieved, Maddie sighed as Jack turned the car around and headed out the gate driving toward Caroline's house.

"Annabelle's no trouble at all," Maddie explained to Jack as they climbed up the Portmans's front steps. "And I'm sure Caroline will be along any minute."

Jack nodded and when Maddie knocked on the door, a young girl answered. "Hello. You must be Sherry. I'm Maddie, Caroline's friend and this is Jack Walker. We're your reinforcements."

"Hi. Come in." The young girl smiled warmly and let them in.

Maddie took two steps into the house before looking up to meet with a swarm of smiling faces that seemed to come out of nowhere. All at once the group chorused, "Surprise!"

A quick tremble passed through Maddie's body for a moment and she backed up right into Jack. He held her arms steady. "Happy Birthday, Maddie."

"B-birthday?" she repeated, stunned. She'd put her upcoming birthday out of her mind completely and never suspected a party, much less, a surprise. She glanced around the room, seeing her friends happily sending her birthday wishes and congratulations amid crepe paper decorations, balloons and birthday signs.

Caroline approached her first. "Happy Birthday, dear friend." They hugged tight, their embrace lasting long enough for Maddie to recover from a truly unexpected surprise. "I had no idea," Maddie said, with tears pooling in her eyes. "This is so…so great."

Little Annabelle tugged on the hem of her dress. Maddie bent to pick her up and give her a gentle loving squeeze.

"Did we surprised you?" Annabelle asked.

"Oh, yes. You and Mommy did a good job of surprising me."

"I helped Mommy do decorating."

"You did a perfect job, sweetie. Everything is beautiful."

Maddie swept her gaze at the guests again, this time really seeing each and every one. Jack, of course, had taken a place next to his father, Monty. Both men grinned at her with twinkling eyes. Kit and his wife stood behind them, along with Brittany and Paul, and a half a dozen of Maddie's closest and dearest clients, people she had come to know very well by treating their animals. Even Darla was here and behind her stood a man, who began to make his way out from the small group.

Maddie set Annabelle down. "Nick!"

He reached her in three strides and Maddie jumped up into his arms, touched that he'd come back to Hope Wells for her birthday. She really hadn't thought she'd see him again, knowing how swamped he was with his own new enterprise.

"I just walked in ten minutes before you did. I almost didn't make it in time."

She beamed him a smile. "I can't believe you're here, but I'm so glad that you are."

"So am I." Nick kissed her cheek. "Happy Birthday."

Overwhelmed and filled with joy, Maddie spent the

better part of the hour making her rounds, speaking with all of the guests and picking at the food on her plate.

Caroline had outdone herself, offering up a dinner buffet fit for a queen. And that's exactly how Maddie felt, like royalty tonight. Everything was perfect except…

Maddie stared at the front door for the tenth time tonight, it seemed, wondering if Trey would show up.

"He's supposed to come," Jack said, in a rare serious tone.

Mortified that Jack had read her thoughts, Maddie fumbled. "Oh, I, uh…I was just wondering if he—"

"He knows about it. He didn't say he *wasn't* coming."

Maddie nodded. Why did it hurt so much that Trey hadn't bothered to come to her party? Why was she fully expecting to see him walk through that door, flashing her his killer smile and wishing her a happy birthday? If she allowed it, her disappointment would swallow her and she'd seem ungrateful to all of the wonderful people who had shown up, who had been kind and gracious to her throughout the year. Each and every one of them meant something special to her. Each, in their own way defined Hope Wells, the small town with the big heart.

She glanced at Nick, who was laughing with Darla at the moment, and wondered if she belonged here in Hope Wells at all, or if she should finally decide to leave town.

She knew that getting in on the ground floor of a new progressive clinic was an opportunity that would only come around once in life. The idea would sweep across her mind at intervals during each day, and each day the temptation seemed greater, like a magnet pulling at her, taking her away from Hope Wells for good. She weighed her options over and over, but unfortunately, Trey Walker's image would always pop into her head, confusing her thoughts, perhaps blinding her to the possibilities.

"Hey, no pickle-pusses around here." Jack made a lighthearted jab at her jaw. "It's time for cake." He took her hand and led her into the dining area and Maddie forgot all about Trey, determined to have a good time with her friends.

"It was a wonderful evening," Maddie said on a long luxurious sigh, hours later as Jack pulled up in front of the house at 2 Hope.

"I'm glad you had a good time."

"I did." She turned to look into Jack's eyes. "You're a good friend, Jack Walker. Even if you lied through your teeth to get me there."

Jack laughed. "You don't know how much I hate lying, but I had to. Trey wouldn't do…uh,"

Maddie sat up straight in the seat and stared at him. "Trey? Was he supposed to bring me?"

"Uh, well…doggone it, Maddie. Sometimes my cousin is just a big jackass. Emphasis on *ass*."

Maddie squeezed her eyes shut. "It's okay, Jack."

"No, it's not okay. Hell, if you weren't head over heels over Trey, I'd be asking you out day and night. He's a damn fool, Maddie. But in his defense, he thinks this is best for you. He really cares about you."

Maddie glanced at the house, noting that Trey's light was still on. "I know he does." And that was why she hurt so much. She feared Trey had deliberately stayed away tonight, for her sake.

"Don't let it spoil your birthday."

"Oh, I won't. I see everything clearly now. If anything, this has helped me make a tough decision."

Maddie leaned over to kiss Jack on the cheek. "Thank you for being a wonderful friend."

Jack smiled. "Anytime."

He walked her to the door lifting a box of gifts she'd received and handed them over to her. "Want me to bring them in for you?"

Maddie shook her head. "No thanks. I've got everything under control."

And Maddie entered the house with newfound determination. She did have everything under control and she knew exactly what she had to do.

Half an hour later, and twenty minutes past midnight, Maddie stood bravely behind Trey's bedroom door. In her hands, she held a small square white box, its inscription on a note card read:

Happy Birthday, Maddie.
Love, Trey

Her eyes had misted immediately upon seeing this small gift lying on her bed, a tied bunch of wildflowers crossing over the box eloquently. She immediately recognized the flowers as the ones that had sprouted up in a patch near the barn. She'd passed them every day, never really noticing their vivid color or sweet scent.

And when she'd opened the box, she couldn't help tears from falling freely, her heart melting like butter on a hot stove. She'd lifted the bracelet out, finding an exact, nearly flawless replica of Aphrodite. The silver shone more brilliantly, but the bracelet matched her Grandma Mae's necklace perfectly.

Maddie had never received a more thoughtful gift.

"Oh, Trey," she whispered, standing behind his door with a rapidly beating heart, wishing things had turned out differently.

She knocked once, her hands trembling. "Trey, it's Maddie."

He opened the door seconds later, his dark hair swept back from his face, wearing jeans that dipped below his waist and nothing else. Maddie's breath hitched, noting the magnificence of his broad shoulders, the luster of his tanned chest and like a jolting shock, she recalled the taste of his skin, the feel of his body pressed against hers. Her mind flooded with memories of making love with him, of being as close as two people can be, sharing more than body heat and desire, but bonding two hearts together and no matter what Trey said or did, Maddie knew that bond to be real and true.

"May I come in?" she asked and Trey opened the door wide to allow her entrance.

She stepped into the middle of his room and looked into the depths of his dark eyes. "I, uh, wanted to tell you, that I've made my decision about leaving for Denver."

Trey swallowed and took a deep breath, nodding his head. "I figured."

There was no question in his eyes, no regret, either, it appeared, but resolute resignation. He didn't ask her intentions and Maddie couldn't bring herself to discuss her decision. Tonight wasn't the time. Trey's bedroom wasn't the place.

"And I wanted to thank you for this." She opened the box she held and lifted out the bracelet. "It came as quite a surprise. The whole night has been full of surprises," she said in earnest. "But this…it's the most precious gift I've ever received. I'll treasure it as much as I'll treasure my time here with…my time here at 2 Hope." She handed him the bracelet. "Will you put it on me?"

His large work-roughened hands fumbled a bit trying to undo the clasp. He leaned in to get a better look and they bumped heads. Both chuckled awkwardly and when he gazed into her eyes, Maddie knew she couldn't leave his room tonight. She couldn't sleep her last night at 2 Hope alone, when Trey was only a few rooms away.

"There," he said, taking her hand and turning it to admire the bracelet. "It fits."

His slight touch alone sent shivers throughout her defenseless body. Maddie smiled up into his eyes. "It does—a perfect match to my necklace."

"The jeweler used a sketch I'd made and well…he did a pretty darn good job."

Maddie touched Trey's cheek with one hand. "You went to all that trouble for me?"

He shrugged a shoulder, in that same way he had of brushing off a compliment but he spoke softly with quiet determination. "No one's more deserving than you."

Staring directly into his eyes, she couldn't doubt his sincerity. Tears she'd held back, fell then, one at a time, slowly, trickling down her face. "It's the best gift I've ever received, but it's not enough, Trey. I guess I'm a greedy woman, because I want more."

Maddie unzipped her dress, allowing the material to skim graciously down her body. She stepped out of it, her gaze never leaving Trey's face. She stood before him in her strappy sandals and her newly purchased bold red underwear. "I want one last parting gift. One more night with you, Trey Walker."

Twelve

Trey's heart slammed into his chest seeing Maddie's tearstained face, realizing that this would be her last night at 2 Hope. This would be their last night together. He'd always known that Maddie wouldn't stay. Hell, he'd done everything in his power to push her away.

And it had worked.

She planned on leaving.

But Trey couldn't push her away tonight. Hell, he didn't have *that* much willpower, not when every cell in his body cried out for her. Not when he ached to hold her in his arms, kiss her adorable heart-shaped mouth and caress her smooth porcelain skin. How could he possibly deny her a last request, when he wanted the same?

Trey knew that in the morning he'd wake up broken, a shattered shell of a man who would feel the loss of her leaving for a long time to come. But that didn't matter because she would move on to something better. She'd carve out the life she'd always wanted. She'd be free of him and the heartache he'd caused her.

He looked at her sweet expectant face, then followed the lines of her body down to each alluring curve and hollow, making a complete and thorough sweep.

"Like I said before, I'd want you with or *without* those sexy things. You're beautiful, Maddie."

Maddie cast him a coy smile. "Without?"

Trey smiled and took her into his arms, pressing her body up to his. Her hands grazed his bare chest then moved up to circle his neck. His groin tightened and his heart pounded like a schoolboy being granted his first kiss. "There's time for *without*. I sorta like the *with*, for now." He toyed with the crimson strap of her bra. "Did you wear them for your party?"

Maddie lifted up on tiptoes and kissed his lips softly, but far too quickly. "No, I put them on afterward. For you."

"God, Maddie. You're killing me. You know that?" This time, he bent his head and kissed her; it wasn't soft and fast, but a long drawn-out kiss, a hot exploration of lips and tongues with bodies meshed together and hearts pounding.

Without another word, Trey took her hand and led her to his bed. He sat down then gestured for her to sit next to him. "I've dreamt of making love to you here, sweetheart."

"I was only a few steps away," she whispered.

"Don't I know it."

Moonlight streamed in, casting Maddie in a soft glow. Trey had always thought Maddie in the moonlight to be a beautiful thing, but never more than tonight. Light shimmered on her coppery hair, framing her pretty face and bringing a lustrous sheen to her smooth skin.

Trey took a steadying breath and plopped down on the bed, his head hitting the pillow with a soft swoosh. "It was all I could do to keep from coming for you in the middle of the night."

Maddie's eyebrows lifted with uncertainty. "Really?"

"Don't doubt it. It put me in more than one sour mood in the morning."

"Trey, why didn't you?"

"Shh." He lifted up to place a finger to her lips. "You know why, but let's not go there tonight, okay?"

She nodded and he kissed her softly on the lips. "We've wasted so much time," she whispered.

"And all we have is tonight."

Trey leaned back again onto the bed, making room for Maddie. He took her hand and turned her toward him. She straddled his thighs and used both her hands to touch his chest, exploring, caressing, wrapping tiny chest hairs around her finger, toying with him.

Trey thought he would die from the pleasure, both physical and visual. He'd never felt or seen anything more enticing, than watching Maddie atop his body, having her way with him.

She leaned down to kiss his lips, her thighs rubbing his, her torso tight against him, her red lace-encased breasts crushing his chest. Trey groaned aloud, his erection pressing the confines of his jeans, and he knew he'd have a walking hard-on for days to come, each time he'd be foolish enough to think about her like this.

Maddie broke off the kiss and wiggled down enough to explore his chest with her lips. She kissed his throat, his shoulders and his torso, then made hot wet circles around his nipples with her tongue.

"Damn, Maddie," he uttered, barely containing another groan.

To Trey, everything with Maddie had been about self-control. He'd resisted her for so long and right now, all he wanted to do was flip her onto her back and drive his hot erection into her until both were sated and spent, but Trey held back. He wanted it all with Maddie. He wanted her to take pleasure and give pleasure all night. He wanted their last night together to be perfect.

"I'm about to bust out of these jeans, honey."

Maddie glanced down and shot him the sexiest, dewy-eyed look Trey had ever seen. It didn't help matters, not at all.

She gestured to his zipper. "Want me to…uh."

"Yeah," he uttered, "although that might make it worse."

"But in a good way," she said, sliding off him long enough to unzip his jeans. She helped him slip off his pants and boxers, then returned to lie down next to him. When her hand cupped his manhood, Trey jerked, more than a little surprised, but all the more pleased.

They faced each other in the darkness as she moved her hands on him, gliding up and down effortlessly. He kissed her again and again as she proceeded to turn his world upside down.

And after several long moments and a near mishap of nature, Trey grabbed her hand and held her still. "How about we do the *without* now?"

Maddie chuckled softly as he reached around and unfastened her bra.

"The *without* is pretty damn good, too, sweetheart," he said, removing the garment entirely to catch sight of

Maddie's breasts spilling out. He cupped her breast in his hand and leaned down to kiss the rosy-tipped crest.

Maddie moaned and wiggled her body. Trey continued to kiss her, using his tongue to moisten each nipple, then suckle gently, until she was hot and wet from his lusty caresses. "So beautiful," he breathed out, holding back, wanting to prolong this pleasure for as long as possible.

There would never be another woman in his life like Maddie Brooks. She was intelligent and wholesome, funny and sexy, innocent and bold as can be. Trey liked the way she gave all of herself to him. He liked the daring side of her. She'd been the best sex partner he'd ever had and she'd probably hold that title for the rest of his life. Hell, there wasn't one damn thing he didn't like about her.

"Trey?" Maddie lifted her head with a question in her eyes. "Did you go somewhere?"

Trey kissed her again, guiding her back down onto his bed. "Just regrouping," he said, realizing he'd lost his focus. He'd been in the middle of making love to a beautiful woman and bittersweet, niggling thoughts had crept into his head. He shoved them away, concentrating on Maddie and making her his, if only for tonight.

He slipped his hand down her torso, his fingers sliding under the red lacy thong and began stroking her softly.

"Mmmm, I like the way you regroup, *baby.*"

Trey groaned. Maddie had a way with that one word that sent his heart racing and his body into overdrive. His strokes became faster and she moved her body with more urgency, until Trey couldn't hold back another second. He knew the time was now.

He reached for the bedside drawer and withdrew a condom. He'd picked them up shortly after their first time together, not trusting himself to keep his vow. At least this way, he'd be responsible, if not rational.

"Old ones?" Maddie asked, her brows lifting.

"New ones," he replied honestly, "with only your name on them." He handed one to her and once she'd fitted it into place, he slipped off her panties with one efficient move and entered her slowly.

Maddie cooed, a soft pleasured sound. "I've missed you, Trey."

Trey slammed his eyes shut, overwhelmed with the very same sentiment. The first time with her had been amazing, but this time their joining meant more than satisfying lust and desire. This time, it counted for more emotions than he could name.

Trey thrust into her, absorbing every sensation, every nuance that was Maddie, committing it to memory. They moved together in sync, wrapped in each other's arms, climbing the limitless ladder of pleasure. And minutes later they climaxed in unison, two bodies joined, two hearts aligned.

Together they sank back to earth, sated and complete. Trey took Maddie in his arms and held on tight with each moment drawing closer to dawn when he'd awaken an empty, hollow, defeated man.

Too soon Maddie woke from a blissful, easy sleep. She opened her eyes to find Trey beside her, one arm draped protectively and provocatively below her waist. She smiled at the man she loved with her whole heart and reached up, not quite touching his face, allowing her fingers to get close enough to nearly caress him. And that's how it was with Trey. Maddie had almost touched him, but she hadn't been able to get close enough to wake him out of his self-imposed sleep. She wanted to shake him and shout that he wasn't cursed, that he was a man she could count on, again and again.

But Trey had to decide that for himself. She knew that now. And she hoped that someday he'd come to that realization before it was too late.

Maddie rested her head against the pillow and sighed quietly. She'd be leaving him soon, the hour nearing dawn. But she took a minute to relive the night, recalling the way Trey made her feel when he touched her, recalling his hands on her body, making magic, creating tingles and shivers. She recalled his lips on hers, so vividly, the way he claimed her mouth with gentle command, forceful and demanding, but also so sweet and tender.

He left no part of her untouched, making her feel treasured and loved. Having his hands on her body seemed as natural as breathing. There was no shame, no regret. Making love with him, having him inside her was like the old cliché, coming home.

Right as rain.

Good as gold.

He'd made her bold, when she'd never been before. He'd made her ache then he soothed her. He'd made her wanton then he sated her. He'd brought out her inner self, the one she kept hidden from everyone else. Trey had filled her body, but he'd also filled her heart and her mind.

He'd done his best to push her away, yet she'd never felt closer to another human being. Her heart cried out for him in the worst way, but she knew that he had to come to terms with his past, to gain his future.

Maddie sighed again, staring at Trey as he slept soundly. They'd made love twice tonight, each time being so different, so compelling, so *earth-shattering*.

A ray of predawn light entered the room, the dusky stream that appeared before the sun lifted high enough to brighten the sky. Maddie knew her time at 2 Hope was up.

She rose from the bed, glancing at Trey one final time, her eyes growing wide enough to hold back tears, then she left his room.

She'd be off the ranch before dawn.

Trey punched open the screen door and stepped out onto the front porch. Sunlight beamed down and slapped him in the face, making him squint. "Damn it."

He'd overslept this morning for the first time in ten years. Old feelings of despair had washed over him, and it had been all he could do to drag himself out of bed today.

Maddie had left 2 Hope.

He'd been successful in his quest to drive her away.

And he hated himself for it.

Trey sat down on the bench seat and hung his head, thinking back on all the mistakes he'd made with her. Kissing her that first time had been his downfall. He'd known better than to get involved with the wholesome, sweet Maddie Brooks. She was a keeper and he couldn't keep her.

God, how his head pounded.

"Headache, boss?" Kit asked, riding up on Julip.

More like heartache. "Nah, I'm fine. Taking her out for some exercise?"

Kit grinned and Trey wondered what the hell he was so happy about this time of the morning. "Something like that. Take a look-see."

Kit rode toward Storm's corral.

Trey stood and called out. "Hey, don't get her too close."

But his foreman pretended not to hear. He rode Julip closer to Storm. Immediately, Trey strode over, thinking Kit had lost his mind. "Careful!"

"Watch this," Kit said and continued until Julip was nose to nose with Storm, from opposite sides of the fence.

Trey reached the fence and stared at the two horses that were eyeing and sniffing each other like childhood sweethearts. He shot his foreman a curious look.

"That's not all," Kit said, still wearing that silly grin. Cued by Kit's soft clicking sound, Julip began to saunter around the perimeter of the corral at a moderate pace. And before Trey could blink his eyes, Storm joined in from his side of the fence, matching Julip stride for stride as if the two were out trotting on a Sunday excursion.

"I'll be damned."

Kit made three circles around each time, Julip allowing Storm to set the pace as the two moved together.

And when Kit returned, a triumphant smile on his face, Trey shook his head in disbelief. "How'd you do it?"

"Not me. Maddie. She asked me to continue working with Julip and Storm. Seems she found a way to settle your wild stallion, without breaking his spirit."

This time, Trey did blink, three times, taking it all in. Maddie hadn't given up on Storm. Even though he'd confronted her, she never quit. He should have known. Maddie Brooks wasn't a quitter.

Storm came up to nudge Trey's hand. The stallion huffed out air and shook his head, so that his ink-black mane shifted. This was the first time Storm had approached him in a nonaggressive way. Trey reached up and stroked his mane, then patted his head with affection. "What a surprise."

"Nah, just nature taking its course, I'd say."

"Yeah," Trey replied, "maybe."

Trey couldn't get over Storm's transformation. Sure, he'd still have his moods—a stallion couldn't change that much—but he had changed enough to make him a true part of 2 Hope. Storm belonged here. He belonged to Trey. In a sense they belonged to each other.

"Then maybe you'd let nature take its course in another way," Kit said.

Curious, Trey asked, "In what other way?"

Kit tipped his hat and smiled. "I was thinking that the right woman could settle the right man. They'd be like soul mates. Sorta like what happened with Storm and Julip. It just takes some smarts to figure it all out, boss." With that Kit spurred Julip into a trot and they headed out.

Trey stared at them as they rode off, his head still reeling. He walked over to the front steps and set himself down. Stretching out his legs, he thought about Storm, his feisty stallion, and realized how wrong he'd been.

Maddie had been right. And he'd been wrong.

Trey wondered what else he'd been wrong about lately, but he couldn't finish the thought because Jack pulled up to the house in his patrol car. He exited the car wearing a tight expression.

"Damn," he muttered. Jack was the last person he wanted to see today. "Nobody's home," Trey remarked, only halfway joking.

But Jack was never one to take a hint. He sat right down beside him and stared into his eyes. "You got the right." He pointed to Trey's head. "Nobody's home in there. Where's your head, Trey?"

"I'm not in the mood, Jack. Say what you came to say, or better yet, just leave."

"You're going to thank me one day for this," Jack said, all sarcasm gone. "Just keep it buttoned. I'm going to do some talking, and you're going to do some listening."

Trey humored him. "Okay, shoot."

"Just a sec." Jack walked into the house and came back holding two beers. He set both down between them.

"It's nine o'clock in the morning."

Jack took his seat on the steps again. "You're gonna need it."

"I thought you were on duty."

Jack smiled. "They're both for you."

Trey grimaced and twisted the cap. "Okay, what?" Then he took a swig. Seemed a cold brew couldn't hurt. He already felt as though he'd been in a train wreck.

"I passed Maddie in town. Her truck was loaded up. She left the ranch, didn't she?"

Trey nodded, like he needed reminding.

"And you just let her go?"

He nodded again and stared at Jack defying him to make a snide comment.

Jack put up both hands in surrender. "I didn't come here to condemn you. I came here to reason with you."

Trey finished the first beer in two gulps then turned to his cousin. "Why?"

"Because any fool can see you're head over heels in love with her, that's why. And Lord only knows why, but Maddie feels the same way. I can't stand by and see you make that kind of mistake. You see, you've been hold-ing onto this lame idea that you are like your father. But,

Trey, let me clue you in, you're not the heartbreaker your daddy was. You haven't got a selfish bone in your body. And I know you're stuck on his last dying words to you. But did you ever stop to think he didn't mean it that way?"

"*Don't make the same mistakes I made, son.* It's hard to misinterpret that," Trey said.

"Right, that's what he said. But maybe he meant that he wanted better for you. He didn't want you to be miserable and lonely without love in your life. It's possible that he knew you were capable of loving one woman and devoting your life to her. He knew he couldn't do that but maybe he wanted to impress upon you that you could.

"Sure we bump heads from time to time, but I've got to tell you, I'm proud to call you my relation. Anybody can see what kind of man you are, Trey. And your father knew you through and through. I'd bet my last dollar that he never meant for you to lose someone as special as Maddie. I think he meant for you to find the right woman and *keep* her. You hit the jackpot, Trey. You found the right woman. You'd never hurt Maddie. I know that and I think you know that, too. So *keep* her."

Trey's head cleared and suddenly, he saw the possibilities. Maybe his father had meant for him to have better, more fulfilling life. Maybe, he had believed Trey capable of love and devotion, something he couldn't quite manage. Maybe his father had thought Trey the better man. But could he look beyond his past and see instead a future with Maddie?

Hell, she'd been the one all along to believe in him even when he didn't believe in himself. She'd tried pointing out all the qualities she admired in him, tried o make him see he had worth and staying power. Maddie had had faith enough for them both.

He slid his hand down his jaw, realizing he'd already hurt her in so many ways. He'd pushed her away again and again. He'd made love to her last night until they could barely move a muscle and then he'd let her leave the ranch. He'd made so many mistakes with her. "It's too late."

"No. She's not gone yet."

"She's not?" An inkling of hope developed.

"I saw her truck parked outside of the Cactus Inn."

"The Cactus Inn?"

"Hey, don't question it, just consider it a lucky break. She's probably still there. I passed her not fifteen minutes ago."

Trey jumped up and gave Jack a big bear hug. "I owe you, cousin."

"Don't kiss me and we'll call it even. Now go."

Trey raced inside to grab his hat and keys, then headed out. He'd figure out what to say once he found her and prayed it would be enough.

Trey thanked his lucky stars that Maddie's truck was still parked outside the Cactus Inn. He entered the motel and strode straight over to the reception desk. "Hi, Jody."

"Hey, Trey. Haven't seen you around much. What brings you in here?"

He and Trey had been buddies in high school and now Jody ran his late father's motel. "I'm looking for Dr. Brooks. You know, Maddie Brooks, the veterinarian."

Jody nodded. "Yeah, I know who she is. You're the third person to come looking for her this morning, and heck, she just checked in after breakfast."

"She checked in?"

Jody nodded.

"Who else came looking for her?"

Jody shrugged. "Don't know their names, but that woman sure has got herself a lot of gentlemen callers. First one, then another. Heck, Trey, you're the third this morning."

Trey grimaced, not knowing what to make of all this. There was only one way to find out. "What's her room number?"

"It's 202 D. Take the stairs then turn right. Boy seems like I've said that a whole lot this morning."

"Thanks. Do you know if anyone is still up there?"

Jody shrugged shoulders that had at one time blocked their high school football team's most competitive rivals. He'd been the best darn tackle at Hope Wells High. "Nope. Sorry, man. Good luck."

Puzzled, Trey climbed the stairs and found Maddie's room. He took in a lungful of air, still not sure what to say exactly and not even sure she'd be alone in there to listen. He knocked briskly. "Maddie, it's Trey."

Seconds ticked by, seeming more like an eternity. Then she opened the door and they stared into each other's eyes. Overwhelmed at seeing her again, at seeing what he might have lost, Trey's body shook powerfully, the tremble coursing the length of him.

Seeing her standing before him, with those curious green eyes questioning him, Trey realized just how much he loved this woman. He realized what a fool he'd been. He'd nearly tossed away the most precious thing that would ever enter into his life. He stood there gazing at her, seeing his future.

"Trey?"

Yanking off his Stetson, he smiled. "Morning."

She smiled back tentatively. Trey couldn't blame her. Basically, they'd said their goodbyes between the sheets last night, so he understood her bafflement. She probably thought she'd never see him again. That was his fault. All of it was his fault.

"Morning."

"Can I come in? Or are you, uh, busy?"

"I'm busy, but of course you can come in."

Trey entered the small, quaint room noticing Maddie's suitcase opened and half of her clothes put up in the closet area. Her other belongings were strewn about the room. Fortunately though, they were alone.

Trey let his gaze wander for only a second or two, before lifting his eyes back to her. He was almost afraid if he took his eyes off her for too long, she'd vanish and he already knew how it felt to have Maddie there one minute, then gone the next. He didn't want to experience that sensation ever again.

"What are you doing here?" she asked quietly.

"I was wrong about Storm."

Maddie blinked. "You came here to talk about Storm?"

God, this was so hard. He didn't want to make her crazy, but Trey had never been great with words. "Not really, but I thought you should know that you were right all along. He's…well, he's as amazing as you are."

Maddie continued to stare at him, her expression softening a little. "Thank you," she said with a small smile.

God, how he loved her. She looked so darn pretty today with her auburn hair pulled back into a ponytail. Wearing nothing special, just jeans and a blouse, the wholesome woman he'd made passionate love to last night, was more beautiful, more sexy, more…everything than any woman he'd ever met. It stunned him how much he'd already missed her presence at the ranch. Trey cleared his throat. "What, uh, what are you doing here?"

"Me? I'm moving in for a while."

"I thought you needed to get to Denver right away?"

Maddie frowned and Trey realized how his comment might appear to her—as if he was eager to see her go. Hell, he really wasn't good at this.

"I'm not moving to Denver."

Stunned, Trey's heart did a somersault. "You're not?"

"No. I never was, Trey." Her eyes met his and they looked at each other for a long moment. "Denver would have been a great opportunity, but it isn't for me. Hope Wells is my home. I realized that yesterday. I have great friends here, a good practice. I have everything I want." Then she glanced away. "Well, almost everything."

Trey kept silent and she went on. "Seems my party wasn't the only surprise I received yesterday. My insurance came through. I have enough funds to rebuild my office. I decided to take some time off to work on the design. I've already contacted an architect and he's going to help me with my plans. I said good-bye to Nick this morning, too."

Maddie smiled warmly and her eyes sparkled. "You see, Trey Walker. You're not the only one around here with *staying power*."

Once again, Maddie had amazed him. He took a moment to recover from her bold assessment then grinned, agreeing with her. Finally. "Damn straight, I'm not. We both have *staying power*."

Maddie let out an uncertain chuckle. "We do?"

He nodded. "Yeah, honey, we do. I just sort of fig

ured it all out. I love you, Maddie. I love you so much that I can barely breathe. I love you so much that if you had gone to Denver, I would have followed you and begged you to come back with me. And it took me all this time to realize it. No, that's not right. *You* made me realize it. You taught me so much. You had the trust and faith in me that I didn't have. You made me see myself in a different light. And if it's not too late—"

"Oh, Trey. It's not too late. It never could be." The guarded look on Maddie's face disappeared, replaced by a soft sweet expression. "I've always loved you."

Trey took her hand in his, weaving their fingers together and holding tight. "I know I've been a fool, but I'm ready to remedy that. I love you, sweetheart. I want to marry you and live the rest of my life with you by my side."

Maddie reached up to caress his cheek. "Yes."

Joyous, Trey flung his hat in the air. "Yes? Yes, you'll marry me?"

On tiptoes, Maddie kissed him soundly on the lips. "Yes. I'll marry you."

Staggered by his good fortune, Trey confessed. "I never thought I'd say those words."

Maddie agreed. "I never thought I'd *hear* those words."

Both laughed as Trey took her into his arms and kissed her long and hard, crushing their lips together. "Move back to the ranch. Live with me. Be my wife. Be my lover."

Maddie's beautiful face beamed. "I'll be all of those things to you, Trey. And more."

Trey couldn't keep from smiling, his heart soaring. "More?"

She nodded and led him over to the bed. "So much more, *baby.*"

Epilogue

"I do." Trey Walker uttered the words slowly, both awed and a little bit frightened. In a million lifetimes he'd never dreamed he'd say those words. Especially not to Maddie Brooks, the auburn-haired beauty directly beside him, her wide eyes filled with love. They sat atop their mounts under an arbor of lush traveling vines in the small garden area behind his house at 2 Hope Ranch. Maddie insisted Storm be a part of the wedding, too, and the feisty yet gentled stallion carried the most beautiful bride Hope Wells had ever seen.

Trey took great pride in his soon-to-be wife. Maddie hadn't given up on Storm. She'd found a way, through patience, careful thought and clever maneuvering, to bring the animal around. She'd read Storm correctly bringing a gentle mare into his corral, one not impressed or intimidated by his wild nature. This was a female unlike all others and Storm, smart creature that he was, came to recognize that fact.

Trey smiled at the similarities, wondering if he really wasn't marrying a sorceress. No, he realized instantly, the magic they made together was real and solid, not something that could be whirled away on a whim.

"I do, too," Maddie said, happy tears welling in her eyes. A gentle breeze blew by, messing her hair enough to give his down-home girl a sexy look.

Trey swallowed hard, intrigued by the young woman who'd be living with him until the end of time. In truth, the petite green-eyed female scared the hell out of him with her innocent looks and wholesome demeanor. He'd never loved so deeply, so completely. Maddie was the exact sort of woman Trey wanted. And he planned to keep her in his heart forever.

Under the minister's guidance, Trey placed the ring on Maddie's finger and spoke his vows, peering deeply into her eyes telling her in a silent message that she'd have no reason to ever doubt his love. His word is good as gold.

Maddie smiled, sealing the deal with vows of her own.

Storm whinnied and sidled up against the mare that had settled him, brushing soft white satin against Trey's leg. He leaned over his saddle, lifted the delicate bridal veil and kissed his new wife.

Life was good again at 2 Hope Ranch.

And it was bound to get even better.

* * * * *

FREE

2 BOOKS AND A SURPRISE GIFT

We would like to take this opportunity to thank you for reading t
Mills & Boon® book by offering you the chance to take TWO mo
specially selected 2-in-1 volumes from the Desire™ series absolut
FREE! We're also making this offer to introduce you to the benefits
the Mills & Boon® Book Club™—

- ★ **FREE home delivery**
- ★ **FREE gifts and competitions**
- ★ **FREE monthly Newsletter**
- ★ **Books available before they're in the shops**
- ★ **Exclusive Mills & Boon Book Club offers**

Accepting these FREE books and gift places you under no obligat
to buy; you may cancel at any time, even after receiving your f
shipment. Simply complete your details below and return the en
page to the address below. You don't even need a stamp!

YES! Please send me 2 free Desire volumes and a surprise gif
understand that unless you hear from me, I will receiv
superb new volumes every month for just £4.99 each, postage a
packing free. I am under no obligation to purchase any books and
cancel my subscription at any time. The free books and gift wil
mine to keep in any case.

D8

Ms/Mrs/Miss/Mr...Initials ....
                                                                                   BLOCK CAPITALS P

Surname ....

Address ....

....

....Postcode ....

Send this whole page to:

The Mills & Boon Book Club, FREEPOST CN81, Croydon, CR9 3WZ